3-Books-in-1!

DON'T MISS THE FINAL INSTALLMENT IN THE *MY TEACHER* SERIES:

My Teacher Flunked the Planet

3-Books-in-1!

MY TEACHER IS AN ALIEN * MY TEACHER FRIED MY BRAINS * MY TEACHER GLOWS IN THE DARK

Bruce Coville

ALADDIN

NEW YORK LONDON TORONTO SYDNEY NEW DELHI

ALADDIN
An imprint of Simon & Schuster Children's Publishing Division
1230 Avenue of the Americas, New York, NY 10020
This Aladdin paperback edition September 2015

For information about special discounts for bulk purchases, please contact Simon & Schuster Special Sales at 1-866-506-1949 or business@simonandschuster.com.
The Simon & Schuster Speakers Bureau can bring authors to your live event. For more information or to book an event contact the Simon & Schuster Speakers Bureau at 1-866-248-3049 or visit our website at www.simonspeakers.com.
Designed by Jessica Handelman
The text of this book was set in Weiss Std.
Manufactured in the United States of America 0316 OFF
2 4 6 8 10 9 7 5 3
Library of Congress Control Number 2015945207
ISBN 978-1-4814-5746-0 (pbk)
ISBN 978-1-4391-1228-1 (*My Teacher Is an Alien* eBook)
ISBN 978-1-4391-1242-7 (*My Teacher Fried My Brains* eBook)
ISBN 978-1-4391-1245-8 (*My Teacher Glows in the Dark* eBook)
These titles were previously published individually by Aladdin.

Contents

MY TEACHER IS AN ALIEN

To my sixth-grade teacher, Florence Crandall,
who told me to write a story

Special thanks to Pat MacDonald,
Leslie Mendelson, and Erin Mendelson

TABLE OF CONTENTS

CHAPTER ONE

MISSING — ONE SIXTH-GRADE TEACHER

"Hey, Geekoid!" yelled Duncan Dougal as he snatched Peter Thompson's book out of his hand. "Why do you read so much? Don't you know how to watch TV?"

Poor Peter. I could see that he wanted to grab the book back from Duncan. But I also knew that if he tried, Duncan would cream him.

Sometimes I wonder if Duncan's mother dropped him on his head when he was a baby. I mean, *something* must have made him decide to spend his life making other people miserable. Otherwise why would he spend so much of his time picking on a kid like Peter Thompson? Peter never bothers anyone. Heck, the only thing he really wants is to be left alone so he can read whatever book he has his nose stuck in at the moment.

That doesn't seem like too much to ask to me. But Duncan takes Peter's reading as a personal insult.

So here it was, the first day back from spring vacation—we hadn't even gone into the school yet—and I could tell by the look on Duncan Dougal's face that the spring fight season was about to begin.

I clutched my piccolo case to my chest and watched as Peter's pale face began to turn red. Peter blushed at almost anything. He was tall and thin and wore thick glasses. And he was the smartest person I had ever met—grown-ups included.

The problem was, it was all book smarts. Peter had absolutely no idea how to deal with a creep like Duncan. Actually, neither did I. If I did, I would have stopped him. But the one time I had tried to come between Duncan and Peter, I ended up with a black eye myself.

Duncan claimed it was an accident, of course. "Susan just jumped right in front of my fist," he said as if I was the one who had done something wrong. To tell you the truth, I think Duncan punched me on purpose. Most guys wouldn't hit a girl. But Duncan doesn't mind. It was his way of warning me to keep my nose out of his business.

As I watched Duncan squinting down at Peter, it occurred to me that sixth grade can be a dangerous place if you don't watch out.

Stacy Benoit was standing a few feet away from Peter, pressed against the school wall and looking nervous. Stacy is this incredibly good kid, who never gets in trouble ever. She hates fights even more than I do.

She had just started edging her way toward me when Duncan ran his foot through a puddle and splashed dirty water all over Peter's jeans.

"Cut it out, Duncan," said Peter.

"Cut it out, Duncan," mimicked Duncan in a whiny, singsong voice.

Anyone who knew Duncan could see he was gearing up for a fight. But it wasn't necessarily going to be with Peter, since Peter usually just took whatever Duncan dished out. I figured Duncan was using him as a warm-up. So I was a little surprised when he tossed Peter's book into the puddle.

Even Duncan should have known that was something you just don't do to Peter.

"Oops!" he said maliciously. "I *dropped* it."

I heard Stacy gasp as Peter launched himself off the wall and bashed his head into Duncan's stomach. Within seconds the two of them were rolling around on the ground.

"I hate it when this happens," said Stacy as the boys surrounded Peter and Duncan in a shouting, cheering circle.

The fight hadn't gone on more than ten seconds when a tall blond man came pushing through the crowd. Without saying anything, he grabbed the two fighters and hauled them to their feet.

Wow! I thought when I saw him lift the two of them right off the ground. *That guy is really strong.*

"Stop!" he said. Then he gave them each a shake and set them back down on their feet.

"Peter started it," said Duncan.

He's such a creep he probably didn't even know he was lying.

Peter wiped the back of his hand across his mouth. "I did not," he said sullenly.

I could see that his hand was trembling.

"No more," said the tall man, as if he really didn't care who started it. "Do you understand?"

"Yes, sir," mumbled Peter. I wanted to shake him. He made it sound as if the whole thing had been his fault.

"Do you understand?" said the tall man again, looking directly at Duncan.

"Sure," said Duncan. "I got it."

"Good," said the tall man. Then he turned on his heel and marched back into the school.

Duncan made a face at the man's back, then wandered off to find someone else to pick on.

"Who was that?" asked Peter as I handed him his soggy book.

"Who knows? I never saw him before. He's probably a new sub. Come on—let's go inside."

Peter and I were usually the first ones into school—but not by much. Our whole class went in early. That's because our teacher, Ms. Marie Schwartz, was so totally great. The thing I liked best about having her was that she was the only teacher in Kennituck Falls Elementary who always did a play with her class. I've always wanted to be an actress when I grow up. But until sixth grade, I had never had a chance to find out what it was like to be onstage. The play would be our last major project, and we had planned to start rehearsals right after spring vacation.

Unfortunately, when we got to our room, Ms. Schwartz was nowhere to be seen. The tall blond man was standing beside her desk, talking to a short, red-faced man who had almost no hair—our school principal, Dr. Bleekman.

Where was Ms. Schwartz?

Peter and I went to our desks. I wasn't happy. I had a bad feeling about this whole thing.

"The sub is handsome," whispered Stacy, who had come in behind us.

"I suppose so," I said grudgingly. "Where do you suppose Ms. Schwartz is?"

Stacy shrugged. "Maybe she's sick. Or maybe her plane didn't make it back on time. That happened to my third-grade teacher once."

I nodded. That was OK. It was disappointing to come back to someone besides Ms. Schwartz, but I could cope with it for a day or two.

The other kids came into the room. Because Dr. Bleekman was there, everyone was super quiet. The bell rang, and we took our places.

"Good morning, class," said Dr. Bleekman. "I want to introduce Mr. John Smith. Mr. Smith will be your teacher for the rest of the year."

The rest of the year! I couldn't believe my ears!

What happened to Ms. Schwartz?

Without intending to, I asked the question out loud.

CHAPTER TWO
NOTE OF DOOM

Dr. Bleekman glared at me. "Susan, if you have something to say, I expect you to raise your hand."

Well, ex-cuuuuse me! I thought. But there was no sense in making things worse than they already were, so I raised my hand. When Dr. Bleekman pointed at me I said—as politely as I could—"What happened to Ms. Schwartz?"

"That is a private matter," replied Dr. Bleekman.

What was that supposed to mean? Was she pregnant? Did she have some horrible disease? Did she get fired? And *whatever* it was, why hadn't she warned us? Why hadn't she said good-bye?

Without thinking about what I was doing, I stood up and said, "I want to know where she is!"

Dr. Bleekman looked at me in surprise. His cheeks got redder. "Do you know the meaning of the word *private*, Miss Simmons?" he asked.

"Yes, sir," I said quietly and slipped back into my seat. While I sat there, fuming, Dr. Bleekman blathered on about how he expected us to behave for our new teacher. Then he turned us over to Mr. Smith and left the room.

As I watched him go, I wondered if Dr. Bleekman had secretly fired Ms. Schwartz. I had always suspected he didn't like her—mostly because she didn't do things "by the book." I had heard them arguing about it once when I came back to school to get some papers I had left behind.

"Ms. Schwartz, I must ask you to show more respect for the curriculum," Dr. Bleekman had been saying when I walked into the room.

Boy, did that set Ms. Schwartz off. "Can't you respect the fact that the kids are learning?" she asked angrily. She grabbed the sides of her head in frustration. Clumps of her frizzy black hair stuck out between her fingers. "Listen, Horace. The kids will get more out of six weeks of doing a play than six months of dittos and workbooks."

Suddenly I wondered if having Mr. Smith meant that we wouldn't be doing our play.

I began waving my hand in the air again.

"Yes, Miss Simmons?" asked Mr. Smith.

Miss Simmons again. Were we going to have to talk like that for the rest of the year?

"Are we still going to do our play?" I asked.

Mr. Smith lifted one blond eyebrow in astonishment. "Play?" he said. "Of course we're not going to do a play. We're here to work!"

I sank back into my seat. Sixth grade was going bad faster than a dead fish on a hot day.

I could hear the other kids start to murmur their protests. Mr. Smith slapped his ruler against his desk.

"Dr. Bleekman hired me to straighten this class out. I can see now that what he told me about you was correct. Things have gotten completely out of control in this room."

Actually, that was only half true. Our room wasn't

out of control; it just wasn't under Dr. Bleekman's thumb. Since most of us had already spent five years in rooms where the teachers did things Dr. Bleekman's way, we knew very well what he wanted a room to be like.

No question about it: Ms. Schwartz's room didn't fit the bill. But as far as we were concerned, things were going just fine. And not just because we were having a good time. We were also *learning* more than we ever had before.

My father claimed we were learning and having a good time for the same reason—Ms. Schwartz knew how to make things interesting.

For example, on the first day of school Ms. Schwartz stood at the front of the room and held up the sixth-grade reading book, *Rockets and Flags* (popularly known as *Rodents and Fleas*).

"This," she said, "is not a good book." She held it away from her with two fingers, like a soggy tissue, and dropped it into the bottom drawer of her desk. "I know a better one," she said. "In fact, I know hundreds." Then she pulled a huge cardboard box from under her desk and started passing around stacks of paperback novels for us to choose from.

We spent the rest of the year reading real books Sometimes we all read the same one, sometimes we all read something different. I remember mornings when we spent the entire reading period arguing about what some character should have done. Kids who had never liked reading before were really getting into it.

Unfortunately, Mr. Smith didn't believe in that kind of thing. In fact, the first thing he did after taking attendance that morning was pass out copies of *Rockets and Flags*.

Ms. Schwartz always read out loud to us, sometimes twice a day. She read wonderful books like *The Hobbit* and *The Sword in the Stone.*

When someone asked Mr. Smith if he was going to read out loud, he gave him a funny look and said it was "a waste of time."

Well, you get the picture. Over the next few weeks Mr. Smith straightened us out all right. But you know how boring a straight line is. We had no more surprises. We pretty much stopped laughing in school. Things weren't terrible—just awfully grim.

Even the playground wasn't so much fun as it had been. Oh, Mr. Smith did keep Duncan Dougal from beating kids up. But he almost went nuts the first time he caught one of us playing a radio. Radios and music players were banned from the playground. Mr. Smith didn't just hate rock music; he hated all music! I could see him shiver every time I picked up my piccolo and left the room for my music lesson.

After the third week of this I said something about it to my music teacher, Mr. Bam-Boom Bamwick. (Actually, his first name is Milton. But everyone calls him Bam-Boom because of his preference for thundering marches.)

Mr. Bamwick sighed. "Susan, you have to understand that not everyone appreciates the finer things in life," he said.

I guess that was as much support as I could expect. You know how teachers stick together.

When I got back to the room that day, it was time for our math test. I finished the test early. I was still feeling cranky about Mr. Smith's reaction to my piccolo, so I decided to write a note about it to Stacy.

"Mr. Smith is a total creepazoid," I wrote. That felt so good I decided to keep going. "He has totally ruined this class. Our whole year has gone down the tubes. The man is a total philistine!"

Philistine was a word I had just learned from my father. It means someone who has no appreciation for art and beauty. I thought it was a neat word, and I was using it every chance I could get.

A few more sentences and I was really wound up. This note was turning into a humdinger! At the bottom I drew an extra-tall, extra-skinny Mr. Smith holding his ears while I played the piccolo.

It wasn't a very nice picture. But when I was all done I felt better. I slipped the note under my test and waited for a chance to pass it to Stacy. I began thinking about how she'd react to my picture. I imagined her laughing so hard she fell off her chair.

Unfortunately, while I was daydreaming, Mr. Smith started collecting our papers. By the time I saw him walking up my row, it was too late to move the note. As I watched in horror, he snatched up my test—and my note along with it.

A wave of terror washed over me. I watched Mr. Smith walk away with my nasty note.

I closed my eyes and swallowed.

I was doomed.

CHAPTER THREE

AN UNEARTHLY NOISE

The only thing I could think about for the rest of the day was how I was going to get that note back!

When we went outside for recess, I pulled Stacy aside to tell her what had happened.

"What am I going to do?" I wailed.

"I don't know," she said. "But you'd better do something because if that note has my name on it, Mr. Smith will get mad at me, too."

"Maybe he won't see it," I said.

Stacy snorted. "Are you kidding? He's checked every single paper we ever handed in."

Stacy was right. She always was when it came to that kind of stuff.

Actually, the heavy-duty checking was probably the best thing about Mr. Smith: he always handed back our papers. Of course, they never had a note or comment on them, just lots of red circles around the mistakes and a grade at the top. I didn't mind that on math papers, but it really annoyed me when it came to my writing. When Ms. Schwartz marked our stories and essays, she had always penciled in comments that showed she was paying attention to our ideas.

When Mr. Smith handed back an essay, it looked as though he'd been sitting next to an ax murderer while he was marking it. The man must have bought red pens by the case. But all he used them for was to circle missing commas and misspelled words. He treated our essays like spelling tests.

I ask you, what's the point of writing something if that's the only response you get?

Finally I decided to try to get back into the building to see if I could snatch my note while Mr. Smith was still outside. If it had been Ms. Schwartz, I would have just asked if I could go to the bathroom. But Mr. Smith didn't believe in letting you off the playground for such a frivolous reason. He said by the time you were in sixth grade, you should know enough to take care of things like that in advance. The first three days after Mr. Smith came we had a line of worried-looking kids standing at the door each time recess ended.

The second-best method for getting off the playground was getting sick.

"I'll see you inside," I said to Stacy. Then I clutched my stomach, squinched up my face, and staggered over to where Mr. Smith was standing.

Later, I remembered that he was looking straight at the sun. But right then I was too worried about the note to pay attention to the fact that what he was doing should have burned out his eyeballs.

"Unnnyh," I moaned, trying to sound pitiful.

Mr. Smith looked down at me. "Is something wrong, Miss Simmons?" he asked.

"I don't feel good," I said. "I want to see the nurse."

Mr. Smith hesitated, then looked at his watch. "It's time to go in now, anyway," he said. "Line up with the rest of us. You can see Mrs. Glacka after we get in."

Now what? If I claimed I was about to throw up, he'd probably let me go inside right away. But if he was bringing everyone else in anyway, I wouldn't have the time I needed to go through the papers and find the note.

"All right," I moaned, trying to sound pitiful. I hoped it would make him feel guilty. I almost wished I *was* going to throw up. I'd make sure to hit his shoes!

Of course, once we were inside, I had to go to the nurse's office—even though I actually felt perfectly fine. Mrs. Glacka told me to lie down. I wasn't surprised. That was her basic cure for everything. So I lay there, staring at the ceiling and worrying about that note.

Finally I decided to follow Mr. Smith home. Maybe I could find some way to get the note back before it was too late. I didn't have any big plan, mind you. I was just desperate.

I wasn't sure where Mr. Smith lived. But I figured it couldn't be too far, since he always walked to school. So after the last bell I hung around on the playground, waiting for Mr. Smith to come out of the building.

I was concentrating so hard I almost jumped out of my skin when Peter Thompson came up behind me and said, "Hey, Susan, what are you doing?"

"None of your business!" I hissed. "Leave me alone!"

Peter's skinny face kind of crumpled, and he looked like he was going to cry.

"Look," I said. "This is private, OK?"

"Sure," said Peter. "I won't bother you." He tucked his book under his arm and walked away, trying to whistle. It was a pretty pathetic sound. I thought about Peter and realized with a shock that I was probably the closest thing he had to a friend.

That made me kind of sad. Not that there's any thing wrong with having me for a friend. But I've got a lot of friends, and I didn't really think of Peter as being one of them. I liked him all right. He just wasn't someone I spent much time with.

I wondered if there was anyone who did spend time with him.

My thoughts were interrupted when I saw Mr. Smith come out of the building. I waited for a minute or two, then began sneaking along behind him. I tried to stay a half a block or so away. When ever I could, I ducked behind a tree or a bush so he wouldn't spot me. I probably looked pretty weird. But that's one nice thing about being a kid: you can get away with this kind of stuff.

Mr. Smith's home was farther away than I had expected. He lived at the edge of town, in an old white house with black shutters. The house was set way back from the street. A thick hedge completely surrounded the lot on which it stood.

I stood outside the hedge feeling stupid. What had I hoped to accomplish by following Mr. Smith?

But I was in luck. As I watched from a hole in the hedge, I saw Mr. Smith set his briefcase down on the porch and go inside. Since it was a warm afternoon, I figured he planned to get something to drink, then come back outside to sit on the porch and correct our papers.

This was my chance! I scooted through a hole in the hedge and onto the porch. I was working up the nerve to open the briefcase when I heard an unearthly howl. It sounded like someone was trying to put a cat in a blender.

Hot as it was, I felt my blood turn to ice. What was going on in there? Had someone attacked Mr. Smith? I wasn't crazy about the man, but I didn't want him to be tortured or anything, which is what this sounded like.

Should I run for help, or go inside?

But what kind of help could I get? All I could say was that I had heard a terrible noise. Nobody was yelling for help, or anything like that.

I didn't think I could get anyone to come.

Then it occurred to me that maybe Mr. Smith really was putting a cat in a blender, or something awful like that. If so, he certainly shouldn't be teaching our class.

I decided to find out.

CHAPTER FOUR

BROXHOLM

The door was unlocked. Trying not to make any noise, I turned the knob and pushed.

The door opened without a sound. I hesitated for just a moment, then stepped in.

I was standing in a hallway. To my left I saw an empty living room—and I do mean empty. Except for curtains, there wasn't one bit of furniture or decoration in the room. The walls and floor were totally bare.

I flinched as another burst of horrible squawking and growling sounded above me.

Taking a deep breath, I began to tiptoe up the stairs. I was glad I was wearing sneakers.

About halfway up I stopped and thought, *What am I doing? I should get out of here while I can!*

You may not believe this, but the only reason I didn't turn back was that I thought Mr. Smith might really be in trouble. Even though I didn't like the man, I didn't want anything horrible to happen to him.

So I swallowed and took another step.

The noise stopped. Was everything over? Would Mr. Smith start down the stairs and find me standing here? I was just about to turn and run when another round of squawking and shrieking made it clear that whatever was happening was still going on.

I still *wanted* to run, but I was afraid to—afraid that if I did, I might read in the paper the next day that something terrible had happened to Mr. Smith. Something I could have prevented. Of course, I was afraid to keep going, but I decided I didn't have any choice. I took another step and then another. I held on to the railing as if it was a life line. The knot in my stomach got tighter with every step I took.

When I got near the top, I lay down on my stomach. I had read somewhere that when you're peering around a comer, you're less likely to be seen if your head is low. So I kept my head as low as *possible.* If I could have pulled out one eye and just stuck it around the corner to take a peek, that would have been fine with me.

The hall was as empty as the living room: no pictures on the walls, no rug on the floor. Through an open door at the end of the hall I could see a small, blue bathroom.

Closer to me, on the right, was another open door. The horrible sound seemed to be coming from there.

I decided low was the way to go. Still on my belly, I slithered down one side of the hall until I had reached the doorway.

I shivered. That noise was like a tiger running its claws down a blackboard; it felt like aluminum foil against my teeth. What could be making it?

When I finally got up the nerve to sneak a look around the bottom edge of the door, I saw Mr. Smith sitting at a little makeup table, looking in a mirror. Stacy was right. The man really was handsome. He had a long, lean face with a square jaw, a straight nose, and cheekbones to die for.

Only it was a fake. As I watched, Mr. Smith pressed his fingers against the bottom of his eyes. Suddenly he ran his fingertips to the sides of his head, grabbed his ears, and started peeling off his face!

I gasped. Fortunately, the horrible noises coming from the room drowned it out. I wanted to get up and run, but I was too terrified to move.

I started to shake instead. Whatever Mr. Smith was, I was pretty sure the face he was slowly uncovering wasn't anything that had been born on Earth! As he stripped away the mask I could see that he had skin the color of limes. His enormous orange eyes slanted up and away from his nose like a pair of butterfly wings. A series of muscular-looking ridges stretched from his eyes down to his lipless mouth.

Soon the handsome face of "Mr. Smith" was lying on the dressing table. The creature that had been hidden underneath it began to massage his face—his real face. "Ahhh," he said. "What a relief!" He smiled at himself in the mirror, showing two rows of rounded purplish teeth.

I had noticed that the horrible noise was coming from a pair of flat pieces of plastic hanging on the wall. But it wasn't until Mr. Smith started "singing" along with the sound that I realized the plastic sheets were speakers. That hideous sound was music! Or at least what passed for music wherever my alien teacher had come from.

I was still trying to find the courage to start backing up when the alien turned down the music and flipped a switch on the table. The mirror began to shimmer. Suddenly the image of "Mr. Smith" was replaced by another alien face, this one just as horrible. Beyond the face I could see a big room, with other aliens bustling around. From the look of things, I figured this must be a spaceship.

The face in the mirror said something that sounded like "lgn rrzznyx iggn gnrrr." The words were low and growly.

"Broxholm reporting," said Mr. Smith.

The face in the mirror made some growly noises.

"It is good to hear our mother tongue," said Mr. Smith—or Broxholm—or whatever his name was. "I cannot wait to return to the ship and have this language implant removed, so I can speak the true tongue, and not this barbaric garble."

Hey! I thought. *Whose language are you calling barbaric!*

But before I could get too angry, I heard something else—something that sent a cold chill down my spine.

"The testing process is proceeding on schedule," said Broxholm. "Before long I will have selected the students I wish to bring back for study."

Bring back for study?

I couldn't believe my ears. My teacher was an alien! Even worse, he had come to earth to kidnap kids and take them into space!

CHAPTER FIVE

HOW STRONG IS AN ALIEN'S NOSE?

The face on the screen smiled—at least, I think it smiled. It's hard to tell with someone who looks like that. Let's just say that all its teeth were showing. Then it made a long speech in that awful language. I felt like someone was grinding metal next to my ear.

I don't know what he said. But it made Broxholm/Smith laugh. Well, I suppose it was a laugh. His shoulders shook as if he was laughing. The sound made my stomach turn.

When Broxholm stopped laughing, or whatever, he reached down and turned off the screen. The other alien faded from view.

Time for me to get out of there! I slithered backward on my belly along the hall and then down the stairs. When I heard the alien music come on again, I relaxed a little.

On the porch I hesitated for a moment. Should I try to recover my note? A noise in the house made up my mind. Compared to what was behind me, any trouble I might get in because of that note was nothing. I jumped off the porch and ran all the way home, praying that Broxholm hadn't seen me.

Did you ever have something awful happen to you, and not really react to it until later? Like, you might almost get hit by a car on your way home from school, but not start shaking until after supper. It was like that with me that afternoon. It wasn't until I got home that what I had seen really began to sink in.

I ran up to my room, plowed my way through the mess, and collapsed on my bed. I lay there until supper, staring at the ceiling and shaking with fear. What was I going to do? What would *you* do, if you found out your teacher was an alien? Go to the principal? Tell your parents?

Think about it for a minute.

Imagine the conversation.

Not a pretty thought, is it?

The only person who might believe me was weird Peter Thompson. I decided to tell him what I had seen. If I couldn't convince him, I knew I didn't have a chance of convincing anyone.

I must have looked pretty bad when I went down to dinner because my mother asked me three times what was bothering me. But then, she tends to be a bit of a fusser. I try never to let her hear me sneeze, because if she does, she decides I've got pneumonia and tries to pack me into bed for a week. All right, that's a slight exaggeration—but not much. She and my dad are always battling about how much freedom they should give me.

"Come on, Margaret," my dad will say. "She's in sixth grade now. You can't treat her like a baby anymore."

"Oh, Edward," my mother will reply, "you seem to think you can treat Susan the same way you would a boy."

Can you believe she actually says that?

Anyway, that night at supper she put her hand on my forehead and clucked about how pale I looked. I think she was actually disappointed that I didn't have a fever. At least then she would have known what to do.

"Are you still upset about Ms. Schwartz, Susan?" she asked, shoveling a load of broccoli onto my plate.

Actually, at the moment I was upset about the broccoli. But Ms. Schwartz was a close second. I nodded weakly.

"Well, I can tell you it wasn't Dr. Bleekman's fault," she said. "In fact, he's very upset that Ms. Schwartz didn't give him more notice. I talked to Helen. She told me Ms. Schwartz didn't even have the courtesy to tell Dr. Bleekman face-to-face that she was leaving. He got a letter the first day of vacation, saying she wouldn't be back. That left him six days to find someone to take her place. I think he did very well to find that handsome Mr. Smith in such a short period of time."

"Mr. Smith is ruining our class," I said bleakly.

"Oh, don't be so dramatic, Susan," said Mom.

I'm planning to be an actress when I grow up.

What should I be? Athletic? Besides, this so-called teacher was going to kidnap some of my classmates and drag them off to outer space. Suddenly I realized that I had been putting off the truth. He wasn't going to kidnap some of my classmates. If he was going to pick *someone* from my class, I might well be on his list. In fact, after he read that note, I might be his number-one prospect.

I swallowed hard. I was dying to tell my folks what I had learned, but I knew they wouldn't believe me.

That night I tried to call Peter. But I couldn't get any answer at his house. "Come on, Peter," I hissed at the phone. "Where are you? I need you!"

I let it ring fifteen times.

No answer.

I tried again an hour later.

No answer.

I was as nervous as a marshmallow at a bonfire. It was even worse when I had to go to school the next morning. I didn't think Broxholm knew I had been in his house. But what if I had left behind some kind of clue? Or what if he had some kind of alien supersenses that would let him know I had been there?

What about that weird, muscular nose? Just how powerful *was* his sense of smell? Would he know I had been snooping by my odor? I watched his nose carefully when I walked through the classroom door that morning. It didn't twitch or anything. But that didn't mean much. Maybe underneath that mask his real nose had sniffed me out. Maybe it was sending him a message even now. There she is. *That's the one who was in the house yesterday!*

I sat down. I was so tense I felt as if I would explode if anyone so much as touched me. I wanted to pass Peter a note asking him to meet me on the playground at recess. But I was in enough trouble because of notes already.

We stood up and said the Pledge of Allegiance. Then Smith/Broxholm motioned me to his desk.

"I think you lost something yesterday," he said.

And then he handed me my note.

CHAPTER SIX

DRAFTING PETER

I sat at my desk and stared at the note. What was going on here? Was Broxholm playing with me?

For a moment the thought that he was actually being a nice guy crossed my mind. I brushed it away. Nice guys don't kidnap sixth graders and drag them into outer space. I decided it was more likely he was just sending me a message. *I've got your number, kid. Don't mess with me.*

I was so wrapped up in trying to figure out what was going on that I could barely concentrate on my work. Most of the time I just sat and stared at

Broxholm's face, trying to figure out how the mask was attached.

When I started to wonder if there was any way I could pull it off, my imagination began cooking up a horrifying scene. In this daydream, I saw myself grab Broxholm's ears and begin pulling on them, trying to unmask him. Only the mask wouldn't come off. So I pulled harder. Suddenly his face began to stretch and twist all out of shape. But still the mask wouldn't come off.

It was gross.

Stop it! I told my brain firmly.

But the vision kept coming back.

Sometimes I wonder about my brain; I mean, it seems to have a mind of its own. If it was really *my* brain, you'd think I would have a little more control over it, wouldn't you?

When you get right down to it, brains are pretty weird.

But not as weird as having an alien for a teacher. By the middle of the morning, I was beginning to wonder if this whole alien business had been a bad dream. It seemed too impossible to believe.

But I knew I hadn't been dreaming. It *was* real. My teacher was an alien.

I couldn't wait to get Peter aside so I could talk to him.

When recess came, I tried to act calm as I wandered over to the wall where Peter usually sat to read. He was sitting on the ground, cross-legged, clutching a book called *A Princess of Mars* in his skinny hands.

I slid down the wall and sat beside him.

He acted as if he didn't notice me. Or maybe he really didn't. He was one of those kids who could get so wrapped up in a book it would take a bomb to break his attention.

I hated to interrupt him. Peter always seemed a little unhappy to me, like he understood that he just didn't fit in with the rest of us. The only thing I knew that made him happy was reading science fiction. He always had a book hidden behind his school book. The neat thing was, it didn't make any difference, because he was so bright that whenever the teacher asked him a question, he always knew the answer. I could never figure out why they wouldn't just leave him alone and let him read. But that's the way school is, I guess.

"So, what's going on?" I said.

What a stupid line! I'm glad I'm a girl, because when I get older the *guys* are going to have to come up with lines when they want to start a conversation. Now there's one job I'll be glad to let them have!

Peter lifted his nose out of the book and looked at me as if I were the alien. He blinked, and I realized he was trying to come back to the real world. I felt bad for interrupting him. In class he had to read with one eye on the teacher. Out here he probably planned on shutting everything out for a while.

I hesitated for a minute. How was I going to say this?

Finally I just decided to jump right in. "I need your help," I said.

Peter looked surprised. "For what?" he asked.

I realized I hadn't jumped in after all. The biggie was still to come.

"Promise you won't laugh at me?" I asked.

Peter shrugged. "Sure, I promise."

"All right, listen. I know you're not going to believe this, but I found out something awful yesterday. Mr. Smith is an alien. He's come here to kidnap a bunch of kids and take them back to outer space."

I held my breath to see what Peter would say. I thought he might laugh, or tell me to get lost, or—and this thought really scared me—shout it out to everyone else. To my astonishment, he didn't do any of those things. He just looked as if he was going to cry.

"What's the matter?" I asked.

"You should know," he said. He sniffed and wiped the back of his hand across his nose.

What was going on here? I had a sudden thought that maybe he was an alien, too. That was stupid, of course. But I had aliens on the brain, and I couldn't figure out what else it might be.

"I *don't* know," I said. "Honest I don't."

He looked at me, and his eyes were so sad they made me want to cry, too.

"I always thought you were the one kid in this class who was on my side," he said. "Like that time you tried to stop Duncan when he was beating me up. I *expect* everyone else to tease me. I just never thought *you* would do it."

Now it was my turn to be mad. "I'm not teasing!" I yelled. Then I lowered my voice. "I'm not teasing!" I hissed. "I'm serious."

Peter stared at me. "Is this some kind of game?" he asked.

I hesitated. If I told him the truth, he probably wouldn't believe me. If I told him it was a game, he might at least help me think things through.

What a fix! The only way I could get him to believe me was to lie to him.

"Yeah," I said. "I thought you were the one guy in this class with enough imagination to play. But now you've ruined it."

"No!" said Peter. "No, we can still play. Just pretend you had to tell me it was a game to get me to believe you."

My head was starting to spin. Peter was using my reason for lying as a reason to pretend that what he believed was a game was for real. Or something like that. This was getting too complicated for me.

This is going to be one of those weeks. I thought. *The*

only person I can count on for help stopping an alien invasion thinks the whole thing is a game!

Well, as my grandmother always says, you make do with what you've got.

And Peter was what I had. I decided to stop worrying about who was believing what and just tell him what had happened.

"Well?" I said when I was done. "What do you think we should do?"

Peter stared at the sky for a minute. He rubbed his chin as if he was thinking really hard.

Then he gave me his answer.

"We've got no choice," he said. "We'll have to break into Broxholm's house to look for evidence."

CHAPTER SEVEN

NIGHT EXPEDITION

Peter was right, of course. That was the worst thing about it.

And what did I say? Now that I had someone who was willing to help me and had actually given me some good advice, did I say, "Thank you very much?"

Are you kidding? I looked at him and said, "You have got to be out of your mind!"

"I am not!" said Peter indignantly. "If we're going to do anything about Broxholm we have to have proof. And the only way to get proof is to get into his house and find some."

I thought about that. I couldn't come up with any way around it. How else could we find proof that we were telling the truth?

Then I thought of something else. "I don't think it will do any good," I said. "There's not much in there. He doesn't have any furniture or anything."

"How do you know that?"

"I told you, I was in there yesterday."

"Oh, yeah," said Peter. "I forgot."

I could tell he still thought I was making this up.

"Did you see the whole place?" he asked.

I shook my head.

"Well, maybe there's something in his bedroom," he said. "Or the attic. Or the kitchen." His face lit up. "That's it!" he said. "The *kitchen*. Who knows what they eat on the planet he comes from? I bet we'll find all kinds of gross alien slime in his refrigerator!"

"Peter, you're brilliant!" I said. I was actually starting to feel hopeful. All we needed was just one thing that would prove I wasn't making all this up.

"Now, when can we do it?" I asked. "We can't let him catch us!"

Peter thought for a minute. "There's a PTA meeting tomorrow night," he said. "I heard Dr. Bleekman say that all the teachers have to be there. That's the only time we can be sure Broxholm will be out of his house."

"Tomorrow it is," I said.

That was Wednesday. By the time Thursday afternoon rolled around, I was a wreck. I had spent two full days sitting in that classroom, staring at Mr. Smith and knowing his handsome face was only a mask—a mask that hid the terrifying face of an alien.

While none of the other kids were crazy about Mr. Smith, they didn't think there was anything really wrong with him. Only Peter knew the secret—and he thought it was a game I had invented. "What about Dr. Bleekman?" he said to me during afternoon recess.

"What about him?" I asked.

"Do you think he's in cahoots with Broxholm? They seem pretty chummy."

I shook my head. "My mother told me Dr. Bleekman was really angry with Ms. Schwartz for quitting so suddenly. He wouldn't have been upset if he'd been wanting to put Broxholm in her place."

Peter looked at me in astonishment. "Don't you know a cover story when you hear one?" he asked. "Of course he acted like he was upset! If he hadn't, it would have been suspicious. The way I figure it, Broxholm asked Dr. Bleekman which teacher he wanted to get rid of the most. Then he zapped Ms. Schwartz so there would be a spot for him to fill."

I felt like there were ants crawling on my skin. Peter was just playing a game. But what he said made sense—too much sense. I still couldn't believe that Ms. Schwartz had just quit without saying anything to us. Something must have happened to her.

My head was whirling. Was Dr. Bleekman really in on the whole thing? Had Broxholm really fried Ms. Schwartz? If so, what would happen if he caught Peter and me in his house? If Broxholm found some way to get himself excused and came home early to catch us rummaging through his house, would he zap us, too?

That last question really terrified me.

But if the ideas Peter was spinning out were true, it was more important than ever that we unmask Broxholm.

"How are you going to get out tonight?" I asked Peter.

"What do you mean?" he asked.

"What do you mean, what do I mean? How are you going to get out of your house tonight?"

I had no problem myself. My parents were officers in the PTA, and they always went to meetings. They had decided at the beginning of the year that I was too old for a baby-sitter, so as long as I was back before they got home, it wouldn't make any difference. I didn't really like sneaking out on them, but this was a matter of life and death.

Peter looked at me in surprise. "Are you really planning to break into Mr. Smith's house?" he asked.

"His name isn't Smith," I said. "It's Broxholm. And, yes, I'm really planning to *search* his house." (I couldn't bring myself to call it a break-in). "I have to have some way to prove what he really is."

Peter looked troubled. He rubbed his hands over

his skinny face. Then he looked me straight in the eye and said, "This isn't a game, is it?"

I shook my head.

Peter's eyes got wide. He swallowed a couple of times. Then he took a deep breath and said, "Don't worry, I'll be there."

I could have hugged him.

That night I met Peter at eight o'clock on the corner of Pine and Main. He was carrying a flashlight, which made me feel stupid, since I had forgotten mine. It was nearly dark. The crickets were singing, and the moon had already risen. Even though it was May, it was cold. Or maybe I was just cold because I was scared.

"Ready?" I asked.

Peter nodded. "Ready," he said.

We each took a deep breath.

Then we set off for the alien's house.

"I was afraid you might not come," I said after we had gone a few blocks.

Peter shrugged. "I didn't want you doing this alone," he said. "For a while I was afraid you were trying to pull a joke on me. I thought when I got to the corner, you and some of the others might jump out and start laughing at me."

"Hey!" I said. "I wouldn't do something like that!"

"I didn't think so," said Peter. "That was one reason I came. The other reason was, I figured if you really were going to break into Mr. Smith's house, this must be for real. You're not the kind of kid who would do something like that unless it was serious."

"Believe me," I said, "this is serious."

"I believe you," he said nervously.

We didn't say anything else until we got to Broxholm's house.

"Well," said Peter. "Here we are."

"Here we are," I echoed.

But neither of us moved. We just stood there looking at the dark empty house. I don't know about Peter, but I was trying to talk myself into taking the next step. To tell the truth, I was so scared I thought I might wet my pants.

CHAPTER EIGHT

THE ALIEN'S LAIR

I don't know how long we stood there, trying to build up enough courage to go in. I do remember looking up at the sky. It was as dark as black velvet, and the stars were like diamonds scattered across it.

Which one of them did you come from, Broxholm! I thought. *And why did you have to come here!*

I heard Peter sigh beside me. "Isn't it wonderful?" he asked, swinging his arm up and out to indicate the entire sky. "Don't you want to go there?"

"You've been reading too much science fiction," I said. "Come on—let's get this over with."

Sharp leaves scraped against our faces as we pushed our way through the hole in the hedge. On the other side we dropped to our hands and knees and crawled across the lawn. Even though we were pretty sure Broxholm wasn't home, we didn't want anyone else to see us and interrupt our mission. The lawn was drenched with dew. By the time we reached the porch the knees of my pants were soaked through and I was freezing.

"How are we going to get in?" whispered Peter.

Good question! It may sound stupid, but I had been so worried about *what* we were doing that I hadn't thought about *how* to do it.

"I don't know," I hissed back. "How do people usually break into places?"

Peter looked at me in disgust. "How would I know?" he asked. "I'm not a burglar."

"Well, neither am I!" I snapped.

I closed my eyes. Fighting wasn't going to get us anywhere. "Let's circle the house," I said. "Maybe we'll find an open window or something."

We crept along the side of the house. As Peter played his flashlight over the windows I felt thankful for the hedge that masked us from the street.

"Nothing on this side," he whispered.

"Check down low," I said. "Maybe one of the cellar windows is open."

But they were all sealed shut.

Peter gestured toward the back of the house. Just around the back corner we found one of those slanting cellar doors. It was padlocked shut.

But the wood was half-rotted, and when Peter shook the lock, the whole thing came loose in his hand. He set it aside and carefully lifted the door. It creaked for an eternity as it came open. I found myself staring down into a well of perfect blackness.

"Dark," I whispered.

"Sure is," said Peter.

Then he took a step forward.

I followed him, wondering if Broxholm had booby-trapped the place. Then I wondered what kind of booby traps an alien would use: lasers that would cut us off at the knees? Stun guns? Freeze rays? Hey, these guys had come here from another star system. Who knew what they could do?

We walked down eight concrete steps. At the bottom we came to a wooden door so old it had a latch instead of a knob. Peter lifted the latch and pushed. Nothing. He put his shoulder against the door and shoved again. It swung open with an eerie creak.

"After you, madam," he whispered.

"Well, at least shine your flashlight in there," I hissed.

He pointed his beam through the door. I couldn't see anything special—just a dusty cellar, the kind you'd expect in an old house.

"Let's go together," I whispered.

Peter took pity on me, and we stepped through the door side by side.

"I don't think we're going to find anything down here," he said, shining his light around the cellar.

I agreed. Except for the furnace, the stairs up to the first floor, and the cobwebs, the space was completely empty.

Without speaking, he headed for the stairway. I ran into a cobweb. I shivered when the wispy, clinging threads brushed over my forehead.

"You don't suppose Broxholm has any friends here, do you?" whispered Peter when we were about halfway up the stairs.

I stopped. "I don't think so," I said after a minute. "He didn't mention any when he was talking to the guy in the spaceship."

Peter nodded. But he had managed to make me even more nervous than I had been to begin with. What if there *was* another alien here? What would he do if he caught us snooping around?

"Where to?" asked Peter when we reached the top of the stairs.

"Let's try the kitchen," I said, remembering his idea about alien food.

But when we opened the refrigerator, all we saw were a bunch of cold cuts, a half-empty carton of milk, a bottle of catsup, and two six-packs of beer.

"He sure doesn't eat like an alien," said Peter. "Are you sure this guy is from another planet?"

"Let's go upstairs," I said. "I'll show you the thing I saw him talking into."

Peter closed the refrigerator door. But before

he would leave the room he insisted on checking the cupboards. He even opened the peanut-butter jar to see if it really had peanut butter in it, and not some kind of extraterrestrial goo.

The second floor had three rooms. I had high hopes for the bathroom; I thought we might find some sort of weird shampoo there or something.

But it was as disappointing as the kitchen. Even the medicine cabinet was filled with typical brand-name items.

"Do you think Mr. Smith really uses Excedrin?" asked Peter. "Or is this just here to convince people he's a teacher?"

"If he was stocking his house to fool snoopers, he'd have put in some furniture," I said.

The only place where we found anything even remotely alien was the room where I had seen Broxholm talking to the man on the ship. The two speakers that looked like pieces of flat plastic were still hanging on the wall. I looked under the dressing table, and found the switch Broxholm had used to tune in his ship. I reached out to touch it, then pulled my hand back. What if I somehow turned it on and the man from the ship saw Peter and me standing there?

"Come on," said Peter. "We might as well go."

"You don't believe me anymore, do you?" I asked sadly.

Peter shrugged. "This place is kind of weird, what with no furniture and everything. But there's nothing that would make anyone think Mr. Smith is an alien. I believe that you believe what you told me. But whether it's true or not . . ." He shrugged and turned to leave the room.

"Wait," I said, following him into the hall. "We still didn't try that door."

Peter swung his flashlight in the direction I was pointing.

"It's just the attic," he said.

I knew that; I could tell by how narrow the door was. But that wasn't the point.

"So what if it's the attic?" I said. "Maybe Broxholm has something packed away up there. Come on, Peter. We've gone this far. We can't give up now."

"Oh, all right," said Peter. He opened the door and started up the stairway. When he got about halfway up the stairs his head passed the level of the attic floor. I was walking so close that I bumped into him when he stopped.

"What is it?" I whispered.

When he didn't answer me, I pushed my way up beside him and cried out in horror.

CHAPTER NINE

THE FORCE FIELD IN THE ATTIC

For a long time neither of us said a word.

"Is she alive?" I asked at last.

Peter didn't answer me.

"Peter," I hissed, pinching his arm. "Do you think she's alive?"

Peter turned to me. I could see his face in the blue glow that came from the thing in the center of the attic. His eyes were glazed and blank. I wasn't sure whether he even knew I was there.

"Peter!" I hissed.

He shook his head. "You weren't kidding, were you?"

"Of course I wasn't kidding!"

"But do you know what this means?"

"Yeah. It means we're in big trouble. Now let's get up there and see if we can figure out what's going on."

"An alien!" said Peter, his voice filled with awe. "Mr. Smith is an alien! We're not alone!"

"What are you talking about?" I hissed.

"Intelligent aliens. Mankind is not alone in the universe."

"Well, I'm feeling pretty alone right now," I said. "Are you going to help me or not?"

Peter closed his eyes and rubbed his face. Suddenly his awe turned to fear. "Oh, my God," he said. "What if Mr. Smith catches us here?"

I rolled my eyes. "Why do you think I've been so scared all night, you yo-yo?"

Suddenly I realized what was going on. "You never did believe me, did you?" I said angrily. "You thought this was all just a joke!"

Peter shook his head. "I believed you," he said. "But I didn't really understand what it meant until—well, until I believed it this way." He shrugged helplessly. "I can't explain it," he said.

It didn't make any difference. I understood. He was feeling the way I felt when I saw Broxholm take his face off.

"Come on," I said. "Let's get up there." Despite my brave words, I climbed the rest of those stairs pretty slowly. Peter climbed up beside me. Standing side by side, we stared at the terrible thing we had found.

In the center of the attic was a column of blue light. It was about three feet across, and stretched from the floor to the peak of the ceiling. And in the center of it stood—Ms. Schwartz. Her eyes were wide open, but they hadn't blinked once in all the time we had been looking at her. Her frizzy black hair was standing straight out from her head, as if she was getting some kind of horrible shock. Her hands were at her sides, palms forward, fingers separated.

I looked carefully, but I couldn't tell if she was breathing.

"Is she alive?" I asked again.

"I don't know," said Peter. "It's hard to tell."

We stepped forward. Ms. Schwartz didn't move. The air smelled funny. My hair started to move by itself. I could feel a strange tingling on my skin.

"It's a force field," said Peter, taking another step forward.

I *knew* he was the right person to bring with me. Only a person who read that much science fiction would know what to call something like this. Now if he only knew what to do about it!

Unfortunately, he didn't.

"If I could figure out where it came from, maybe I could turn it off" he told me. "But I don't see any equipment. Besides, I'd be afraid of hurting Ms. Schwartz."

I nodded. "Do you think she's OK in there?" I asked, blinking back a tear.

How had Broxholm done this to her?

Maybe the handsome creep had tricked her into going out on a date with him. What a treat—a date with an alien. I could just imagine his line: *Let's go see a film. Then I'll take you back to my house and lock you in a force field.*

What a rat!

"Oh, Ms. Schwartz," I moaned. "What are we going to do?"

I couldn't stand seeing her trapped like that. I

stepped forward and tried to reach out to touch her.

"Don't!" cried Peter, when he saw what I was doing. But it was too late. I had already laid my hands against the blue light. I felt a tingle run through my body. For a terrible instant I thought I was going to be drawn into the force field, too. But it didn't happen.

What did happen was I heard a voice inside my head. *Susan, don't worry about me. You've got to warn the others!*

It was Ms. Schwartz.

"Peter!" I yelled. "Come here. Touch the force field. You can hear Ms. Schwartz!"

I suppose it sounded crazy. But by this time he was ready to believe anything. He pushed through the heavy air that surrounded the force field and put his hands next to mine on the column of light.

Hello, Peter, said Ms. Schwartz.

"Telepathy!" whispered Peter in awe. "These guys are amazing."

Yes, they are, said Ms. Schwartz inside our heads. *Amazing, and dangerous.*

"What do they want?" I asked.

You! she said.

I yelled and jumped back from the force field. The air around me felt so thick. It was hard to move through it. I realized I had lost my connection with Ms. Schwartz. Pushing forward, I pressed my hands back against the force field.

I'm sorry, said Ms. Schwartz. *I didn't mean to frighten you.*

I looked at her face. Her eyes were staring straight ahead. It was weird to hear her voice inside my head when she was standing there like that, looking as if she had been frozen.

Don't worry about me, she said. *Your job right now is to warn the others.*

"Warn them of what?" asked Peter.

About Broxholm! His mission here is to find five students to take back with him. He plans to select the best, the worst, and the three most average kids.

"What's he going to do with them?" I asked.

The voice inside my head sounded worried. *I don't know for sure. The plan is to bring them back here and head out into space on the night of May twenty-sixth.*

"But that's next week!" I cried.

Ms. Schwartz moaned. *I didn't know so much time*

had gone by, she whispered inside our heads. *I can't keep track inside here. Listen, you have to unmask him somehow. If you don't, you're all in terrible danger.*

Just then we heard the front door open and close.

Talk about terrible danger.

Broxholm was back!

CHAPTER TEN

SOLO EFFORT

My mouth went dry. My hands started shaking. Peter's eyes were so wide they looked like ping-pong balls.

Shhh! cautioned Ms. Schwartz. *Don't make a sound.*

I appreciated the advice, but I had already figured that much out on my own.

What are we going to do? I thought.

To my surprise, Ms. Schwartz answered me.

Wait till he reports in, she said. *Then you can sneak out.*

Did you just read my mind? I thought.

Just the message you sent me, she replied. That was

a relief! There's a lot going on inside my head that I don't want anyone to know about—not even Ms. Schwartz.

I looked around the attic. If Broxholm came up here, we were sunk. I couldn't see a single thing to hide behind.

Suddenly I heard that horrible music again.

"This is our chance," I whispered. "He must be in his dressing room. I bet he's taking off his face and getting ready to report to the ship."

"Then let's go," said Peter.

"Wait," I said desperately. "What about Ms. Schwartz? We can't leave her here like this!"

You have to, she thought at us. *I'm all right for the time being. The best thing you can do for me is unmask the alien.*

I still hesitated.

GO! she shouted inside my head. The message was so powerful I staggered back from the force field.

Casting a last look over my shoulder, I took Peter's hand. He didn't pull away. This wasn't romance, it was terror. Each of us needed someone to hold on to as we sneaked down the stairway.

When we reached the bottom, Peter opened the door as quietly as he could. The tiny click was lost in the awful screech of the alien music. Moving slowly, he peered around the edge. "No one in sight," he whispered.

"Then let's go!"

My heart was pounding in my ears. I don't think I've ever been so frightened in my life. I had a feeling Broxholm would jump out and grab us at any second. For one horrible instant I wondered if the mirror on his dressing table might be at the right angle to show our reflections as we stepped out of the attic. I imagined him racing into the hallway, his Mr. Smith face hanging down around his chin, ready to turn us into a pair of puddles on the floor—or whatever a person from his planet did to kids he caught snooping in his attic.

The screeching music continued.

Still moving slowly, Peter closed the door behind us. That seemed like a waste of time, until I realized he was afraid that if he didn't secure it, the door might swing open after he let go of it.

One noise like that and we were dead meat. Dropping to our hands and knees, we crawled along the edge of the wall. I couldn't help it—when I was opposite the door of Broxholm's room, I glanced in. Broxholm was sitting there, peeling off his face. I prayed that he wouldn't see me, and crept forward.

We slid down the stairs, slipped out the front door, and ran for all we were worth. After about three blocks we stopped to catch our breath. But not for long. In addition to everything else, I was worried that since Broxholm was back my parents might be home, too.

But when we reached my house I could see that I had made it back first. That wasn't too surprising. My folks often stayed to gab with the other parents after the formal meeting was over. It was even possible that the meeting was still going on, and Broxholm had managed to slip out early.

Peter walked me to my door. I thought that was brave of him—especially when I watched him walk off into the darkness and realized how frightened I would be if I had to go home alone. That skinny kid had more courage than anyone I knew.

As for me, I was terrified. I went around and turned on every light in the house. (Don't ask me what good I thought that would do. All I know is it made me *feel* better.) Then I sat in the living room, waiting for my parents to come home and worrying that Broxholm might show up first.

All in all, I decided it had been a good night's work. Even if I hadn't found anything to prove my story, at least one other person now knew what was going on. Even more important, we had found Ms. Schwartz.

But what should we do now?

The crucial thing was to reveal Broxholm for what he really was. But how could we do that without getting turned into puddles on the floor? Our only advantage was that he didn't know we knew his secret. If we could make whatever we did seem innocent, he might not guess what we were up to.

Of course, the most obvious thing was just to pull off his mask.

But how do you pull a mask off an alien's face?

I spent the whole night trying to find the courage to do what I knew I had to do the next day.

Mr. Bamwick had scheduled me for an extra lesson that morning. As usual, Smith/Broxholm shuddered when he saw me pick up my piccolo. Let him shudder! If he kidnapped me, maybe I'd play the piccolo all the way to the next galaxy.

The reason for the extra lesson was that Bam-Boom wanted me to work on a solo he had asked me to play for the spring concert. We were doing the greatest march of all time, "The Stars and Stripes Forever" by John Philip Sousa. (If you don't know it, you should go to your library and get a record of it so you can listen to it. It's great.) Anyway, the high-point of the march is this incredibly neat, incredibly difficult piccolo solo.

Mr. Bamwick had told me way back in February that he had wanted our band to do this march for seven years. He said he had just been waiting until he had a piccolo player good enough to handle the solo, and now he thought he had one. Me.

I was flattered that he had so much faith in me.

The problem was, I didn't have that much faith in me. Oh, I could do most of the solo right—most of the time. But there was one trill near the end that I always messed up. Let me tell you, if you're going to play something in concert, you don't want to get it almost right. You want it perfect.

But Mr. Bamwick was determined we would play "The Stars and Stripes Forever" that spring, or die trying. The way my lesson was going that Friday, it looked as if we were going to die.

"Come on, Susan," said Mr. Bamwick after I messed up for the third time. "The concert is next week! Did you practice last night?"

I shook my head. "I didn't have time," I said.

I knew it sounded pretty lame. But how could I tell him I hadn't practiced because I had been prowling through my teacher's house, trying to find evidence to prove he was an alien?

I could see Mr. Bamwick trying to control himself. I have to give him credit. He knows that it doesn't do any good to make a kid feel stupid. But I could tell he really wanted to explode. By the time I left his room, I was pretty upset myself.

That wasn't *all* bad. Being angry gave me the strength to do what I knew I had to do. Taking a deep breath, I marched back to my room. I paused outside the door and took another deep breath.

Then I went through the door, staggered over to Mr. Smith's desk, and pretended to faint.

On the way down, I grabbed for his ear.

CHAPTER ELEVEN

PARENT CONFERENCE

Failure! I had hoped to hit the floor with Mr. Smith's face in my hand and Broxholm's real mug exposed for all the world to see. Instead, I ended up with a handful of air and a bump on the head.

The other kids in the class shouted and jumped to their feet. Smith/Broxholm waved them away. He told Mike Foran to go get the nurse. Then he knelt over me to see if I was all right. He was acting so tender and concerned that I almost felt bad about trying to pull off his face. But all I had to do was think of Ms. Schwartz trapped in that force field in his attic, and any guilt I might have felt just floated right away.

"Susan! Susan, are you all right?" he asked, fanning my face.

I moaned and fluttered my eyes. "What—what happened?" I asked.

"You fainted," said Broxholm. He patted the side of his head. "Almost took my ear with you," he added. He gave me a cute little smile that showed the dimple in his right cheek.

Between the two of us, the air was thick with fake innocence. Was it really possible he didn't know what I was up to?

A minute later Mike came running back with Mrs. Glacka puffing along behind him. She checked my pulse, felt my forehead, and then helped me to her office to (surprise!) lie down.

She also decided to call my mother. This meant that I had to go home, and then to the doctor's, and then spend the rest of the afternoon in bed with my mother fussing and worrying.

She even decided that I had to spend the evening in bed, too, after she brought my supper to my room.

"Gracious, Susan," she said when she burst through

the door. "This place looks like an explosion at a garage sale. Can't you keep it a little neater?"

"I was planning to clean it today," I said. "Only I didn't feel up to it after I fainted."

"Poor baby," she said, setting the tray on my nightstand.

She seemed so pleased I decided not to tell her I had been kidding. She never could understand that I liked my room the way it was.

After supper I slipped out of bed and went to see my father.

He was sitting in his den, building a model of the Empire State Building out of toothpicks. That's his hobby—making famous buildings with toothpicks. If you ask me, it's pretty weird. But it keeps him happy, which is more than I can say for most adults I know. So I guess I shouldn't complain.

"Hi, Pook," he said when I walked in. "Feeling better?"

I nodded, not wanting to tell him I hadn't been feeling bad to begin with. I sat down next to him and started handing him toothpicks.

"So, what's on your pre-pubescent mind to night?"

he said, holding up a toothpick and dabbing a bit of glue onto the end of it.

"Dad!" I said. But that was all I could think of. I tried, but I just couldn't bring myself to explain the situation. After a full minute of silence he turned to me and said, "Are you all right, Susan?" I knew he was really concerned, because he let the glue on the end of his toothpick dry out while he was waiting for my answer.

"I'm fine," I said at last. "Well, not exactly fine. I've got a problem."

"What kind of problem?" he asked. He put down his toothpick and gave me his full attention.

This was terrible! Can you imagine trying to tell your father that your teacher is an alien? He was going to think I was out of my mind.

But I had to do something. So I took a deep breath and said, "It's about Mr. Smith."

He nodded, inviting me to continue.

Look, I tried. I really did.

But I just couldn't bring myself to say the words, "My teacher is an alien."

After a long, uncomfortable silence I finally said,

"I don't think he likes me very much."

Dad looked appropriately worried. "Why not?" he asked.

"Well, he shudders whenever he sees me go to my music lesson." I hoped that might sound weird enough to get him to ask another question.

Come on, Dad, help me! I thought. *Ask the right questions.*

But he just laughed. "As long as Mr. Smith doesn't actually say anything, I don't think you can complain too much," he said. "Maybe the guy just doesn't like music. Not everyone can be as cultured as we are, you know. He's probably just a philistine."

Yeah, I thought, *a Philistine—from the planet Philis!*

But all I said aloud was, "Yeah. A philistine."

Figuring he had solved my problem, Dad turned back to his toothpicks. "I wouldn't let it get to you, honey," he said. "The school year's almost over. You can tough it out till then. Now, you better scoot back to bed before your mother catches you out here."

I gave him a hug and trudged back to my room.

Now what? If I was going to do anything about this mess, I had to get some proof, and fast.

I was still trying to figure that all out when Peter called.

"Nice try today," he said. "You're really brave. I just hope Broxholm didn't figure out what you were up to."

Great! That was the last thing in the world I wanted to think about.

"I wasn't brave," I said. "Just desperate. What I want to know is what are we going to do next? We've got to find some way to prove the truth about Broxholm."

"Actually, that's why I'm calling," said Peter. "I wanted to know if you had a camera."

"Sure. Why?"

He hesitated, then said, "Well, are you game for another expedition into Broxholm's lair?"

I smiled for the first time that day. "So we can take a picture of Ms. Schwartz! Peter, you're brilliant. Only when can we be sure he won't be there?"

"How about during school?"

"Peter, I can't skip school! My mother would kill me!"

"Would you rather get kidnapped by aliens?" he asked.

I sighed. "All right. I'll bring my camera to school on Monday. We'll talk about it then."

I hung up and tried not to think about the fact that in two days, I was going to go back into the alien's den.

In fact, I spent most of that whole long, sleepless night trying not to think about it.

CHAPTER TWELVE
THINGS GET WEIRDER

I didn't think it was all that weird when Stacy Benoit called me Saturday morning to see how I was doing. After all, she's my friend, and she did think I had fainted in school the day before. I didn't realize when I laughed and told her there wasn't anything wrong with me that I was only confirming her worst fears.

I didn't figure *that* out until Monday morning, when our class turned into something from the Twilight Zone.

Until that point, I had other things to worry about—like what to do about Ms. Schwartz.

Since my mother still wouldn't let me out of the house, I spent a long time discussing this force field thing with Peter over the phone. He told me he was pretty sure Ms. Schwartz was actually safer inside that thing than she would be walking the streets.

"She probably doesn't like it in there," he said. "I know I wouldn't. But nothing's going to hurt her."

"Well, doesn't she have to eat or go to the bathroom, or something?" I asked nervously.

I could almost see Peter's shrug over the telephone line. "I don't think so," he said. "I have a feeling time is pretty much holding still inside that thing. So unless she had to go to the bathroom when he put her in there, she's probably fine." He paused, then added, "Come to think of it, that force field could be a woman's dream—she won't age a bit!"

"Don't be a male chauvinist piglet," I said angrily. "This is serious."

"I know it's serious," snapped Peter. "But we can't do anything about it this weekend—unless you know of a time when we can be sure that Broxholm won't be there."

"I suppose you're right," I said.

But the thought of Ms. Schwartz trapped in that force field gnawed away at me for all the rest of the day and all of Sunday, too. I had to get her out of there!

I was still stewing about that on Monday, until things got so weird that I forgot about Ms. Schwartz for a while.

It started with Duncan Dougal, who walked into class carrying the biggest apple I had ever seen in my life.

"Good morning, Mr. Smith," he said. "How are you today?" His voice was so syrupy-sweet it made me want to throw up.

I looked away, then looked back again so fast it put a crick in my neck. *Duncan?* I thought in astonishment.

The class bully put his apple on Mr. Smith's desk, then went to his own desk, sat down, and folded his hands neatly in front of him.

I squeezed my eyes shut and then opened them again to see if anything would change. But the apple was still there, and Duncan was still sitting at his desk, smiling like a little angel.

What was going on here?

When I opened my desk, I found a note that said, "I think you are the bravest person I have ever met." It was signed, "A friend."

Who had it come from? And why?

I looked around the room, but the others were all bent over their desks, working busily away.

I turned back to my work, trying to figure out what was going on. But even the weird stuff that had happened so far hadn't prepared me for what came next.

"You pig-faced baboon!" yelled a familiar voice.

Stacy? Stacy Benoit? The girl most likely to be declared a saint while still living?

I turned around and saw Stacy standing beside her desk, shouting at Mike Foran—the only kid I had ever heard of who had never, I mean NEVER, gotten in trouble with a teacher.

"Shut up!" yelled Mike. "Shut up, you creep!"

When Stacy slapped him across the face I almost fell out of my chair. Of course, Stacy couldn't slap that well, having never done it before. So it was kind of a wimpy little slap. But this was *Stacy Benoit,* for heaven's sakes.

"Stacy!" yelled Mr. Smith, who was sitting at the back of the room with a reading group. "Michael! What is going on up there?"

He started for the front of the room. But he was too late. When Stacy slapped Mike, he jumped up so fast he knocked his desk over. His face was red. I didn't realize until later it was from stage fright.

"You mother wears—uh, uh—your mother wears—"

I wanted to prompt him. It was pathetic to see the nicest kid in the class try to come up with a withering insult, and even more pathetic when he finally finished up with, "your mother wears polyester!"

But it seemed to do the trick. Stacy began to shriek in outrage.

Mr. Smith reached them just in time to keep them from going for each other's throats.

"The rest of you stay in your seats," he ordered. "I'll be back in a minute."

Then he walked out the door, dragging the

two best-behaved kids in sixth grade along with him. They were kicking and screaming every step of the way.

I closed my eyes and shook my head. I was sure I was awake. So what was going on? Was this the same planet I had gone to sleep on?

I couldn't wait for recess so I could talk to Peter.

CHAPTER THIRTEEN

RUMORS

"Stacy and Mike did a good job, didn't they?" said Peter, when we got together on the playground at recess.

"What are you talking about?" I asked.

"Stacy and Mike. Didn't you think that fight they put on was pretty good?"

"The fight they *put on?*" I echoed.

Peter sounded impatient. "Stacy and Mike are afraid Broxholm will decide one of them is the best kid in the class and then try to kidnap whichever one he chooses. So they decided to fake a fight—you know, mess up their reputations a little."

All of a sudden everything came clear. "That's why Duncan brought Mr. Smith an apple this morning!" I said.

Peter giggled. "Pathetic, isn't it? But it might work. Right now Duncan is a sure pick for worst kid in the class. But if he works really hard, he might actually manage to pull himself off the bottom of the list. Since he knows that no matter what he does, he's never going to push himself into the most average category, if he can improve at all, he's probably safe. The problem is, he's been so bad all year that it's going to take a major effort to get out of the bottom spot."

Peter paused, then added, "I intend to have some fun with him over the next three days."

Three days! That was all the time we had before Broxholm was scheduled to kidnap five of us into space.

"That's not very nice," I started to say.

But then I remembered the way Duncan had tormented Peter for the last six years. I decided I couldn't blame Peter if he wanted to get a little of his own back while he could. Any decision to be a nice guy about this was going to have to come from inside himself.

I decided to change the subject. "Tell me," I said. "Just how did they know about all this?"

"I told them," said Peter.

"And they believed you?"

Actually, it made sense. If they were going to believe anyone, it would be Peter. He had a reputation as being the most honest kid in the class, which was one of his problems. He didn't know how to tell the kind of "little white lies" that keep people from getting mad at you.

But I doubted that even his reputation for honesty would convince people this story was true.

Peter smiled. "Actually, you're the reason anyone believed me. It started with Stacy. She just didn't believe you had really fainted—or that if you had, you would have tried to grab the teacher's ear on the way down. So she knew something was going on. Later she cornered me on the playground and demanded to know what you were up to."

"Why you?" I asked.

Peter blushed. "You're going to hate this," he

said. "There's a rumor going around that you're my girlfriend because we've been spending so much time talking on the playground."

"Yuck!" I yelled. "Yuck! Yuck! Yuck!" Suddenly I realized what I had just done. "Don't take that personally," I said.

"I won't," said Peter. "Since I feel the same way."

Hey! I thought. What do you mean, you feel the same way?

But we didn't have time to work that out right then.

"Anyway," said Peter, "Stacy was convinced I must know what was going on. And since I did, I told her."

"The whole story?" I gasped.

Peter nodded. "She didn't believe me at first, of course. But when she talked to you on Saturday and you told her there was nothing actually wrong with you, she figured it must be true." He laughed. "That was all it took. By Saturday afternoon, the phone lines were humming all over Kennituck Falls."

"How come you know all this?" I asked. "How come no one asked me?"

Peter shrugged. "That's not the way rumors work.

People never check with the source. They always ask someone else. Don't ask me why, but it's true. Lots of stupid things are true. Anyway, Stacy told Mike, and Mike told someone else, and that was it. It's the kind of story that travels fast."

"And they all believe it?" I asked.

Peter shook his head. "I don't think so—at least not yet. Except for Duncan. He's so dim he'll believe anything—especially if Stacy and Mike believe it. He thinks they know everything. That's why he hates them so much."

"I see," I said, though some of this was coming a little too fast for me. "Well, do you suppose if enough of us start to believe it, the adults will pay any attention to us?"

Peter looked as if I had just suggested Mickey Mouse was likely to be the next president of the United States. "Get real, Susan," he said. "They'll say it's just another crazy kid rumor. Do you remember last year, when half the people in this school were convinced that the president was coming to Kennituck Falls to make a speech?"

I nodded. I had almost believed it myself—half

because so many of my friends did, half because I wanted it to be true. I also remember how my father had laughed when he heard about it. "Just because a thousand idiots believe something, that doesn't make it true," he had said.

Which was true, I guess. But it certainly didn't help us now.

That was when Peter decided to complicate things with a new problem.

"What are you going to do about this yourself?" he asked.

"What do you mean?"

"Well, since one of the things on Broxholm's shopping list is the best kid in the class, if we can't unmask him you've got a good chance of being picked yourself."

That was the best laugh I'd had in days. "You're nuts," I said. "There's no way I could be picked for top kid in the class!"

"There is too. It all depends on how he's making his choice. The way I see it, there are four of us that might be considered best in the class—Stacy, Michael, you, and me."

"You're nuts," I said again.

"Listen to me! Stacy and Michael are your basic perfect students. But they just did a good job of taking themselves out of the running—though to tell you the truth, I don't think Broxholm would have chosen either of them, anyway. They're real bright, but they don't *think* that much. They believe everything the teacher tells them. I'm sure Broxholm is bright enough to know that doesn't make a great student."

He paused. "Then there's me," he said. "I'm real bright. But I'm not motivated. And I'm not very social. You know how it goes: 'Peter is a good student, but he's not very well rounded.' I hear it every year. That leaves you, Susan. You get good grades. You get along with everyone. You're in all kinds of activities. Let's face it, you may not be the best in any one thing, but when you look at everything together, you make a pretty good pick for top of the class."

I stared at him in horror. "You're not kidding, are you?"

He shook his head.

CHAPTER FOURTEEN

WHAT CAN DUNCAN DOUGAL DO?

I couldn't believe what I was hearing. I had been worried that Broxholm might want me for one of his "average" slots. It never even crossed my mind that I could be considered the top student in the class.

"Peter, what am I going to do?" I wailed.

Peter shrugged his skinny shoulders. "Don't worry," he said. "I've got a plan."

I thought he meant the camera. He didn't, but I didn't know that then. The plan he actually meant was so weird I never would have thought of it.

I took a deep breath and tried to settle down. "I'm glad you mentioned that," I said, referring to the camera. "I think I've figured out the best time for me to get back into Broxholm's house."

"You mean *us*," said Peter.

I shook my head. "I mean *me*," I said. "I'm going to do it tomorrow morning, during my music lesson time. That way Mr. Smith won't suspect anything when I leave the room. I figure if I use my bike, I can make it to his house and back before I'm really missed. I'll get in trouble later, but at least I'll have the proof we need."

"You're not going alone," said Peter.

"Yes, I am," I said. "If we both take off, it's going to look suspicious—especially considering the amount of time we've spent together lately. Maybe suspicious enough that Broxholm will pretend he's sick, just so he can check up on us. We don't want him walking in on us while we're taking the photos. I doubt we could manage to sneak out of his house without getting caught a second time—especially if he's actually looking for us."

"Then I should go instead," said Peter. "You might not have enough time. I'll just skip school altogether."

"Now, how can you do that?" I asked.

Peter sighed. "I keep trying to tell you, it doesn't make any difference what I do. As long as I don't get in trouble with the law, no one cares."

"Peter, that's not a very nice way to talk about your parents," I said.

"I don't have parents," he snapped. "I've got *a* parent. Period. And he doesn't care what I do, as long as I don't get in trouble."

I felt stupid. Here I had known this kid for six years, and I didn't even know he only had one parent.

"All right," I said. "We'll go together."

"Why don't I just go alone?" said Peter.

I shook my head. "I got this whole thing started. It's my job."

Actually, I wasn't really feeling all that noble. I wanted to see Ms. Schwartz again—to make sure she was OK, and also to get some advice.

Peter shrugged. "You're the one who's going to land in hot water. If that's the way you want to do it, it's OK with me."

Then it was time to go back inside. Even though the major weirdness was over for the day, you could sense a kind of nervous energy in the classroom. The other kids didn't *really* believe the rumors about Mr. Smith being an alien—at least not yet. But after the little show Stacy and Mike had put on, they were starting to take things pretty seriously.

It would have been funny, if it wasn't so scary. The next morning I rode my bike to school, carrying my piccolo and camera in my backpack. As I was putting the lock on my front wheel, Duncan Dougal came sidling up to me and said, "If you and Peter are pulling some kind of joke on me, I'm going to turn you into peanut butter."

Strange as it may seem, Duncan's threat made me feel better. At least I knew there were some things in the world that I could still count on.

"It's no joke, Duncan," I said, drawing a cross over my heart with my fingers.

He looked at me suspiciously. Then he nodded. "OK," he said. "Now, what are we going to do about it?"

Now that was something I *hadn't* expected: an offer of help from Duncan Dougal. *Think quick,* I told myself. *This may not happen again for another ten years.*

I looked at Duncan. "How would you feel about skipping school today?" I asked.

He grinned, showing the big gap between his front teeth. "I love skipping school," he said.

He wasn't telling me something I didn't know. One of the things that made it possible to survive having Duncan in our class was the fact that he was out of school so often. We all knew his older brother wrote his excuses for him. But none of us were about to tell; we weren't crazy enough to do something that would put Duncan in our classroom any more often than necessary.

Besides, if one of us told and Duncan found out who did it, he would massacre that person.

But it might be useful to have him along—if I could be sure of one other thing. "Can you go someplace with Peter without picking on him?" I asked.

"Sure," said Duncan. "I like Peter."

I looked at him. To my astonishment, he looked like he really meant it.

I shook my head. What can you say to someone like that?

"All right," I said. "You go do whatever it is you do

when you skip school. I'm going to sneak out of the building at quarter after nine. I want you to meet me at the corner of Pine and Parker. You'll need a bike."

I thought about telling him not to steal it, but decided that might seem too insulting.

Duncan nodded his head. "Where are we going?" he asked.

I looked him right in the eye and said, "Peter and I are going to break into Mr. Smith's house and take pictures of the force field where he's holding Ms. Schwartz prisoner. I want you to stand outside and be our lookout, in case Mr. Smith gets wise and comes back to stop us."

I hesitated, then added, "I hope you won't mind facing an alien death ray."

I suppose that was a rotten thing to say. But the look on Duncan's face made it worth it.

CHAPTER FIFTEEN

HOOKEY FOR THREE

I was so nervous that I didn't even look at Mr. Smith when it was time to leave for my lesson.

Forgive me, Mr. Bamwick, I thought as I headed away from his room, toward the side door.

Peeking out to make sure there was no one around, I sprinted to my bike, unlocked it, and headed out of the schoolyard as fast as I could.

Duncan was waiting at the corner of Pine and Parker, sitting on a blue five-speed.

"Follow me!" I said and kept riding for the edge of town.

I checked my watch. It had been twelve minutes

since I left the class. If I could make it back just as fast, that would give me sixteen minutes to take the pictures.

Peter was waiting in front of the hedge at Broxholm's house. I could see his smile quickly turn to a frown when he saw who was with me. His pale face turned even paler as we drew up.

"What's *he* doing here?" demanded Peter.

I was impressed. It took a lot of nerve for Peter to say that in front of Duncan.

To my surprise, it was Duncan who tried to make peace. "I just came to help," he said. He did say it kind of belligerently, but he was holding up his hands with the palms out to show that he meant peace.

"He's going to be our lookout," I added, hoping that Peter would see the wisdom of this.

He hesitated for a moment, then nodded. "OK," he said grudgingly. "I guess you can stay."

Duncan looked as pleased as a naughty puppy who's just been let back into the house. "What do you want me to do?" he asked.

"Stand right here," I said, indicating a spot just

inside the hedge where he could have a good view of the sidewalk. "If you see Mr. Smith coming, run up on the porch and pound on the door to give us a warning. Then run for your life!"

Duncan nodded seriously and took his place. I looked at Peter. He gave me a nod, and we headed for the back of the house.

To my relief, the broken lock was still where Peter had jammed it back in place after our last adventure here. I had figured that as a temporary tenant, Broxholm probably wouldn't keep that close an eye on things that needed repair around the place. It was nice to find out I had been right.

We opened the door, and headed back into the alien's lair.

I felt a little more at ease this time. After all, we could be pretty sure that Broxholm would stay at school. We knew exactly where we were going. And we had a lookout to keep us from being surprised.

How could we go wrong?

The answer to that question was even worse than I expected.

For the first few minutes everything went as

smooth as could be. We made it out of the cellar and into the attic with time to spare.

Nothing had changed. The column of blue light was still there. And poor Ms. Schwartz was still trapped right in the middle of it.

I rushed over to it and placed my hands against the force field. Almost instantly I could hear Ms. Schwartz's voice in my head. *Hello, Susan. What are you doing here?*

We came to take some pictures of you, so that we can prove what's going on, I thought back at her.

Her reply scared me. *Weren't you just here a few minutes ago?* she asked. She sounded confused.

I bit my lip. Was she all right?

Of course, since the thought was about her, Ms. Schwartz picked it up.

I'm not sure, she responded. *It's getting so it's very hard to think in here.* She paused for a moment, then asked, *What day is this?*

It's Tuesday, I thought. *Tuesday, the twenty fourth of May.*

Her reaction almost knocked me over. *You must do something!* she thought desperately. *It's only two days until Broxholm is planning his pickup. Susan, you have to do something!*

I know, I know! I replied. Her fear was coming through as clearly as her thoughts, and it was making me afraid, too.

Our conversation was interrupted by Peter. "Susan, we can't just stand here and chat. We've got to get these pictures taken!"

He was right of course. *Hang on, Ms. Schwartz, I thought. We'll get you out of there somehow!*

Peter had already started flashing.

"That's good," he said. "Let me get a couple more of you standing next to her. Then move away from the force field so I can get some of Ms. Schwartz by herself."

I was glad Peter was there. I might have gotten so wound up talking to Ms. Schwartz that I wouldn't have taken the pictures in time to get back to school. But he was working fast. In a few minutes he had used up most of the camera's memory, taking some pictures with flashes, some without, working from all different angles. I helped, and we did everything we could think of to make sure we got at least one good shot.

We were just trying to figure out the last angle when we heard a terrible scream from downstairs.

"Ahhhhhh! Ahhhh ahhhhhh ahhhhh!"

I couldn't make much sense of the words. But I recognized the voice. It belonged to Duncan Dougal.

CHAPTER SIXTEEN

DUNCAN'S DISASTER

Peter looked at me. I looked at him. I wondered if he was as terrified as he looked. I wondered if I looked as terrified as I *felt*.

"What's he doing in here?" I whispered.

"And what's happening to him?" hissed Peter.

And what are we going to do about it? I thought.

We hesitated for only a second and then began to creep down the stairwell.

Duncan was still screaming.

We had left the door to the attic open, in case we needed to make a quick getaway. Poking my head around the edge, I looked in the direction of the screams. They were coming from the room where Mr. Smith sat to take off his mask every night.

I reached for Peter's hand. "What should we do?" I mouthed to him.

He pointed down the hall and started off with me following close behind.

After a couple of steps, we dropped to our bellies and slid up to the door and peeked around the edge.

I couldn't believe it—Duncan was all alone. He was standing in front of the "mirror," screaming for all he was worth.

I can't say that I blamed him—the communicator was on, and Duncan was looking into the bridge of Broxholm's starship. And one of those hideous aliens from the ship was looking back at him, talking to him in that language of growls and shrieks.

I took a deep breath and slithered into the room, crawling across the floor as fast as I could move. I scooted right under the table and hit the switch I had seen Broxholm use to turn the set off.

It made a crackling noise and then fell silent. Duncan stopped screaming.

"You idiot!" yelled Peter, jumping into the room. "What are you doing in here?"

"I got bored," sniveled Duncan.

Talk about a short attention span. He couldn't have been out there more than five or ten minutes.

"And I wanted to see if you were telling the truth or not," he continued. "So I went around the house and came in through the cellar. This was the only room with anything in it, so I came in. When I touched the switch, that—that—that *thing* showed up and started growling at me."

Duncan was blubbering now, with big tears cutting clean paths down his dirty face.

He turned to me and said, "Is that what Mr. Smith really looks like?"

I nodded my head.

Duncan's eyes rolled back in his head—and he fainted.

By the time we got him on his feet and out of the house, I only had ten minutes to get back to school.

"Maybe I shouldn't go back," I said.

Peter shook his head. "You have to," he said. "We can't afford to be more suspicious than we already are.

Anyway, I don't think the aliens actually saw you—at least not your face. You stayed down low enough."

"What about me?" blubbered Duncan. "What about me?"

Peter hesitated. "You'll have to hide out at my house," he said. "It's the last place anyone would think to look for you. If you stay there, you may be safe. Get *going*, Susan; you've got to get back to school as soon as possible. Don't worry about the pictures; I'll take care of that. Just move!"

I hopped on my bike and headed for school. By riding extra hard I got there just about the time my lesson was supposed to be ending. But I was all hot and sweaty when I sneaked back in. Even worse, I ran into Mr. Bamwick the moment I walked through the door.

He was furious. "Susan, where have you been?" he shouted. "I've spent the last forty minutes waiting for you. We've got a concert in two days, and my star soloist can't even show up for her lesson!"

I did the only thing I could think of: I started to cry. It wasn't hard to do, since I was on the edge of tears, anyway.

"I'm sorry, Mr. Bamwick," I sobbed. "I'm just so frightened I couldn't come to my lesson."

Wow! So far so good. I was actually managing to tell him something that was pretty close to the truth.

But then I felt bad, because Mr. Bamwick, who really is a good guy, got upset about scaring me and started apologizing for putting me under so much pressure.

In the end it worked out better than I could have imagined. Mr. Bamwick went to Mr. Smith and explained that there had been a problem with my lesson, and since we had this important concert coming up, would it be possible for him to keep me for a little while longer, and so on.

It was great! I had a real excuse, and I even got to work on my solo.

Back in class things were pretty quiet, until just before the end of the day when Mike Foran started throwing spitballs at Stacy. I wondered if the two of them weren't actually enjoying themselves. After all, they had been so well behaved for the last several years that maybe this was the perfect chance for them to let off a little steam.

But it wasn't Stacy and Michael who were asked to stay after school that day.

No, that honor was reserved for yours truly. I was sitting at my desk, thinking that maybe we had actually gotten away with our little photo session when Mr. Smith walked up to me and said, "Miss Simmons, I want you to stay after school. I need to talk to you."

It was amazing how two such simple sentences could teach me whole new levels of fear.

CHAPTER SEVENTEEN
TEACHER CONFERENCE

The other kids had left. I was alone with the alien.

At least Stacy had lingered at the door for a few minutes—until Mr. Smith turned to her and said, "It's time for you to go, Miss Benoit. I want to speak to Miss Simmons in private."

Stacy looked at me with an expression that said, "I *tried*." Then she hurried away.

Broxholm/Smith walked over and straddled the chair in front of my desk. He leaned toward me. "I know what you did today," he said.

"Oh" was all I could manage. I felt as if someone had dropped an ice cube into my heart. The worst thing was, I couldn't even be sure what he meant. Did he know I had skipped my piccolo lesson? Or did he know I had been inside his house?

I looked at the door and wondered if I would ever go through it as a living person again.

"Well?" said Broxholm.

"I'm sorry," I whispered. It was about all my voice was good for at that point. It was also just as vague as his first statement. I wasn't about to say what I was sorry for.

Broxholm looked at me. "I don't understand why you dislike me so much, Susan," he said. "I'm just trying to do what is right for this class. Yet you've been hostile to me from the moment I walked through the door."

What an actor! I wondered if I would ever be that good. It was amazing how he was still pretending to be just a teacher who was having trouble with one of his students.

Suddenly he rose and crossed the room to close the door. "Now," he said, sitting down in front of me again, "let's be honest with each other, shall we, Miss Simmons?"

Should I say something? Should I tell him I knew his secret?

"Why are you here, anyway?" I said at last, still playing his game of not saying anything that couldn't be taken at least two ways.

"I'm here to learn," he said smoothly. "After all, isn't that what school is for?"

Creep! I thought. But out loud I said, "I thought you were supposed to be the teacher." I tried to keep my voice from cracking. But it did, anyway.

Broxholm shifted in his chair. "A good teacher is always learning," he said. "Education is a process of give and take. I have to *take* certain things in order to learn. Look at all I've taken from this class already. I've taken a lot of nonsense. I've taken a lot of snottiness."

Suddenly he turned and looked directly at me. "And I'll have to take a few MORE things in order to learn all I can—if you *take* my meaning, Miss Simmons."

I shrank back in terror.

I don't know how he did it, but I could actually see his alien eyes beneath his mask, as if they were burning with a light of their own.

"And I won't *take* kindly to any interference with

my educational mission," he said in a voice without any emotion.

He had picked up a copy of *Rockets and Flags* as he talked. Now he began to squeeze it. I watched his fingers sink right into the cover, compressing the paper with the power of his grip.

I heard a horrible thumping sound. I glanced around to see where it was coming from, then realized it was the beating of my own heart.

"The universe is a very big place, Susan," said Broxholm gently.

He dropped the book. His fingers had left dents half an inch deep in the cover. If only I could get the book out of there, I would finally have proof of what he was. But, of course, he had no intention of letting me have the book. He picked it up and carried it to his briefcase.

"A very big place indeed," he said. "And there are more things going on in it than you can possibly imagine. It's important to learn all we can. Otherwise, terrible things can happen. Terrible things. That's my job—to prevent terrible things. Can you understand that, Miss Simmons?"

I shook my head. Maybe I should say I shook my head *harder,* since I was already shaking all over.

He sighed. "Well, perhaps someday you will," he said. "For now, I simply want you to know that it is wisest—and safest—not to interfere with your elders."

He closed his briefcase. "I will see you tomorrow, Miss Simmons," he said. "I trust that you will spend the entire day here in the classroom—and not enter my home again!"

I almost fell off my chair. He knew. He had known all along! Before I could say anything, he went out the door, leaving me alone.

CHAPTER EIGHTEEN
CONCERT CONCERNS

It took me almost twenty minutes to get home. I cycled along the sidewalk slowly, watching every corner. I kept expecting aliens to leap out of the bushes and grab me.

When something *did* jump out of the bushes, I screamed so high and so loud, I was surprised I didn't break the glass in the street lamp overhead.

But it was only Peter.

"Are you trying to give me a heart attack?" I asked, straddling my bike and glaring at him.

"It would serve you right for bringing Duncan along today," he said.

I wasn't up for a fight, and I said so. Peter was mad enough that he might have kept it going, anyway, but when I started to tell him what had happened after school he got so interested he forgot about being angry. He insisted that I try to remember every word Broxholm had said.

"Where's Duncan?" I asked when I finished my story.

"Hiding in my closet," said Peter with a wicked grin. "We called his folks, and he's going to spend the next couple of days at my house."

"Didn't they ask any questions?"

Peter laughed. "If you were Duncan's mother, wouldn't you be glad to have him out of the house for a while?"

I didn't think that was very nice, but I let it pass. "Will *you* be able to stand him till this is over?" I asked.

"My problem is trying not to take advantage of him," said Peter sadly. "It's not easy. I'd really love to get back at him for some of the things he's done to me. But he's so terrified I don't dare have any fun with him. I really think if I popped a bag near his ear he would have a heart attack and die."

I laughed in spite of myself.

"What about your father?" I asked.

Peter grimaced. "He won't even notice Duncan is there," he said. "By the way, I still have that memory card with the pictures. We can look at them after school tomorrow."

"If we live that long," I said.

"Relax," said Peter. "Broxholm and his friends are here to collect people. I'd be really surprised if they actually kill anyone."

That made me feel a little better. But it was only the thought that this whole mess might be over when we got the pictures that kept me from losing my mind that night. Even so, I was so frazzled I couldn't think about anything else.

By morning I was such a wreck that my special session with Mr. Bamwick was a total disaster. "No, no, no!" he kept yelling. "It's B flat, Susan. B *flat*!"

"Well, I can't get it right if you keep screaming at me," I said, trying not to cry.

I couldn't blame poor Mr. Bamwick. The concert was only a day away, and I was getting worse by the minute. But I just couldn't concentrate on the music. How could I, when I knew what else was supposed to happen? Could you play the piccolo, if you knew some of your friends—or maybe even you—were about to be kidnapped by aliens?

"Aren't you worried?" I asked Peter that afternoon on the playground.

"Not really," he said. His pale face split into a wide grin. "I told you, I've got an alternate plan."

"Listen, Peter," I said, taking his arm. "This isn't one of your science fiction books. And you're not Buck Rogers. Don't get carried away."

He shook my hand away angrily. "This is the greatest thing that's ever happened in this town," he said. "And don't you forget it, Susan!"

At that point Stacy and Mike went running by, yelling bad words at each other.

We started to laugh. "I heard Stacy say that her mother is going nuts," said Peter. "I bet Mike's mother is, too."

I nodded. I almost felt sorry for them. It can't be easy to have a kid who hasn't been in trouble since kindergarten suddenly turn into a maniac.

"Of course, Stacy and Mike don't have much choice," I said.

"Sure they do," said Peter.

"What do you mean by that?" I asked.

But he wouldn't answer me. "Just watch," he said. "You'll figure it out soon enough."

CHAPTER NINETEEN

PETER'S CHOICE

That afternoon I finally began to understand Peter's "alternate plan."

Actually, it took me a little while to figure it out. I knew there was something strange going on when Peter—the kid who always knew the answer but never bothered to give it—started raising his hand for every question that came along.

And suddenly it all came clear to me. Peter *wanted* to be picked by Broxholm. He had decided that this was his big chance to live the kind of science fiction adventure he had been dreaming about. He figured if he really tried, he might just be able to make it from "bright, but unmotivated" to being, without question, the best student in the class.

You could almost see the gleam in Broxholm's alien eyes when Peter unleashed his mighty brain.

We were having a history lesson at the time, and Peter started to answer every question perfectly.

Broxholm started asking harder questions, but Peter never blinked; he just kept reeling off the answers. Even I had no idea how smart that kid was. (And as for Broxholm, I swear, that alien must have memorized an encyclopedia; or maybe he had one transplanted into his head. Who knows what these people could do?)

When school was over I dragged Peter off to the side of the playground. "Are you crazy?" I hissed. "What are you doing?"

"Plan B," said Peter. "If we can't unmask Broxholm, I want to be one of the ones to go on the ship."

"Forget Plan B!" I yelled. "You don't know what they're going to do to you up there. They're bad!"

"You don't know that," said Peter.

"They kidnapped Ms. Schwartz!"

He shrugged. "That still doesn't mean they're bad.

They may be so far above us they think of us like we think of ants or something."

I didn't say a word. But he could tell by my expression that I thought that was stupid.

"Maybe they're scared of us," he continued.

That made me laugh.

"I'm serious," said Peter. "Think of that conversation you had with him yesterday."

"I can't," I said. "It still scares me."

"No, *think* about it," said Peter again. "Maybe these people are really peaceful. Maybe they've seen how much we fight, and they're afraid if we get much farther into space, we'll cause some huge war."

"You don't know that," I said stubbornly. "Anyway, maybe we won't have to worry about it. Let's go to the drugstore to get our pictures."

It took all our money for the pictures. I thought about explaining to the girl behind the counter that we were trying to stop an alien invasion, but I figured she probably wouldn't buy it.

We forced ourselves not to open the envelope until we were in the park.

"You open it," I said, handing the envelope to Peter.

He hesitated for a moment, then tore the envelope open and pulled out the pictures.

His face fell.

"What is it?" I asked.

Without saying a word, he handed me the photos.

My heart sank as I flipped through them. Peter had done a good job. The beams and timbers of the attic showed up perfectly. The focus and exposure were fine. But the force field with Ms. Schwartz in it had come out as nothing but a blue streak—that was all, just a blue streak down the middle of each picture. It looked like a flaw in the film, or maybe some trick of the light. You couldn't see Ms. Schwartz at all.

"These aren't going to do us any good," I moaned.

Peter nodded. "I'm sorry," he said.

"It's not your fault," I replied. But I knew he didn't believe me.

By Thursday the whole school seemed to be on the brink of nervous breakdowns. Stacy got caught drawing dirty pictures on the blackboard. Mike tried out a new word he had learned from his uncle, who was a sailor. And Peter waved his hand like crazy every time Broxholm/Smith asked a question.

The ones who were really having a hard time were the kids in the middle. See, by this time, everyone was starting to believe the rumor about our teacher being an alien. I think the fact that Peter and I knew it was true, combined with the fact that we weren't *trying* to convince them was what really did convince them. They figured if it was a joke, we'd be trying to fool them. Since we weren't, it had to be for real. Or something like that.

Anyway, the kids in the middle were going nuts because they knew Broxholm wanted the three most average kids in the class. But what was an average kid? No one knew. So none of them knew how to behave to keep from being kidnapped. Most of them just acted the same as usual, except that they were really nervous. Every time one of them answered a question, you had the feeling they were trying to decide whether they should answer it right or wrong. It was like they were asking themselves: "Will a right answer get me a one-way trip in an alien spaceship?"

"I'll be glad when this is over," I said to Peter that afternoon during recess.

"Me too," he said. But I didn't like the kind of dreamy way he said it.

"Aren't you scared?" I demanded.

"I'm terrified," he said. "But that doesn't change my mind."

School just got wackier as the day went on. By the time the last bell rang I got the feeling every kid had heard there was supposed to be an alien invasion at the concert that night.

If I wasn't so worried, it would have been funny. "Did you hear about the invasion?" kids would say. "Did you know that the aliens are coming tonight?"

I wanted to say, "No, the aliens aren't invading. They're just coming to kidnap some of us." Although, for all I knew, the reason they wanted to study us was so that they could invade sometime in the future.

I felt sorriest for Mr. Bamwick. He had hoped to have the best spring concert ever. Now it was beginning to look as if it would be the biggest disaster of his career.

"I'm cutting 'The Stars and Stripes' from the program," he told me that afternoon. He was trying to be nice about it, but I could tell that he was really disappointed.

"I'm sorry," I said. "I just couldn't get that trill."

"No, it's not just you," said Mr. Bamwick sadly. "The whole band has fallen apart. I don't know what I've done wrong."

How could I tell him that he hadn't done anything wrong—that his concert was just another casualty of the alien invasion.

CHAPTER TWENTY
PICCOLO POWER

The alien-invasion rumors had reached the adults, too—as I found out that night at dinner.

"My goodness, Susan," said my mother as she was dishing up my broccoli. "I hope *you* don't believe any of this nonsense."

Believe it? I thought. *I started it!*

But I didn't say that. Instead, I put down my soup spoon and looked at her. "What if I did believe it?" I asked. I tried hard to sound like I was interested, not like I was challenging her.

"Well, I suppose we'd have to get you counseling," she said.

I could have cried. Obviously, there was no point in asking my parents to help out with this mess.

I went upstairs to get ready. *Which ones will it be?* I wondered as I slipped into my dress. *Just who is the alien going to steal?*

I looked in the mirror and crossed my fingers, praying that it wouldn't be me.

My parents drove me to the school. They dropped me off and went to find a parking place.

I wonder how he's going to do it, I thought as I walked through the door. *Will he just freeze everyone here on the spot? Will his ship use some sort of tractor beam to lift up his targets? Or will he wait until later, when everyone is asleep, and then sneak into their homes and snatch them?*

The school was fairly zinging with nervous energy. The rumors about the alien invasion had spread to all the grades. The third graders were walking around in pairs, checking over their shoulders every other step. If I hadn't been so scared myself, I would have laughed. I wanted to grab them and say, "Stop worrying. The alien's not after you."

"Hey, Susan," called Peter. "Wait up!"

Peter was in the chorus. The chorus was bigger than the band; almost every kid in the sixth grade was a member. They would be singing last of all.

Peter looked very nice. He had on a white shirt and a red tie. His pale blond hair was slicked down.

"Is your father here?" I asked.

He just stared at me. "Are you kidding?" he asked.

We walked on until we came to a private place. "What are we going to do?" I asked.

Peter shrugged. "What can we do? Keep our eyes open. Be ready to call for help when there's something we can prove. Other than that, I can't think of anything. Is Broxholm here?"

I nodded. All the teachers had to come to the concert to keep us under control while we were waiting to perform. I figured Broxholm wasn't ready to blow his cover yet.

Peter glanced at his watch. "We'd better get into the gym," he said. "No sense in getting in any more trouble than we have to."

The gym was where we had to wait for our turn to perform. It was across the hall from the combination cafeteria and auditorium where we put on our concerts. The third-grade chorus was about to go on when Peter and I walked in.

"Get over here, you two," hissed Miss Tompkins, the world's oldest living fifth-grade teacher. "They're ready to start."

As we walked across the gym I heard the third-grade chorus begin to sing. They had only gotten through about three notes when the music stopped. I grabbed Peter's arm. Had it started?

Not actually; as it turned out, Cindy Farkis had fainted. The chorus teacher, Miss Binkin, stopped the program while two parents helped Cindy out. Then the singing began again.

"False alarm," said Peter with a grin.

I nodded. But I didn't feel like smiling. Suddenly I heard a familiar voice. "Band members. Band members, over this way."

It was Mr. Smith. He was standing at the far end of the cafeteria, holding up his hand. "Band members, over here!" he shouted. "We're going down to the primary wing. Mr. Bamwick wants you to meet there to tune up."

"You can bet Broxholm won't stick around for

that," said Peter. "Not the way he hates music."

Well, that gave me an idea. I might not have done it if I hadn't been feeling so crabby. But between the fact that we hadn't figured out any way to stop Broxholm from kidnapping some of our class and the fact that he was still holding the best teacher I had ever had prisoner, I was pretty mad. I decided if I couldn't beat the alien, I'd settle for annoying him.

So before we started down the hall I took my piccolo out of its case and put it together. Most of the other kids already had their instruments ready. Everybody was nervous. And it wasn't just preconcert jitters. About half the band was made up of sixth graders. They were the *most* frightened, of course—especially the ones from our class.

"All right, follow me," said Broxholm as he started down the hall.

Holding my piccolo behind my back, I positioned myself at the front of the group. When we got about halfway down the hall, I started to play a scale.

"Stop that!" shouted Broxholm before I had played three notes.

"Just practicing," I said.

"Well, don't," he snapped.

I had never heard him sound so cranky before. I must have really gotten to him!

I began to wonder if I could break through his false front, get him to show himself for what he really was. I put the piccolo to my lips and began to play again.

"Miss Simmons, stop that!" he ordered again. But this time I didn't stop.

"Please!" he said, clapping his hands over his ears. "Miss Simmons, please stop!"

I couldn't believe it. He was in agony. I began to play louder.

"Susan," he howled, bending over. "Stop!"

I took the piccolo away from my lips for just an instant. "Not on your life—Broxholm!"

Then I started to play again, the best piccolo music I knew—the solo from "The Stars and Stripes Forever."

"Stop it!" shouted Broxholm, stumbling down the hall ahead of me. "Stop, stop, stop!"

"Help me, you guys!" I said. That was a big mistake. As soon as I took a pause from playing

Broxholm spun around and snatched at my piccolo. But I pulled it back to safety before he could tear it from my hands.

"Take this, you alien creep!" I cried. And then I trilled him with a high C.

He backed away, holding his hands to his ears. I went back to "The Stars and Stripes," starting at the beginning. I heard Mike Foran join me on his saxophone. Then Billy Gootch brought in the trumpet. We advanced on Broxholm, playing for all we were worth. He retreated down the hall, his handsome face twisted with pain.

Now the clarinets were coming in. And the rest of the trumpets. Then came the drums. And finally, deep and low and powerful, the sousaphone.

We sounded fantastic.

Mr. Bamwick came running out of the room where he had been waiting for us. "They're playing it!" he cried in joy. "They're playing it!"

But now I heard Dr. Bleekman charging down the hall behind us. "What's going on out here?" he roared. "Smith! Bamwick! Can't you keep those kids under control?"

"They're playing it!" cried Mr. Bamwick joyfully. "Seven years I've been waiting for this."

"Stop that!" roared Bleekman.

"No!" cried Mr. Bamwick. "Don't stop now! Let me hear it!"

We couldn't stop. We were on a roll. We had never sounded so good. And Broxholm was crumbling before us. "Stop," he pleaded. "Stop, stop!" Adults were crowding out of the auditorium and into the hall. "What's going on?" they shouted.

"What's happening out here?"

We reached the big finale. I played that trill like I had never played it before. We kept advancing on Broxholm. Soon the new Kennituck Falls Elementary School Marching Band had the alien cowering in a corner.

"What do you want?" he pleaded.

I didn't dare stop playing. I knew my piccolo was keeping him at bay. But Mike stepped in. "Take off your mask!" he shouted.

"Your mask!" cried the others. "Take off your mask!"

"Anything!" said Broxholm. "Just stop that noise."

"First your mask!" cried the band.

Even Dr. Bleekman could see that there was something weird about his favorite teacher now.

He waited in silence.

I played my trill again.

Broxholm reached behind his head, and began to peel off his face. Behind us people started to scream. Someone cried, "What is it? What's happening?"

"Oh, my God!" yelled someone else. "It's Mr. Smith—he's—he's—an alien!"

CHAPTER TWENTY-ONE

OUT OF THIS WORLD

I thought it was over. But I was wrong. Broxholm was still crouched against the wall, about two feet from the doors to the outside. The rest of us were about ten feet away from him, staring in horror at his strange alien features.

Suddenly the door to the left of Broxholm opened. It was Peter. He must have run out the front doors and circled around.

"Broxholm," he shouted. "This way. Run!" The alien jumped to his feet and took off as if he had rocket-powered roller skates. As soon as he was through the door, Peter slammed it shut.

The rest of us started to run, too. Then Broxholm pulled something that looked like a thick pencil out of his pocket. He pointed it at the doors and fried them shut.

I started to tremble. He could have pointed that thing at me if he had really wanted to! He probably could have melted my piccolo to my lips.

Maybe old Broxholm wasn't so bad after all, I thought as I stood with my face pressed against the window, watching the alien and my best friend disappear into the night.

My best friend? I thought in surprise. But I knew it was true. Peter *was* my best friend.

And now he was gone.

Someone had called the police. Pretty soon their cruisers came screeching into the school yard. My mother was flapping her hands and worrying that I might have some alien disease.

With all the yelling and shouting, it took the police a while to figure things out. But soon they put me in a patrol car and we hightailed it out to Broxholm's place.

We were only a block from his house, when we

heard a roar, followed by a high whine. Then this thing—this beautiful huge silvery sphere with a wheel of lights spinning around it—lifted into the air ahead of us.

"Stop the car," I said.

I don't know why, but they did—probably because the ship was so amazing. I pushed my way past the policeman on my right and stood in the road, watching the ship rise on a column of purple light into the black night. "Goodbye, Peter," I whispered. "Have a good trip!"

I felt as if something hard had become stuck in my throat as I watched the ship soar higher and higher, until it was lost among the twinkling of the stars.

The police sealed off the house, just in case there were any aliens left inside. When they finally decided it was safe, I took them to see where Ms. Schwartz had been held prisoner.

I was afraid Broxholm might have taken her along. But when we climbed up into the attic, we found her sitting on the floor saying, "This is the worst headache I have *ever* had!"

"Ms. Schwartz!" I cried. I ran to her. She held out her arms and I fell into them. The two of us cried for a long time, which I think kind of confused the policemen.

The rest of the house was empty, except for a note from Peter we found stuck to the refrigerator door. He asked us not to worry and said that he would probably come back again someday.

And that was that. Things are back to normal now—at least, as normal as they ever get around here. Duncan has been picking on everyone he can. Mike and Stacy have regained their angelic reputations. (Though to tell you the truth, I wouldn't be surprised if they decide to get into a little mischief now and then just for the fun of it.)

As for me, I'm doing fine—except when I play my piccolo. That's when I think of Peter.

Sometimes I go outside at night to look at the stars. I try not to think about how far away Peter is. I only remember how much he wanted to go there. I do wonder where he is and if he's seeing all the wonderful things he used to imagine when he was reading those crazy science fiction novels.

Of course, I never *really* wish I had gone with him. After all, I've got a family that loves me. I like my life here on Earth.

But I wonder, sometimes, what it would be like to travel the stars with aliens.

Or maybe with *earthlings*. I've been studying my math pretty hard lately. I've kind of changed my mind about being an actress. I'm thinking maybe I'll be a scientist when I grow up.

I'd like to invent a ship—a ship that would take us right out of the solar system—out to explore all those distant stars that fill the sky at night.

Worlds where *we* would be the mysterious aliens.

Wouldn't that be something?

MY TEACHER FRIED MY BRAINS

To Byron,
because the first one changed my life—
and because he asked for it

Special thanks to Pat MacDonald, Tisha Hamilton,
and Adam and Cara Coville

TABLE OF CONTENTS

CHAPTER ONE

FIRST DAY BLUES

I was standing in the bathroom, brushing my teeth, when I looked up and saw a horrible green face in the mirror.

"Hey, Duncan," rasped a voice from behind me, "what time is it?"

A wave of terror washed over me. "Go away!" I yelled, spattering toothpaste foam across the mirror.

"Wrong answer!" shouted the face. "It's not go-away time, it's *bopping* time!"

A strong arm wrapped around my neck. "Help!" I screamed. "Aliens!" But even as I was screaming,

I saw in the mirror that the arm holding me was a strong human arm.

"Patrick!" I shouted, mad now instead of terrified. "Come on, Patrick, cut it *ow*!"

I said "OW!" instead of "out" because Patrick had just landed a major noogie on my skull. I would tell you why my big brother was beating on me if I could, but I can't, because I don't know. He just does that sometimes. I do it to other people. You know how it is: you get upset, things build up inside you, and suddenly you BOP! someone.

Or maybe you don't. But that's how things work in our family.

Patrick gave me another noogie.

"You creep!" I screamed, trying to wriggle out of his grip. "Get out of here!"

"Quiet up there!" shouted our father.

I would have yelled for him to make Patrick leave me alone, but it wouldn't do any good. Dad's theory is that life is rough, and I might as well get used to it. That may be true, but I've noticed that when I hit kids in school none of the teachers say, "Why, Duncan, what a good lesson you've just given little Jimmy in the fact that life is rough." What they usually say is, "Look, you little jerk, I've had about enough of your antics. One more stunt like that and you're heading straight to the principal's office!" Or if they're feeling particularly nice they might say, "Now, Duncan, that's not how we solve our problems, is it?"

It is in our family. What planet are these teachers from?

"What planet are they from?"—a good question, considering what had been going on around our town.

See, things had been pretty tense in Kennituck Falls since last spring, when this alien named Broxholm kidnapped weird Peter Thompson and took him off into space. Even though Broxholm was gone, people were still frightened—as if they thought there were aliens still lurking around, waiting to grab people.

With the grown-ups that scared, you can be sure kids around here had about the worst summer ever, mostly because parents were afraid to let their little darlings out of the house. It seemed like the town motto was, "I don't want *you* disappearing like that

Peter Thompson." (Well, my parents didn't say that. But most of the others did.) I bet a hundred years from now people in this town will still be telling their kids that if they don't behave an alien boogeyman will get them.

To make things worse, Peter Thompson's father—who didn't really give a poop about Peter when he was here—had decided that he really missed his son.

Mr. Thompson had come up to me in the park one day. "You know where he is, don't you?" he said. "You know where they took my boy."

I had stared at him for a moment. Mr. Thompson was skinnier than he used to be, and there were dark circles under his eyes. Then I remembered what Peter had said when he let me stay in his house to hide from the alien: "Don't worry about my father. He won't mind. He won't even know!"

It had been true. Mr. Thompson was almost never there, and when he was, he didn't pay any attention to Peter at all.

So I had looked at him, all skinny and sad, and said, "What do you care where he is?" Then I ran away because I was afraid he was going to hit me. I suppose it was a pretty rotten thing for me to say, but I had a feeling that the main reason Mr. Thompson was so upset was that everyone else thought he should be.

To tell you the truth, I kind of missed old Peter myself. Everyone used to think I hated him. That wasn't true. I just picked on him because I didn't know what else to do with him.

Well, maybe I did hate him a little, because he was so smart and I was so dumb. Except I wasn't really dumb. I just *thought* I was. Of course, my family and my teachers had given me a lot of help in coming to that conclusion.

I was feeling plenty dumb when I got to school that morning. First of all, I was late because of the fight with Patrick. Second, my head hurt where my father had whacked me afterward. (At least he whacked Pat, too. He always treated us both the same way when it came to that.) Third, I couldn't find my classes, so I kept walking in on things that were already in session.

The reason I couldn't find my classes was that it

was the first day of school, and I had never been in the building before.

The reason I had never been in the building was that I had played hookey the day we had our junior high orientation tour. I'd figured there was no point in going, since I hadn't expected to pass the sixth grade. (I think the only reason I did pass, which was kind of a shock, was that after what happened with the alien the school decided to pass our whole class out of sympathy or something.)

Well, the first day in a new school is hard enough if you get there on time and have some idea of what's going on. You don't really need things like walking in late and having some big, tall man with black hair and eyes like coal grab your arm and say, "Not off to a very good start, are we, Mr. Dougal?"

"Aaaahh!" I shouted. "Leave me alone!"

That seemed to startle the man. (Actually, it startled me, too. But the way he grabbed me reminded me of the first time I had met Broxholm, when he was pretending to be a substitute teacher and stopped me from beating up on Peter Thompson.)

"Stop that!" said the man, giving me a shake.

I stopped, mostly because I had recognized him. He was the assistant principal. His name was Manuel Ketchum, and he had come to work at our school last spring, after the old assistant principal had a nervous breakdown. According to my brother Patrick, Mr. Ketchum was a real beast. Most kids called him "the Mancatcher" when he wasn't around.

I guess the Mancatcher must have heard of me, too.

"I've been warned to keep an eye on you, Mr. Dougal," he said. "I can see why already."

He asked me for an excuse for being late, which I didn't have. Then he gave me a lecture about punctuality and responsibility, which made me even later for where I was trying to go.

I had to stick my head into three rooms before I found the one where I belonged. Each time I did, I could hear kids snickering when I left. That really fried me. I *hate* it when people laugh at me.

It was almost as bad when I finally did find the right room. It was home economics class! I couldn't believe they had scheduled me for home economics.

Fortunately the teacher was a real babe. And she smiled when she saw me come in! That was the first nice thing that had happened all day.

"Are you Duncan Dougal?" she asked in a kindly voice. When I nodded she smiled again and said, "My name is Miss Karpou. I'm glad you finally made it."

"She'll change her mind once she gets to know him," someone whispered.

The people who heard it started to laugh. I started to blush. If I could have figured out who said it, I would have whapped the jerk.

I did notice it was kind of nervous laughter. In fact, the whole seventh grade seemed a little twitchy that day. Kids are always a little nervous the first day of school, of course. But this was something more. I think being back in school had everyone thinking about the alien again.

Miss Karpou went back to what she was talking about, which was how to use the equipment without hurting ourselves. Except she wasn't very good at it, because she managed to burn herself almost immediately.

"Ouch!" she cried. She popped her finger into

her mouth, then spun around and bent over the counter. For a minute I was afraid she was going to cry. Instead, she turned and ran out of the room.

I felt bad. Miss Karpou was young, she was pretty, and she had been nice to me. I didn't want her to be sad.

The class got a little rowdy then, and pretty soon the Mancatcher came in to shut us up.

Naturally, he blamed everything on me.

As if things weren't bad enough already, at lunchtime this huge eighth grader named Orville Plumber (which is probably half his problem anyway) came up to my table and said, "Hey, kid—you Duncan Dougal?"

I looked up and said, "What about it?"

Orville smiled, a big, nasty, gap-toothed smile, and said, "I'm gonna turn you into dog meat."

CHAPTER TWO

AN ALARMING SITUATION

I've been held back a couple of times, so I'm bigger than most kids in my class. But Orville was like a small mountain. I swallowed hard.

This Vietnamese kid named Phon Le Duc started to giggle. "Go get him, Duncan," he said.

I could have killed Phon for that. The problem was, I nearly *had* killed him a couple of times last year, since I used to beat him up about once a month. So I could see why he would have been happy to watch Orville cream me.

"What did I do?" I asked, stalling for time.

"Nothing," said Orville. "I just don't like your

face. Come on outside so I can rearrange it."

"Oh, shut up and sit down," said a voice from behind me.

It was Susan Simmons—the girl who had unmasked the alien last spring.

Susan Simmons, one of the five best-looking girls in seventh grade.

Susan Simmons, who was probably the smartest kid in our class, now that weird Peter Thompson was gone.

Susan Simmons, who walked up to Orville Plumber and said, "Go away." That's all she did—just said, "Go away."

You want to know the amazing thing? Orville went. Actually, the first thing he did was turn pale. *Then* he went.

I turned to Susan. "How did you do that?" I asked.

She shrugged. "Ever since last spring a lot of people have been afraid of me. The dumber they are, the more they're afraid. Orville probably thinks I stole some secret weapon from Broxholm and I was ready to use it to drill a hole through his skull."

"Is that true?" I asked, remembering the way Broxholm had melted the school doors shut when he was making his getaway. I also remembered how much time Susan had spent exploring Broxholm's house. Maybe she *had* found something there.

She just smiled and said, "What do you think, Duncan?"

Then she turned and walked back to her own table.

I was frustrated. I wanted to talk to Susan some more. I felt good when I was with her. But she had her own group of friends, and just because I had helped her fight the alien didn't mean she was going to let me in. OK, I guess I hadn't really helped. But I'd been involved! Me, Susan, and Peter—we were the only ones who had really known what was going on. You'd think that would count for something.

I was also embarrassed, since it doesn't look good to have a girl save you from being turned into dog meat.

Things didn't get any better after lunch. I still hadn't figured out how to get around the building, so I was really late for my sixth-period class, which was math. I tried hard to find it—I really did. I had promised myself I would do better in school this year. (So far that idea wasn't working out very well.) Also, I knew kids would laugh if I came in late again, especially if they had already heard about Susan saving me from Orville. To top things off, I knew from Patrick that the math teacher, Mr. Black, was pretty cranky.

So I really wanted to get there on time.

I kept running up and down hallways, looking for Mr. Black's room. My brain felt like it was melting. I couldn't make any sense of the building. When I finally did find the room I was panting and my heart was pounding.

"Ah, Mr. Dougal, I presume," said Mr. Black when I walked in. "I will accept your lateness today. However, in the future either be here on time or plan to spend the period in the office."

I had had it. Between my brother, my father, the Mancatcher, and Orville Plumber, I just wasn't ready to have anyone else dump on me—especially when I had been trying so hard to do something right.

Does your mouth ever do things without getting

your permission first? Mine does. It did it right then. I looked at Mr. Black and my mouth said, "Bug off, pinhead!"

About three seconds after the words came out of my mouth I realized what I had done. My skin turned cold. At the same time I felt a hand grab my arm.

"What did you say?" asked Mr. Black, yanking me around and staring into my face.

"Nothing," I whispered. "I didn't say anything."

Mr. Black pulled open the door and shoved me through it. "You can try again tomorrow, Mr. Dougal. For today, I think you'll be better off out here."

Inside I could hear the kids laughing.

I really hate it when people laugh at me.

If Mr. Black thought I was going to stand in the hall until the end of the period, he was wrong. I was getting out: out of his hall, and out of his school.

I was heading down the hall when I saw the fire alarm. I figured since I was leaving, everyone else might as well leave, too.

That's not true. I don't know what I figured. I just know that I reached out and pulled it.

The bell started to clang. Doors flew open. Screaming kids poured out of the classrooms. "It's the aliens!" they cried. "The aliens are back!"

It should have been funny. It would have been funny, if not for one terrible fact: when I pulled the alarm, it sprayed purple ink all over my hand! It didn't take much brainpower to figure out that the ink was to mark people who turned in false alarms.

I had to wash the stuff off. I ran for the boys' room.

Duh! Brilliant move, Duncan. That's exactly what they expect you to do—which shouldn't have been too hard to figure out, except I was either too scared or too stupid to manage it. Fortunately, my brother had warned me about this.

I shot back into the hallway. Things were still in an uproar. Some kids were actually crying because they were convinced the alien invasion had begun. Teachers were shouting and trying to get them out of the building.

As fire drills go, this was a total disaster.

Jamming my purple hand in my pocket, I pushed through the confusion and headed for the back door of the school. The door opened onto a loading dock. Three or four empty cardboard boxes were stacked at the far end. Closer to me stood a big green dumpster, already starting to stink in the afternoon heat.

What I really wanted to do was take off and run. But since about half the school was outside already, I couldn't do that without being caught. I had to hide someplace.

Well, at least I wasn't in the boys' room. I figured the Mancatcher was there right now, looking for a kid with a purple hand.

I pulled my hand out of my pocket and stared at the purple stain. It was like a big sign that shrieked, "Duncan did it! *Duncan did it!*"

Where could I hide? I peeked back around the door. Things were quieter now. Maybe I could hide someplace inside until school was over.

I opened the door, slipped through, and almost swallowed my tongue.

The Mancatcher was heading right toward me.

CHAPTER THREE

AN EXTRA HAND

I shot back out the door and looked around in desperation. Where could I go?

I could see only one place where no one would look for me.

The dumpster.

The Mancatcher would be coming through the door soon. No time to think—only to do. I ran across the loading dock, grabbed the lip of the dumpster, and swung my leg over the edge.

When I looked down inside I almost changed my mind. Four feet below me waited a smelly mass of banana peels, bread crusts, half-eaten hamburgers, and things too gross to mention. I considered turning back. Then I heard the door start to swing open.

Taking a deep breath, I swung my other leg over and dropped into the dumpster.

My feet sank several inches into the trash. A cloud of fruit flies swarmed around my head. It was like jumping into a swamp. The only thing I didn't get was the smell. That was because I was holding my breath.

I crouched there in the trash, listening for Man-catcher sounds. After a few seconds I heard him say, "Is somebody out here?"

I let out a sigh of relief. (A soft sigh.) If the Man-catcher had spotted me, he would have been calling my name, not just asking for "someone." So he hadn't seen me—at least, not well enough to know it was me. It was the first break I had had all day.

In a little while I heard the door open and close again. I started to relax. But suddenly I realized he might be trying a trick—making it sound like he had gone, so anyone out here would think it was safe to stop hiding.

I decided I had better stay right where I was. The only move I made was to shift around slightly so I could sit down. As I did, I could feel stuff smearing all over me. Something wet started soaking through my jeans. This was revolting! But it was better than getting nabbed by the Mancatcher.

I gave up holding my breath and sucked in a load of fresh air. Well, "fresh" wasn't quite the word for it. Let's just say that if I didn't have to breathe, I would have quit right then.

It was hot in the dumpster. Not surprising—the thing was made of dark green metal. I began to feel like I was in a big, smelly oven. Sweat started pouring down my face.

How long was I going to have to stay here? When would it be safe to sneak out?

I heard the all-clear buzzer sound. Kids began to shout and laugh. No aliens after all!

I began to relax. Everyone would be inside soon. Maybe then I could get out of the dumpster or out of here without getting caught.

Unless, of course, the Mancatcher was still lurking around outside.

Soon I realized I was hungry. I also realized I was surrounded by food. I wondered if there was anything I could eat in here—maybe something that had just gotten thrown in.

If I have a good fairy, she has rotten timing. I can think of a dozen wishes I would rather have had come true that day, such as that I had never gotten out of bed to begin with that morning. No sooner had I started thinking about food than I heard a sound. Without thinking, I looked up just in time to see the round mouth of a garbage can being lifted over the edge of the dumpster. Down it came, right over my head—a garbage shower of soggy napkins, pickle bits, orange peels, ketchupy french fries, and who knows what else, all swimming in leftover chocolate milk.

I wanted to scream and shout, but of course then I would have been found and dragged off to the Mancatcher's office. My stomach was trying to add my own lunch to the pile of stuff in the dumpster, but I managed to hold things down.

I heard scraping noises. Another garbage can appeared above me. I scrambled back across the trash on my hands and knees. It was slick, and I had gone only a few feet when one hand plunged down into a soft spot and I dropped face first into the goop.

That was disgusting, but not terrifying.

What was terrifying was what I spotted only six inches in front of me as I was going down.

It was a hand. A human hand, lying between a ball of aluminum foil and a leaky, half-eaten jelly sandwich.

The garbage muffled my scream. When my heart stopped beating so fast, I lifted my head and looked again. That was when I realized the thing I had seen was more like a glove than a hand. A *skin* glove. Maybe a better way to describe it is to say it was like a mask for someone's hand.

It reminded me of Broxholm's mask—the one he had used to make him look human. When my brother had tried to fool me that morning, it was his human-looking arm that had tipped me off that he wasn't an alien. Until now, I hadn't thought about it the other way around. But since Broxholm was really green underneath his mask, then the rest of his skin must have been green, too.

Or maybe it wasn't. Who can tell with an alien? Maybe his different parts were all different colors. But whatever color they were, you can bet his hands didn't look like human hands. So he must have been hiding them some way—*such as with a glove that looked like human skin.*

Only Broxholm had been gone since last May.

Everything in the dumpster had been put in over the last couple of days.

Which meant this glove was fresh garbage.

Which could mean only one thing.

We still had a teacher who was an alien.

CHAPTER FOUR
HONEY FLINT

The way I figured it, whoever owned the glove got left behind when Susan and the school band drove Broxholm out of town. But why hadn't the aliens come back for him? (Her? It?)

Had he/she/it been abandoned?

Or was the mission still on?

Whatever the case, I figured we had to do something about it. But first I had to get out of the dumpster. Except I was really afraid to do that, because if the alien, whoever it was, saw me climbing out, then he/she/it might wonder if I had found the glove. And in that case he/she/it might decide it was no good having me around.

I remembered the way Broxholm had fried the school door shut. Maybe I should just leave the glove where it was. But if I did, I couldn't prove what I had found. On the other hand (so to speak), if the alien somehow caught me with the glove, I was dead meat for sure.

I crawled farther into the dumpster to think. Settling onto a pile of used french fries, I stared at the glove, trying to decide what to do. The only thing I knew for sure was that I didn't want to mess around with these guys!

After what seemed like hours the final bell rang. I could hear kids shouting and screaming as they ran out of the school. The back door scraped open. One of the janitors dumped more stuff into the dumpster.

By now my clothes were soaked with sweat—among other things. (At least I wasn't wearing nice new clothes, like most of the kids.) I would have traded almost anything for a breath of clean air. Closing my eyes, I leaned my head against the side of the dumpster. Ouch! The metal was hot. I scrambled over to the other side, the side in the shade, and tried again. That was better; not cool, but not burning, either.

I think I dozed off for a little while (who knows—maybe the fumes knocked me out). The next thing I knew, I was jolted awake by a horrible clanging noise. Someone was bouncing a basketball off the side of the dumpster! If I was into headbanger music, it would have been great. I'm not. It was terrible.

I heard another noise, and screamed as a huge rat scurried across my leg. Fortunately, my scream came at exactly the same moment as the next thump of the basketball, so I don't think anyone heard me.

"Get out of here!" I hissed at the rat.

It ignored me.

I grabbed a half-eaten apple and threw it as hard as I could. I missed, but the rat ran away—about a foot away. Then it went back to examining the garbage.

I decided if it left me alone, I would leave it alone. Except I found that whenever it got out of my sight, I started to feel nervous.

By the time the mad basketball player was done

bouncing his ball off the Dumpster, I felt like someone had been working over my head with a sledgehammer. I listened, which wasn't easy considering the way my ears were ringing. I couldn't tell for sure, but I thought the parking lot was empty.

I stared at the glove again and decided I had to take it with me. I knew that if I didn't, no one would believe me when I told them about it. And I had to tell people. If I didn't, who knew what the alien might do to our town?

Feeling nervous, I crawled to the front of the dumpster and poked my head above the edge. Fresh air! It was glorious. That was the single best breath I have ever taken.

It was also almost the last, since the next thing I saw was the Mancatcher. He was walking across the parking lot.

I dropped back into the dumpster and waited to hear the sound of his car pulling away before I tried again.

This time the coast was clear. Straining, I pulled myself up on the edge of the dumpster. It wasn't easy—the heat had drained my strength. Finally I got my leg up over the edge and dropped back onto the loading dock. I felt as if there should be little odor lines in the air around me, like in the comic strips. I smelled worse than my brother's socks—which he usually wears for three days straight.

I was almost as confused as I was smelly. What should I do first? Who should I talk to about the hand mask I had found?

The answer to that one was simple. I had to talk to Susan. She would believe me.

But when I got to Susan's house and rang the bell, her mother opened the door. She took one sniff at me and told me to go home and get cleaned up. She wouldn't even tell Susan I was there.

So I didn't tell her that I was afraid to go home.

I was stinking my way down Pine Street, trying to figure out what to tell my mother, when a woman stepped out of the bushes.

I shoved my purple hand into my pocket. I didn't want anyone to see the evidence that I had pulled the fire alarm.

The woman was very pretty. She had long blond hair tied back in a ponytail and eyes as blue as my father's Buick. Her figure looked like someone had taken one of those Greek statues I like to look at in the encyclopedia and put clothes on it. A camera dangled from a strap around her neck.

"Hello, Duncan," she said, putting out her hand. "My name is Honey Flint."

I was dying to shake her hand, only I couldn't because I didn't want her to see the purple stain.

"How do you know who I am?" I asked.

She smiled, which probably should have been against the law since there wasn't much a guy could do to defend himself against it. "I've been paying attention," she said. Then she wrinkled her brow—and her nose—and added, "What happened to you?"

"I don't want to talk about it."

That wasn't really true. I did want to talk about it. But I was afraid she would laugh at me.

Honey shrugged. "I guess boys just have all kinds of adventures," she said. "Which is what I wanted to talk to you about. I understand you've had some adventures with an alien."

I felt a little prickle of fear. People in town had been keeping quiet about the alien situation.

According to my dad, they figured no one would believe what had happened, so they just weren't talking about it. The police reports simply showed Peter as missing, either a runaway or a kidnap victim; they didn't mention anything about an alien.

So how did this woman know about what had happened? Was she one of the aliens? Did she know I had found the hand mask? Had she come to try to get it back from me?

"How do you know about the alien?" I asked nervously.

Honey smiled. "I have my sources," she said. Then she put her hand under my chin, so that I had to look up into those blue eyes, and said, "How would you like to be in the news, Duncan?"

"What news?" I asked, more interested now.

Honey smiled again. "The *National Sun*!"

Now *that* was exciting. My father loves the *Sun*. He makes my mother buy a copy every week when she does the grocery shopping. I like it, too. It has great headlines, things like "Elvis Ate My Baby" and "Walking Zombies Terrorize Town."

As soon as Honey mentioned the *Sun*, I felt

I could trust her. I figured if she was an alien she would have said she worked for the *New York Times* or something. What kind of an alien would claim to work for the *National Sun*?

I also thought how amazed my father would be if his favorite paper did an article about me.

"Well?" asked Honey.

"Sure," I replied. "I'll talk to you. I like your paper. My whole family likes it. We keep it in the bathroom."

Honey blinked, then smiled and said, "Why don't you just tell me what happened to you last spring?"

Then it hit me. Honey was my answer. This was what to do about the skin glove.

Reaching into my pocket, I said, "Honey, have I got a story for you!"

CHAPTER FIVE

HOW TO HIDE A HAND

My interview with Honey Flint went fine until I suddenly began to wonder if she was the alien after all. I mean, nothing said these guys were limited to one face. For all I knew, old Broxholm had carried a whole box full of masks, one for every occasion.

So when Honey asked if she could take the glove, I didn't know what to do. Maybe she had spotted me climbing out of the dumpster and was looking for a way to get the glove back without putting me on ice. (Not that I thought the aliens were kind and sweet or anything. But I could see where this one might not want to create more suspicion by having another kid disappear.)

Of course, if Honey was telling the truth about being a reporter, she might be able to help me convince the world that we still had an alien teacher in town. But if she was lying to me, if she was really the alien in disguise, then I would be handing over the only piece of evidence I had.

Finally I told Honey that she could take a photo of the glove. She seemed unhappy that she couldn't have it, but I didn't know if that was because she was secretly the alien, or just because she wanted it to prove her story to her boss. (That's one problem when you start to get suspicious; you can't trust anything anymore.)

On the other hand, she did seem really thrilled with the story. "This is great," she kept saying. "Oh, Duncan, this is just great."

When we were finally done talking it was almost dark. Honey told me she would like to take me to get a milkshake or something, but that she didn't think any place would let us in the way I smelled, and she really didn't want to put me in her car, either. I suppose I should have been offended. But she said it real nice, and besides, it made sense.

I wasn't all that thrilled about walking home alone in the dark, especially since I was half expecting an alien to jump out of the bushes and grab me at any moment. Also, I didn't know what was going to happen to me when I got home. Being late wasn't a problem—my parents didn't really care that much what time I got there. But the garbage thing might be an issue.

Finally I stopped at old man Derwinkle's house. Mr. Derwinkle has the best lawn on the block, mostly because he's always watering it. I figured the odds were good that I would find a hose lying in the driveway.

I was right.

Old man Derwinkle is pretty deaf, so he didn't hear me spraying myself down. The first water was hot, from the hose lying in the sun all day. Once I got past the water that had been in the hose, the rest was cold. I didn't care; hot or cold, it all felt great. I didn't realize how much stuff had been stuck in my hair until I saw it coming out in the water that ran off my head.

So now my clothes were soaking wet, and stained in several places, but not nearly as smelly as they had been.

The same was true for me.

The only problem was that when I got home Patrick spotted me and bellowed, "Ma! Duncan's dripping all over the floor." So my mother made me go out back and take off all my clothes and put on a bathrobe before I could come inside.

Patrick snuck out back and took a picture of me while I was naked, which shows you what a booger he is.

I spent almost an hour that night trying to get the purple stain off my hand so I could go to school the next morning without getting in trouble. I wondered how long it would take to fade away. I considered asking Patrick, since he knows about this kind of stuff, but I couldn't count on him not to say something to my father.

Of course I could always stay home sick (I know four different ways to make myself throw up) or play hookey, but that's a little tricky the first couple of days of school. Later on, once you know the routine, it's different. But skipping at the beginning can really mess you up.

I suppose if I had been smarter I would have seen the answer sooner. It wasn't until I went back to my bedroom, which I have to share with Patrick-the-booger, that I thought of the alien glove. If it could hide the alien's hand, why not mine?

I pulled the glove out of my pocket and looked it over. What if it was full of alien germs or something? I decided to wait until morning to decide whether to use it.

When morning came my hand was as purple as ever. So I went into the bathroom, where no one would see me, and pulled on the glove.

It was like magic. The glove fit my hand perfectly, almost as if it was adjusting its shape while I was pulling it on. What was even weirder was that as I was putting it on, it changed color to match my other hand—as if it were a chameleon or something.

I had only two problems. First, the fingernails were too clean. So I grubbed them up a little. Second, there was a small hole at the end of one of the fingers.

I suppose that's why the alien threw it away. I put a bandage over the hole. I have to wear a lot of bandages, so that looked pretty natural. Even so, if you had looked closely, you would have known it wasn't really my hand. But unless you give them a reason to, most people don't look at stuff very carefully. That's one reason a guy like me can get away with a lot of things; people just don't see what you do.

My mother and father didn't notice my new hand at all. I didn't give Patrick a chance to see it.

I was really happy when I started off to school that morning. Things looked a lot better than they had the day before.

The Mancatcher was standing at the door when I came in. I knew he was looking for a kid with a purple hand, so I waved at him when I walked up.

"Hiya, Mr. Ketchum!" I said cheerfully.

He scowled at me. I knew he thought I was the one who had pulled the alarm. But when I waved my hand in front of him like that, it looked as if I had nothing to hide. So he didn't even bother to look at it closely.

Things would have been just fine if not for the

fact that sometime during science class my fake hand started to fall apart. I tried to shove my hand into my desk, until I realized all we had were those stupid desks that have only a writing surface and no place underneath to keep stuff. I'm glad no one saw me flopping my hand around, trying to hide it in a space that wasn't there.

Finally I jammed my hand into my pocket. But my pants were a little tight, so strings of flesh-colored material bunched up around my wrist.

I stared at them in horror.

Normally, I might just have been kind of upset. But I had spent a lot of time the night before thinking about who the alien might be. I had even asked Patrick which teachers were new to the school since last winter. I asked that because I figured that, like Broxholm, this alien would be someone who hadn't been around for a long time.

Patrick's response had been typical. "What do you care?" he snarled.

"Eat dog meat, fuzzhead," I replied.

I said that because if I told Patrick why I really wanted to know, or even let him think that it really mattered, he wouldn't tell me. This way he just punched me, and then told me what he knew.

As far as he could remember, our school had four new people. The first was none other than Manuel "the Mancatcher" Ketchum, who had started working there last January. The other three were teachers—Mr. Black, the math teacher; Betty Lou Karpou, who I had for home economics; and Andromeda Jones, the science teacher.

The same Andromeda Jones in whose class I was sitting at that very moment.

CHAPTER SIX

A HAND OUT

I began to pluck at the strands of fleshlike stuff around my wrist, hoping I could get rid of them before the bell rang. I didn't have a chance to find out if I would have made it. Ten minutes before the period was over the phone on the wall started to buzz.

Ms. Jones picked it up. She listened for a moment, then turned to me and said, "It's for you, Duncan. You're wanted in Mr. Ketchum's office."

I swallowed. It wasn't that I had never been sent to the principal's office before. The secretary in our old school used to say that she saw more of me than she did of her own kids. She claimed that if I ever left for the junior high, she was going to have a special "Duncan Dougal Memorial Name Tag" put on the chair where I used to sit while I was waiting to see the principal.

Unfortunately, Mr. Ketchum was a lot tougher than our old principal. And he had already taken a dislike to me.

My plans for doing better this year were going down the toilet fast.

"Duncan," said Ms. Jones sharply, "they're waiting for you!"

I sighed and stood up.

"Ee-yew," said the girl sitting next to me, when she saw the stuff around my wrist. "What's that?"

"Skin disease," I snapped. "But it's not catching, unless you get too close to it." Then I lurched toward her so I could watch her jump. I figured it was the last fun I would have that day. Maybe that week. Maybe forever, considering that Mr. Ketchum was one of the people on my alien suspect list.

As I walked out of the science room I wondered if I was being called to the office for the fake fire drill, because of the alien glove, or for some other reason altogether. More important, I wondered if I would ever leave Mr. Ketchum's office alive. It would be easy enough for him to do some alien nastiness to me and then claim that I had never showed up after he called for me.

Suddenly not showing up seemed like a good idea. I turned and headed for the back door of the school. I had only gone about four feet when I heard a deep voice say, "Thinking of leaving us, Mr. Dougal?"

I swallowed. Hard. Had the Mancatcher read my mind? Or did he just know the kind of thing I was apt to do? Either way, things were getting worse by the moment.

"Me? Leave?" I asked, trying to sound innocent. I turned to face him, then started a story about going to the bathroom before I came to the office. I could see by the look on his face that he knew it was baloney, that he knew I knew it was baloney, and that he knew I knew he knew.

So I shut up and followed him down the hall.

"Take your hand out of your pocket," he said once we were inside his office.

"I can't."

"Why not?"

"Skin disease," I said. "It's really awful. You don't want to see it."

The Mancatcher gave me a look of disgust. "I have a strong stomach. Take your hand out of your pocket."

"No!"

The Mancatcher looked frustrated. "All right, we'll come back to that. Right now I want to move on to other things. This morning I received a phone call from a woman named Honey Flint. Do you know her?"

I was so excited about the fact that Honey had called the school, I didn't stop to think. "Sure!" I blurted out. "I met her last night."

The Mancatcher nodded. "And when you met her, did you tell her about what happened here last spring?"

I nodded. I started feeling nervous again. Something was wrong, but I wasn't sure what.

Mr. Ketchum steepled his fingers in front of his face. His dark eyes glared at me. "That was a very foolish thing to do, Mr. Dougal."

Yikes. Was he mad because the school was trying to keep it a secret—or because he was the alien?

"I've got a right to tell the truth," I said.

The Mancatcher laughed, as if the idea of me telling the truth was too silly to even discuss. "No one is questioning your right to tell the truth, Mr. Dougal. What I want to know is if you consider spinning some cockamamie story about alien hand masks and an ongoing invasion part of telling the truth!"

I got mad. "You call *this* cockamamie?" I shouted, pulling my hand out of my pocket and waving it in front of him.

"No," said Mr. Ketchum, "I call it purple ink, the mark of a person who has pulled a false alarm. Two false alarms in this case, since the nonsense you spun out for that newspaper woman counts as a false alarm as well."

I stared at my hand in horror. The glove was gone; every last shred of it had disappeared. The only thing left on my hand that didn't belong there was the purple stain.

"Did you do that?" I asked, staring at the Mancatcher.

He looked at me in puzzlement. "Do what?"

"Make the glove disappear. You know it was there. *You know it.*" I was shouting now, partly because I was frightened and partly because that's what I do when I get in trouble.

The Mancatcher stood up from behind his desk. "Settle down!" he said sharply.

"You leave me alone!" I shouted in terror.

"Duncan, *sit down*!" he bellowed.

I sat.

Then the talking started. First the Mancatcher lectured me about the danger of false alarms. Then a policeman came in and lectured me. Then a fireman came and did the same. By the time they were done we all knew that I was an antisocial jerk with no sense of responsibility and that I was probably going to wind up in prison.

By then I knew even better than they did how dangerous false alarms can be. Because of that stupid fire drill, no one was willing to believe me about the alien. Every time I tried to bring it up, Mr. Ketchum accused me of trying to take advantage of a "tragic situation" (meaning Peter's kidnapping) and told me to shut up.

Was he doing that because he didn't believe me—or because he was the alien?

After the police department and the fire department were done with me, Mr. Ketchum brought in my mother. Mom was crying, which I hate, and she asked me why I did it, which I couldn't really explain since I wasn't sure myself. Then she went on about how she didn't know what my father was going to do. I knew that was true. Based on past experience he would either beat me, or laugh and say, "Boys will be boys."

When they finally let me go I wasn't sure whether I should go home or run away. It would have been nice if I had had someone to talk to. But when you've been the class bully for several years, there aren't too many people who want to hear your problems.

I was walking down Pine Street, trying to figure out what to do, when I spotted Susan talking to Stacy Benoit and Mike Foran. It was like a little convention of good kids. I should have known I didn't belong there, but I tried to join the conversation anyway. (Stupid, right?)

"Hey, it's the Mad False Alarmer," said Mike when I walked up.

So I punched him in the nose.

Susan and Stacy were still yelling at me when I started to run. I didn't stop until I got home. I ran up the stairs and into my bedroom. But I couldn't cry because Patrick was there.

So I just lay in my bed, staring at the ceiling, wondering why I had been born.

CHAPTER SEVEN
ANDROMEDA JONES

Even though I went to school every day. I didn't see the inside of a classroom again until the middle of the next week. That was because I had to sit in the Mancatcher's office for the next five days. The teachers sent down work for me, but I didn't understand it, so I don't know what the point was.

On Wednesday Mr. Ketchum decided he had had enough of me, and said I could start going to class again. Like it was a big gift or something.

He personally delivered me. I was hoping we would go during first period, so I could go to home economics. I didn't hate the class as much as I had expected to, and I really liked Miss Karpou, since she was a little goofy and made funny mistakes. I think she liked me, too, which was a nice change from most teachers, I want to tell you.

As things worked out, I had to wait until second period, because first period the Mancatcher was busy bawling out Orville Plumber. I thought this was pretty funny. Only I didn't laugh about it because if Orville had heard me, he would have plugged me good later.

"Ready for your grand return to society, Mr. Dougal?" asked the Mancatcher when he was done with Orville.

I nodded. The Mancatcher nodded back and gestured toward the door. I went out first.

When we got to science class, the teacher, Andromeda Jones, was getting ready to do a demonstration of static electricity.

"Now, class, I need a volunteer," she was saying as we walked in.

I had no intention of volunteering. After all, Ms. Jones was one of the new people to come on staff since last year, which meant that she was a prime candidate for being the alien. So who knew what that machine was really for?

Besides, I thought the way she dressed was silly. She wore a lot of that safari stuff—you know what I mean, khaki clothes with more pockets than an eighth grader has zits. I had heard a rumor that she claimed she dressed that way because teaching junior high was more dangerous than making a trek through the jungle, but I don't know if that was true or not.

Anyway, after about twenty seconds went by without anyone volunteering, the Mancatcher pushed me forward. "Duncan will be glad to participate in your demonstration, Ms. Jones," he said cheerfully.

"Not me! Uh-uh. No way."

The Mancatcher leaned down next to me and whispered, "Duncan, you haven't begun to learn how unpleasant I can be. Unless you want to spend the next five days in my office learning a new definition of misery, get up there and participate in this experiment."

I sighed and walked to the front of the room. People started to giggle and snicker, which only made things worse. I started to blush. It's just as well the Mancatcher was there. Otherwise I probably would have bopped someone.

"Listen up, everyone," said Ms. Jones. "The purpose of this demonstration is to give you an idea of how free-flowing electricity can affect things." She motioned to a black kid sitting in the second row and said, "Marcus, I want you to crank the generator."

Marcus smiled. "Sure thing, Ms. Jones."

I wasn't surprised that Marcus was smiling. One night last spring my father had gotten drunk and done some things that were pretty mean. I was still in a bad mood when I came to school the next day, and when Marcus had said something to me that I didn't like, I knocked him down and jumped on his lunch pail. So of course he was happy to crank the generator for Ms. Jones.

Once Marcus was in place, Ms. Jones put a huge helmet over my head. It was made of clear material, with a couple of jagged lightning bolts painted on the front. Lumpy knobs extended from the sides and the top.

Once the helmet was in place, Mr. Jones told Marcus to start cranking.

My scalp began to tingle. My hair started to move, as if a slight breeze were blowing through it.

Within a few seconds everybody was laughing like crazy. I suppose I did look pretty funny, with my eyes wide and my hair standing straight up.

Funny or not, I *hate* it when people laugh at me. I was so mad I wanted to bop someone. Only I couldn't, because the Mancatcher was right there.

So I held what I was feeling inside. But I had had it. Forget trying to save the world. For all I cared, the aliens could come and take everyone away.

Suddenly I stopped thinking about people laughing at me. Something else was going on, something weird. The *inside* of my head was starting to tingle. I felt like I had ants walking around inside my skull.

"All right, Marcus," said Ms. Jones. "That's enough."

Marcus gave the machine an extra crank or two for good measure.

"Marcus!" snapped Ms. Jones. "I want you to stop now!"

Looking like someone had just stolen his candy, Marcus stopped cranking. I promised myself I would bop him as soon as I got a chance.

The class was still laughing. My cheeks were burning as I headed for my seat.

I sat down and tried to listen, but my head was still tingling from the demonstration. I don't think they should be allowed to do things like that to kids.

After school I had an idea. That was kind of neat, since it didn't happen all that often. I decided I would go talk to Ms. Schwartz over at the elementary school. Since the alien had put her in a force field last spring, she might believe me when I told her about what I had found in the dumpster.

On the way, I saw a bunch of kids from the seventh grade standing in front of Sigel's Pharmacy. They were talking and muttering, but when they spotted me they began to hoot and holler.

Susan Simmons stepped out of the group and walked over to where I was standing. She poked her finger into my chest and said, "I knew you were a creep, Duncan, but even I never thought you would sink this low. I've met earthworms that I respect more than I do you."

I looked at her in shock. Now what had I done?

CHAPTER EIGHT

"DUNCAN DOUGAL, BOY HERO"

"Don't give me that look," said Susan.

"What look?"

"You know what I mean," she said. "Your 'What? Who, me? What did I do?' look. I've seen you use it on teachers a million times. All it means is that you're guilty."

Sheesh. You know you're in trouble when you can't even get a look on your face without people deciding you're guilty of something.

Before I could protest, Susan shoved a newspaper in front of my face. "Look at this!" she ordered.

I looked. I groaned. It was the *National Sun*. Across the top, in huge letters, it said, "TEEN HERO SAYS ALIENS STILL LURK IN SMALL TOWN!" Next to the headline was my picture.

"Listen to this," commanded Susan. "'Duncan Dougal, the heroic teenager who foiled last spring's attempt by aliens to take over a typical American town, says that the entire planet remains in danger of an alien invasion.'"

"It's true!" I said.

"Oh, really?" said Susan. "*You* stopped the invasion? If I remember correctly, about the only thing you did was stand in front of Broxholm's viewer and scream."

I tried to explain that I meant it was true about the invasion. But before I could say anything Susan was quoting the newspaper again. "'My friends were pretty scared last spring,' Dougal told *Sun* reporter Honey Flint. 'But I kept my cool. That's how I was able to figure out how to drive off the alien.'"

She looked at me. "*You* figured out how to drive off the alien?"

I blushed. Susan was the one who had done that, of course.

"Duncan Dougal, boy hero," called Stacy, her voice mocking.

"Oh, Duncan, save me!" shouted another girl.

"Shut up!" I yelled. "Just shut up, all of you!" Then I started to run.

What was I going to do? I knew one of our teachers was still an alien, but after Honey's article, there was no chance that anyone would believe me. I didn't mean to lie when I talked to Honey. I just tried to tell my side of things. I guess I got carried away.

"Duncan Dougal, boy hero!" The mocking words still rang in my ears as I raced through the front door of our house.

Patrick was already there. He was reading a copy of the *Sun*. "Nice bunch of lies, buttface," he said when he saw me come in. "Your friends are going to love you for this one."

What friends? I thought miserably. *I don't have any friends.*

But I wasn't about to say that to Patrick. So I told him to shut up, and ran up the stairs into our room. I could hear him laughing downstairs.

It was even worse when my father came home

and saw the paper. He was thrilled. He went out and bought twenty copies of the paper, and started calling all our relatives. It was the first time he ever acted like he was happy that I had been born, and it was all because of a bunch of lies I had told some stupid reporter.

Patrick was jealous about Dad being excited, so he spent the evening giving me noogies when no one was watching.

I had terrible dreams that night. People I knew kept turning into aliens. I woke up sweating and terrified.

I wanted to skip school the next day, but I didn't have a chance because my father insisted on driving me.

"I want to have a little talk with your principal," he said.

Actually, Dad's presence saved me for a little while. As we walked down the hall I could tell that kids were laughing. But with my father there, they didn't say anything out loud. They knew you didn't mess around with my dad.

Our visit to the principal's office was really embarrassing. We didn't see the Mancatcher, since my father insisted on going straight to Dr. Wilburn, the head principal.

"Look, what are you going to do about this alien situation?" asked Dad once the secretary had shown us in.

Dr. Wilburn was a tall, elegant woman with silver-gray hair. She looked at my father and said, "To tell you the truth, Mr. Dougal, we are still trying to decide. We had thought about suing Duncan for slander. However, since he is a minor we chose not to follow that option. I will be bringing the matter up at the Board of Education meeting later this week, where I will note your concern. An apology from Duncan would, of course, be useful."

My father looked like someone had smacked him in the face with a dead fish. When he demanded that Dr. Wilburn find the alien and get rid of him or her, Dr. Wilburn replied that there was no way the school was going to pay attention to the rantings of a disturbed seventh grader who had a long history of lying and was using last spring's tragedy to bring attention to himself.

"What about the glove?" demanded my father, his face red with anger.

Dr. Wilburn folded her hands in front of her. "Show me the glove, and I will take action," she said.

"Duncan," said my father, "where's the glove?"

"It's gone," I whispered. "It fell apart."

The look on his face said it all. My father felt I had totally betrayed him.

Dr. Wilburn asked us to leave. Actually, she told us that if we didn't go, she would consider having us arrested.

I felt like a bug on the windshield of life. I felt like dog poop. I felt like blowing up the universe.

My father went off, and I went to my first period class, which was home ec. I was looking forward to seeing Miss Karpou, since she was usually so cheerful, but she was all upset because the refrigerator was broken, and it had messed up her lesson plan for the day.

Plus, everyone started to laugh when I came in.

"Quiet, class!" said Miss Karpou.

No one paid any attention (which was what usually happened when poor Miss Karpou tried to get us to shut up). They just kept laughing and mocking me.

Too bad for them. Because a few hours later, when I finally got a clue as to who the alien was, I decided to keep it to myself.

Oh, I had my reasons. For one thing, I knew no one would believe me. For another, by then I didn't give a bat's butt about what happened to any of them anyway.

Besides, what gave me the clue was something so big, so tremendously exciting, that I knew it might be the most important discovery in the history of the planet.

Given the way everyone was treating me, I decided it was going to stay my secret.

CHAPTER NINE

HOW TO FRY YOUR BRAINS

My discovery happened during math class. Mr. Black was explaining something about changing fractions into decimals, which was about the same thing as explaining how to make snoods into farfels as far as I was concerned, when suddenly I started to understand what he was talking about.

Now that may not seem like much to you. But it was the first time it had ever happened to me. I never got *anything* in math the first time around. Of course, I didn't usually listen real hard, but that was mostly because there didn't seem to be much point in listening, since I knew I wasn't going to get it anyway.

That day was different. As I listened to Mr. Black, all the things I was supposed to have been learning about math over the last eight years suddenly began to fit together. I was amazed. This stuff actually made sense! It connected. It was almost *beautiful*, in a weird sort of way.

My brain was tingling.

And then the next amazing thing happened. Mr. Black asked a question, and *I knew the answer*! I thought about raising my hand, but that seemed too weird. Besides, if I answered the question, I knew people would just figure I was cheating somehow, and I had already had enough attention for one day.

It didn't take me too long to guess what was happening. Even a moron could have figured it out, and I was no moron—at least, not anymore.

It was simple: Andromeda Jones was the alien, and that machine she had used on me the day before was some sort of alien brain fryer—a brain fryer that made you smarter.

And if it could make me smarter once, maybe another dose would make me even smarter. Wouldn't that be cool? Forget Duncan Dougal, boy hero. I was going to be Duncan Dougal, boy *genius*!

I couldn't wait for the day to end. I had my plans already made. All I had to do was hang on and not bop anyone before the final bell rang. It wasn't easy, since I was still getting a lot of flak about the article in the *Sun*. But I didn't care anymore. I was going to be better than those jerks, better than all of the clods who had laughed at me all these years.

When the last bell rang I headed for the boys' room. I slipped into one of the toilet stalls and stood on the seat, so no one would see me if they looked underneath the door. Normally it wouldn't be a problem to stay after school; lots of kids stay after for different activities. But since I was known as a troublemaker, the school didn't want me around. If anyone spotted me, I would be sent home.

While I was standing there waiting, I found myself wishing that I had brought a book to read.

The very thought made me blink. Why in heaven's name would I want a book?

The answer was simple. My brain was hungry.

This being-smart thing was going to take some getting used to!

After about an hour I left the rest room. By that time most of the teachers had gone home, so I knew the halls would be a little safer. Besides, I was worried that one of the janitors would be coming in to clean the toilets before long.

How soon did I dare go use the brain fryer?

Not soon. The more I thought about it, the more I knew I didn't want to be interrupted. I didn't want any teachers or kids to catch me at this. It was going to stay my secret.

And I sure didn't want the alien to catch me.

Of course, the question I should have been asking myself was, why had she used it on me in the first place? I had probably gotten smart enough to think of that question. But I was too excited about the potential of all this to really worry about that idea. I didn't want anything to stop me—not even the possibility that this was a trap of some kind. If it was, the bait was worth it. I was tired of feeling stupid.

I began sneaking down the hall toward the science lab. I figured I might as well hide in there, even if I was going to wait until later to use the brain fryer.

After about three steps I decided to take off my sneakers, which aren't all that great for sneaking no matter what you call them. They're not bad, but they can give you a surprise squeak if you're not careful. Socks, even filthy ones, are quieter.

I heard a noise and scurried into a classroom. Lying on the floor, I watched as a whistling janitor pushed a broom down the hall. I tried to time him in my head and see how long it took before he came back. I counted a hundred and eighty elephants—about three minutes.

I decided to wait right where I was, which was probably as safe as anywhere. Then I realized that I was across the hall from the library. That would be more interesting.

I waited for the janitor to go past again, then scurried across the hall and through the library door.

That was the first time I had been in the library this year. It might have been the first time in my *life* I had gone into a library without being forced. I found a book that looked interesting, something about cars, and crawled under a table in the corner.

I had enough light, but just barely. It didn't make

that much difference. Even though I really wanted to read the book, I couldn't. I just couldn't figure out what the words said.

I had to get another zap of that brain fryer.

I tried to read for a little while longer. My eyes got heavy. My head sagged forward. Soon I was asleep.

When I woke the building was pitch dark. I crawled out from under the table and listened. Silence.

Well, near-silence. My stomach started to rumble, which wasn't surprising since I hadn't had anything to eat since lunchtime.

Trying to ignore my stomach's pleas for food, I stepped out into the hallway. It was kind of spooky being in the school all by myself. Kind of fun, too. Normally I might have decided that this was the time for a little mischief. Now I only had one thing on my mind: getting smarter.

Wow. Getting smarter in school. That was the first time the idea had ever occurred to me.

I tiptoed down the dark hall to the science lab. I paused at the door. The room was pitch dark. What if the alien was inside? For all I knew, she slept here—maybe she folded herself up and spent the night on the shelf. Who could tell with an alien?

My stomach rumbled again. I wondered if Ms. Jones had anything to eat in the lab refrigerator. I figured if I was going to get smart, there was no point doing it on an empty stomach.

I felt my way to the lab refrigerator and pulled open the door. The little light inside seemed terribly bright after all the darkness. At first glance, it wasn't very encouraging. Most of the bottles had either little dead animals or small green plants. None of them looked like they were meant for human stomachs.

But at the back of the fridge I found a square Tupperware container that looked promising. I pulled it out. Hoping there would be something inside that might make my stomach stop complaining, I pulled off the lid.

Then I started to scream.

CHAPTER TEN

POOT!

I probably wouldn't have screamed if the stuff in the container had only been glowing. Even if it had only started to wobble, I might have been able to control myself, telling myself that I had accidentally shaken the container.

But when the glowing, jellylike mass I had uncovered began to ooze over the rim of the Tupperware and up along my arm, it was more than I could handle. I not only screamed, I dropped the container onto the counter.

But the blobby stuff was attached to me. It stretched, extending from my wrist to the container.

I backed away, still screaming. The stuff continued to stretch, dragging the container with it. Suddenly the container slid off the edge of the counter. The goo inside pulled out with a horrible sucking sound, then snapped onto my hand, almost like a rubber band.

Then it started to whine.

"Aaaahh!" I screamed. "Aaah! Aaah! Get off! Get off!"

I shook my hand, trying to get rid of the glowing goo. The stuff stretched to the right, and then to the left, bulging with my movements. Suddenly it came loose from my hand. It sailed through the air and landed on the counter with a *splat*!

It sat there whimpering for a minute. Then it slowly reshaped itself until it looked something like a two-foot-long slug. A glowing slug. The slug-thing lifted its front end (at least, I assume it was the front end) several inches into the air. It turned so that it was pointing at me.

And then it burped. It burped right at me, as if it wanted me to know how disgusted it was with me.

Then it collapsed onto the counter.

I wanted to run. But if I did, if I left that stuff lying on the counter, Ms. Jones would know that someone had been snooping around. And then I would never get to use the brain fryer. And I *wanted* to use it.

Suddenly I got an idea, which sort of shows you the effect the brain fryer had already had on me. The idea was this: if I used the brain fryer first, maybe it would zap up my mindpower enough so that I could figure out what to do with the slug next.

"You stay there," I said, pointing at the slug and trying to keep my voice from trembling.

It lifted one end and said, "Poot." But it said it in kind of a weak little voice. I felt a twinge of fear. Did this thing have to be in the refrigerator to stay healthy? Was it going to die if I left it out on the counter? If it did, what then? Andromeda Jones would *know* that someone had been fooling around in the lab, and with her alien science it probably wouldn't take her long to figure out who it was.

Then another thought hit me. The worst one yet. What if I was *supposed* to come in here and fry my brains? And what if the reason was that this thing I had found in the refrigerator was some alien brain-eater that needed a supercharged brain for a snack every now and then, or else it would starve to death? Suddenly the phrase "brain food" took on a horrible new meaning.

I couldn't decide if I was glad I was smarter, because it let me think of things like this, or if I wished that I wasn't so smart, so such awful ideas wouldn't cross my mind.

Well, I had gone this far. No point in stopping now. Unless there was some way to put that machine in reverse, I was going to have to keep getting smarter just so I could stay alive.

Of course, none of this was going to make any difference if I couldn't find the thing. It suddenly occurred to me that maybe Ms. Jones had taken the machine home with her rather than leave it around in the school, where someone like me could get ahold of it.

That is, assuming she had a home, and wasn't curled up somewhere on a shelf in the science lab, just waiting for me to finish making a fool of myself by making a genius of myself so that she could feed me to the refrigerator slug.

I tried to remember what she had done with the machine after Marcus had finished cranking it the day before. At first I had no idea, which made sense, because I had been so mad at everyone that I wasn't really paying attention to what happened with the machine.

But then some images began to form in my head. I was remembering. I was *really* remembering! I hadn't even paid attention. But the images were stored in my brain.

I wondered how much else was stored in there.

This getting smart had its advantages after all!

I went to the walk-in closet where Ms. Jones had put the machine after her demonstration was over. My heart began to pound. What if she was inside waiting for me? My imagination created a vivid image of her hanging upside down from the ceiling, like some giant bat, just waiting for me to open the door so she could grab me.

I shook my head. I guess I was also getting more creative. Too bad courage wasn't also part of the package.

I was dying to turn on a light. But that was impossible. It would have been like standing on the roof and shouting that someone was snooping around in the building.

Taking a deep breath, I began to open the closet door. Slowly. Very slowly, standing not in front of it but beside it, in case anything came charging out of the darkness.

Nothing. Silence.

Holding my breath, I began to peer around the edge of the door. Suddenly I felt something touch my ankle.

I learned it doesn't take brains to invent antigravity, just fear. I was halfway to the ceiling before my scream hit my lips. "Aaaaah!" I cried, just like before. "Aaaaahh!"

"Poot?" asked a small voice.

I was standing on the doorknob. I looked down and saw the glowing slug-thing on the floor beneath me. One end was lifted in the air, waving in a slow circle.

"Poot?" it asked again.

My heartbeat went from jackhammer level down to bass-drum level. For a moment I wondered what would happen if I jumped on the slug. Maybe I would kill it. Or maybe it would just split into a jillion little slime balls, each one of them hungry, angry, and out to eat my brain.

Scratch that idea.

"Go away!" I yelled.

"Poot!" answered the slug, sounding as angry as me.

I decided to take a chance. I jumped down from the doorknob, landing about two feet from the slug. "Scram!" I screamed.

"Poot!" it cried in panic. Then it formed itself into a circle and began to roll back across the floor to the lab table.

I didn't have much time. And after all that noise, there was no way I was going to sneak up on anyone (or anything) waiting in the closet. So I just walked in.

I didn't spend long looking for the thing. Actually, I didn't spend any time *looking* for it, since the closet was too dark inside to see anything. But I hadn't groped my way more than two feet past the door when I bumped into a rolling table, the kind teachers usually keep movie projectors on.

This one didn't have a projector; it had Ms. Jones's brain fryer.

Trembling with excitement, I rolled the machine back into the lab. Working in the dim light (half from the moon, half from street lamps) that came through the windows, I began to set up the machine. At one point I closed my eyes, trying to remember how the helmet had been connected to the generator. In a few seconds my brain sent me the image.

I smiled. This being smart was good stuff.

I looked around for the slug. It was lurking over by the lab table.

Placing the helmet carefully on my head, I got ready to fry my own brains.

CHAPTER ELEVEN
ZAP!

I concentrated hard, trying to remember everything Ms. Jones had done that first time. After all, I sure didn't want to put the machine in reverse and make myself dumber.

Finally I was ready. Leaning one hand on the table next to the generator, I took the crank in my other hand and began to turn it—slowly at first, then faster and faster.

For a moment nothing seemed to happen. Then I felt a familiar sensation, as if a breeze were ruffling my hair.

I turned the crank a little faster.

My hair stood up. The ants started to crawl around inside my head.

I could almost feel myself getting smarter.

Now I started to really crank. "Come on, machine," I whispered, "come on, baby, do your stuff. Make me the next Einstein!"

Sparks of lightning began to flash through my head. Colors seemed to flicker around me. My hand was a blur as it turned the generator's crank faster and faster.

"Poot!" cried the slug-thing in alarm.

I thought I smelled something burning. I wanted to stop, but it was as if my hand were on automatic pilot, and my brains were too busy getting fried to give it a new order.

Z-A-A-A-P!

That sound, like an enormous spark sizzling through the night, is the last thing I remember. I blacked out and fell to the floor.

"Duncan," whispered a voice in my head. "Duncan, wake up."

I knew that voice; it belonged to weird Peter

Thompson. But it couldn't be Peter. He was gone, off in space with Broxholm somewhere. Which meant that I had to be dreaming. Which meant that I was asleep.

I tried to wake up.

My body didn't cooperate.

All right—I'll stay asleep, I thought.

Peter's image materialized in my brain, looking just as he had the last time I had seen him, the night of our spring concert; the night Susan had used her piccolo to drive off the alien teacher.

It hadn't surprised me that Broxholm couldn't stand the sound of her piccolo. I didn't like it much myself.

But I had never quite gotten over the fact that as near as any of us could tell, Peter had *chosen* to go into space with the alien. I mean, the rest of us were terrified that we were going to get kidnapped. Old Peter couldn't wait to get his butt up into that spaceship.

Peter Thompson, tall and skinny, his brown eyes lost behind the thickest pair of glasses in the sixth grade.

"Duncan," he whispered again. "Do you remember how many times you beat me up in the last three years?"

I shook my head—in my dream, that is.

"Lots," said Peter with a nasty smile. Then his face began to change. His skin started to turn green: pale green first, then darker and darker, until it was the color of limes. His eyes stretched out until they looked like butterfly wings, huge and orange.

Broxholm!

"Get away from me!" I screamed.

And then I woke up—which didn't improve things any, because when I opened my eyes I saw myself staring back at me. Only my face had no color. No color at all, only a pale, greenish-yellow glow.

I blinked. The other me blinked, too.

I shouted in terror.

The other me said, "Poot!"

"Yeeaaah!" I cried, rolling away. It was the slug-thing. It had climbed/crawled/oozed its way to the underside of the lab table, where I had landed when I blacked out.

I didn't mind so much that it had been hanging

over me, though that was pretty disgusting. What had me worried was the fact that it had imitated my face. I hoped it wouldn't do that when I wasn't around. It would be like an announcement that I had been here.

Could the slug only copy something that was in front of it? Or once it had copied something, would it be able to repeat that image over and over again? Who could tell? It's not like there's been a lot written about the mental ability of alien slugs that live in Tupperware containers kept in the refrigerators of junior-high science labs.

Of course, that was only one of the important questions I was facing at the moment. The others included (a) how was I going to get the slug back into the refrigerator? (b) how long had I been asleep? (c) had the brain fryer worked? (d) if it *had* worked, just how smart was I? and (e) what should I do next?

I decided the first thing to do was put the machine back. As I was packing it up I kept an eye out for the slug, which had crawled down from under the lab table and was watching me (I guess you could call it watching) from a spot on Andromeda Jones's desk.

"Stay there," I said, trying to sound menacing.

"Poot!" it replied.

I put everything back in place and rolled the cart toward the storage area. As I closed the door, I wondered if the machine had some sort of meter that would let Andromeda Jones keep track of how much brainpower it had passed out. I figured I must have gotten smarter, since that wasn't the kind of thing I would have thought of before. Of course the thought didn't serve any purpose other than to make me nervous. But at least it showed I was thinking.

I also wondered if Ms. Jones had used the machine on anyone else.

And I wondered why she had used it on me. I didn't think it was out of the goodness of her alien heart.

That thought made me really nervous. It also convinced me that I had done the right thing. If Ms. Jones had fried my brains as part of some alien experiment, the best thing I could do to protect myself would be to get smarter as fast as I could.

I stopped and closed my eyes. How much smarter

was I? It was hard to tell. I didn't really have any way to test it. And the last brain fry had taken a while to really have an effect. I did feel a tingling in my skull. Maybe the machine had stimulated my brain so that it was growing new synapses or something.

I blinked. Why in the world did I know a word like *synapses*?

Must be the brain fryer had worked after all. Except I couldn't figure out where I had found the word to begin with. Was the thing putting new information into my head, like those subliminal messages in records that people keep worrying about?

I shivered.

"I'll think about it tomorrow," I said to myself. "Just like Scarlett O'Hara."

I blinked. It was happening again. Other than "Make my day," I had never quoted a movie or a book before. Where was this stuff coming from?

Never mind. I had to get out of the lab. No more fooling around. I grabbed the Tupperware container and its lid and headed for the slug.

"Inside!" I ordered, holding the container in front of it.

"Poot?" it replied, sounding pitiful.

"Inside!" I repeated, trying to sound fierce.

It made a little pooty sigh, then slumped forward and oozed into the container. I slipped on the cover, then sighed myself. Remembering how my mother used these things, I pressed the edges of the lid in place, then pushed down on the center to get rid of the extra air. This is called "burping" the Tupperware.

Only the sound that came out was a tiny "poot."

I put the container back into the refrigerator, which reminded me that I still hadn't had anything to eat.

Stomach rumbling, I stared around the room. As far as I could tell, everything was back in place.

Now to head for home, I thought. I decided to put on my sneakers. I figured that with the amount of screaming I had done already, if there had been anyone else in the building, they would have caught me by now anyway.

Even so, I walked quietly. Being alone at night in a building where you don't really belong will do that to you. Also, I still had a slight fear that the alien was going to jump out and nab me. That may not have made much sense, but you live through what I had lived through in the previous few days and tell me how much sense *you* make!

I went to one of the back doors, since I didn't want some late-night driver who happened to be passing by to spot me slipping out of the building.

The moon had disappeared behind a cloud. Its absence made the sky darker and the stars brighter. I looked up into the darkness and wondered which of those points of light Andromeda Jones called home. As I stood there staring into the night, I suddenly remembered that there was a constellation called Andromeda. Was that where she had gotten her fake human name? Pretty nervy of her.

Of course, it was pretty odd for *me* to remember the name of any constellation. But I barely noticed that fact. I guess I was already getting used to being smarter.

I walked around the school. The grass was soaked with dew, and so were my sneakers by the time I got to the front of the building. I could hear crickets singing in the distance.

I like being out in the night. The time is quiet and private, and you can feel more like yourself than you do in the daylight.

I heard the town clock begin to chime. Two hours past midnight. I figured I had better get moving.

I had only walked a couple of blocks when a car pulled up beside me and a deep voice said, "Get in, Duncan."

CHAPTER TWELVE

ACCUSED

Once my heart started to beat again, I realized that I knew the person driving the car.

It was Peter Thompson's father.

"Get in," said Mr. Thompson again. "I'll give you a ride home."

I hesitated. Not because I didn't trust Mr. Thompson. I just didn't want to hear him whine on about how much he missed Peter now that he was gone.

On the other hand, I was tired and hungry, and getting a ride home instead of having to walk was very appealing. I decided I could listen to Mr.

Thompson for a few minutes if it meant getting to my house—and my refrigerator—faster.

Actually, it was the refrigerator that was topmost in my mind. I was hoping I could find something in there that I could eat without having to worry about whether or not it was still alive. Of course, there was no guarantee on that matter. My father calls our refrigerator Resurrection City, because my mother puts in stuff that's dead and three months later takes it out covered with new life. Whenever Dad says that my mother replies, "Look, Harold, if you don't like it, you can clean the refrigerator yourself, since last time I looked you didn't have two broken arms—though you might if you don't watch out."

Life at my house is not exactly like life on *Leave It to Beaver*.

"So, what are you doing out at this time of night?" I said as I climbed into the car.

The instant I said it I realized what a dumb question it was for a kid to ask an adult at two o'clock in the morning on a school night. But then, I've noticed that for most people, their tongue is the last part of their body to get smart.

I wished I hadn't asked. I wished it even more when Mr. Thompson answered, because depending on how I took it, what he said was either terribly sad or as scary as anything that had happened so far that night.

But I had asked, and Mr. Thompson answered.

"I'm looking for Peter," he said.

I closed my eyes. Even though my tongue was running ahead of my brain, I was smart enough to know that "Grow up, Jack, your kid took off for outer space because he couldn't stand you," was not the right thing to say under the circumstances.

Actually, I could think of several dozen things that were not the right thing to say under the circumstances. What I couldn't come up with was anything that I *should* say.

So I kept my mouth shut, which was probably the best proof I had had so far that the brain fryer was making me smarter.

"I know he's around here somewhere," said Mr. Thompson as he began to drive. "I just don't believe he's gone that far away. He's too smart to think he could survive someplace like New York

City, even though he always wanted to live there."

This was sad. Mr. Thompson's idea of far away was several trillion miles short of where his kid had really gone.

"Do you know where he is, Duncan?" asked Mr. Thompson. "I know you were his best friend, because you were the only one who ever stayed overnight at the house. He must have told you where he was going. Tell me. Please tell me."

A car passed us, going in the other direction. In the glow of its headlights I could see that Mr. Thompson had tears running down his cheeks.

"Peter didn't like me as much as you think he did," I said truthfully, which was sort of a new experience. "He only let me stay at your place because I was in trouble."

Mr. Thompson nodded. "Peter would have done that," he said. "He was a good boy."

I felt like asking Mr. Thompson if he had ever bothered to tell Peter he thought he was a good kid while he was still around. I decided it wasn't the time.

I really didn't like seeing him so sad. So when he

stopped the car in front of my house I said, "Listen, if I hear from Peter, I'll be sure to let you know."

"Thanks, Duncan," said Mr. Thompson. "You're a good boy, too."

I swallowed. My throat started to hurt. I don't know why, for sure, except that no one had ever said that to me before.

When I went inside everyone was asleep except Patrick, who was sitting up watching an old movie. "Ma's mad 'cause you didn't call," he said.

I nodded. She always said she was mad when Patrick didn't show up, too. But usually she was really just relieved.

I went upstairs and got into bed.

But I didn't go to sleep.

Mostly I stared at the ceiling, trying to figure out the answers to questions I had never asked before I got so smart.

If I didn't know how to take Mr. Thompson, my teachers began having the same problem with me. It started two days after I gave myself the second dose of the brain zapper. Mr. Black, the math teacher, called me in at lunchtime and said, "Mr. Dougal, I am going to give you one chance to confess. Otherwise you will be going straight to the principal's office."

I looked at him. "Confess to what?" I asked.

He glared at me. "Mr. Dougal, I cannot abide cheating. I want to know how you passed the math test I gave you yesterday afternoon."

Sheesh! What was I going to tell him? That I passed it because I had gotten my brain fried and I was probably smarter than he was? I was smart enough to know that was a bad idea, even if I hadn't been smart enough to realize that suddenly passing a test was going to get me into trouble.

I closed my eyes and thought fast. "I'm turning over a new leaf," I said, trying to sound sincere. "I really studied for that test."

Actually, that was a lie. I had barely studied at all. I didn't need to; my brain had just absorbed the information.

From the look on his face, Mr. Black might have found the fried-brain story more believable.

"I want the truth," he said.

"Mr. Black, I didn't cheat. I can prove it. Give me

some more questions, right now, and I'll do them for you. You'll see. I really know the stuff. I do!"

Mr. Black smiled, as if he knew I had really gotten in over my head. "All right," he said. "Have a seat."

I sat down in the first row. Mr. Black went to his desk and took out a sheet of paper and a pencil. He scribbled down a few numbers, then brought the paper over and set it in front of me.

I wanted to kick him. The problem he had written down was harder than anything on the test. He *wanted* me to get it wrong.

Brain, I thought, *don't fail me now.*

CHAPTER THIRTEEN

THE SOUND OF MUSIC

I stared at the problem. For a moment my mind seemed to go blank. Then I could almost feel the ants start crawling around inside my head. Without looking up, I reached for the pencil Mr. Black was holding. He handed it to me, and I began to figure.

Thirty seconds later I had the answer.

When I handed the paper to Mr. Black he was staring at me as if I had just sprouted wings and flown around the room a couple of times.

"How did you do that?" he asked.

"Must be you're a great teacher," I said. It was a nasty crack, but I was really mad.

Mr. Black sat down at his desk. He looked at me, at the paper, and then back at me. "You can go, Duncan," he said at last. "Please keep up the good work."

I should have learned my lesson from that little scene. People don't want you to change too fast. Some people don't want you to change at all, because then they have to think when they deal with you.

But I was too excited about my new brain to hide my light under a bushel for the moment. When I left Mr. Black's room I went straight to the library.

The librarian looked at me suspiciously. "We don't circulate the swimsuit issue of *Sports Illustrated*, Duncan," she said when I walked through the door.

"That's all right," I said. "I want to read a book."

The look on her face was even better than the one on Mr. Black's had been.

It wasn't until I got to science the next morning that I realized I had better be careful about this. Home economics had been fun. Even though I was doing better there, people just figured it was because I had settled down for a couple of days. No one thought that much of my intelligence because I didn't ruin the eggplant, though Miss Karpou gave me a big smile and thanked me for my good work, which made me feel kind of warm inside.

But when I sat down in science class it suddenly occurred to me that if I showed off too much, Ms. Jones would be bound to know what I had been up to.

On the other hand, since she was the one who had fried my brains in the first place, I shouldn't have to act entirely stupid in her class, either.

The ones who really had a problem coping with me were the other smart kids. They had known me as Duncan the Dunce for so long that they didn't know how to react when I started answering questions that some of them couldn't figure out.

Part of the reason I was getting smarter so fast was that I was reading my brains out. Or in. Or something. It only took me a day or two to realize I needed to do that in secret. The first time Patrick saw me reading a book he pulled it out of my hand and asked me if I was turning into a geekoid. I couldn't believe he could be such a jerk.

Then I remembered how I used to treat Peter Thompson.

My father was no better. He told me he thought reading was a complete waste of time.

So I had to do all my reading where no one could see me.

Two nights later I stayed after school and gave myself a third zap with the brain fryer. I looked in the refrigerator for the slug-thing, but it was gone. I wondered if Ms. Jones had eaten it or something. To my surprise, the idea made me a little unhappy. Despite the fact that it had terrified me, I had gotten kind of used to the little guy.

Between the third session with the brain fryer and the fact that I was reading hundreds of pages a day, I could feel myself getting smarter faster and faster. Something I hadn't expected was that the more I learned, the more things made sense. Sometimes learning one thing made three other things suddenly come into focus. I was starting to find the connections that made learning fun.

Sheesh. Listen to me! Who ever thought I would use the words *learning* and *fun* in the same sentence?

Even though I was having fun, there were a few things still bothering me. Number one was the question of what Andromeda Jones was up to. Why had she fried my brains to begin with? And why hadn't she said or done anything about it since? Was I some kind of experiment? Had the aliens gotten together and said, "Hey, let's see what happens if we make a bozo bright"? I didn't particularly like that idea, though from my point of view it was working out OK for the time being.

But what if when the experiment was over she decided to take the smartness back? That was the most frightening idea of all. I didn't think I could stand going back to being what I used to be.

The second thing bothering me was the way the other kids were acting. No one knew what to think about me anymore. The only one who didn't treat me like a complete freak was Susan.

My third problem was that I was getting so smart that I didn't know what to do about it. If a kid like me, or like I had been, suddenly announced that he had figured out how to create world peace, would you pay any attention to him? More important, would the President and Congress? But that was exactly the situation I found myself in.

When I described a brilliant plan to end world hunger, my social studies teacher said it was silly.

The next day I figured out cold fusion—only I didn't dare tell *that* to my science teacher, since I didn't want her to know I had been tampering with her brain zapper.

But can you imagine how frustrating it was? Think about it. Wrapped inside my magnificent brain was information that would have solved every one of earth's energy problems, eliminated most of our pollution problems, and made me a billionaire in the process. And there wasn't a darn thing I could do about it!

I tried. I even sent a letter to the Department of Energy telling them I would *give* them the information. They sent back a very polite note letting me know in the nicest possible terms that they thought I was an idiot.

That was one more thing I learned once I got smart: no one wants to listen to a kid with an idea. Sometimes I thought I could understand why old Peter had decided to go with Broxholm that night.

Even so, I was feeling pretty good about myself,

and about what had happened—until the night that I went to bed and couldn't get to sleep because of the radio.

At least, I thought it was the radio.

"Come on, Patrick," I said. "Turn it off so I can go to sleep."

"Turn what off?"

"Your radio!"

"My radio is broken, Duncan Dootbrain, so shut up and leave me alone."

I blinked. Patrick was telling the truth. I remembered hearing him complain to my mother the day before about his radio being broken.

So where was the music coming from?

I rolled over, and the station changed. Instead of Madonna, I was getting a blast of Beethoven. I rolled back, and Madonna's voice came back on.

Or maybe I should say back in. Because what I had figured out was this: the music was inside my head.

Most people have five senses. Suddenly I had six. I had fried my brain one time too many, and turned it into a radio receiver.

CHAPTER FOURTEEN

INVISIBLE INFORMATION

I didn't get much sleep that night. Every time I moved my head I got a different kind of music playing inside it.

Finally I found a station that played truly boring elevator music that should have put me to sleep almost instantly. It probably would have, if I hadn't been so terrified about what I had done to myself.

Lying in bed while elevator music plays endlessly in your head and you sweat with fear about what you've done to yourself—that's about as bad as life can get.

At least, that was what I thought at the time. The next day I realized that I was wrong.

I had forgotten about TV.

It started shortly after home economics class, when I closed my eyes and found myself watching a rerun of *The Donna Reed Show*.

You might think having a TV receiver in your brain sounds like fun. Believe me, it's not. For one thing, I couldn't turn it off. The shows were always there. If you think about how smart I had become, and how stupid most television is, you'll see how painful this was for me.

I had read enough by this time to guess what was going on. To understand, you have to start by realizing that the air around us is filled with invisible information. That may seem weird, but it's true. Think about it for a moment. Whenever you smell something, you're pulling information out of the air. When you hear something, you're pulling information out of the air. What are you smelling? What are you hearing? You may be able to see the object, but you can't see the smell itself; it travels to you in the form of incredibly tiny molecules. The sound comes to you in waves of vibrations moving through the air.

Invisible information.

The thing is, we know how to interpret that information. Our noses and our ears take the molecules or the sound waves and translate them so that we can say, "Ah, rotting fish" or "squealing tires."

Now, we know that we don't take in all the information around us. For example, our noses aren't built to process smells the way a bloodhound's can. When a bloodhound tracks someone down by following their smell it's using invisible information we could use, too, if only we could perceive it.

Now think about your radio. You turn it on, and you get instant music. (Or news, or idiotic disk jockey chatter, or whatever.) Where is the music coming from? Inside the radio? That would be true if you were playing a tape or a compact disc. But when you turn on the radio, it pulls the music out of the air.

The music was there all along; you just couldn't get at it.

The same is true for the TV set. You turn it on, and bang! sound and pictures both. And where are they coming from? Unless you're playing your VCR, they're coming from radio waves that the television pulls out of the air.

Those same kind of waves are passing through your head all the time. Right now, even as you read these words, an incredible amount of information is passing *right through your skull*. Broadcast waves from four or five television stations. A dozen kinds of music. News reports, police calls, CB radio chatter—they're all passing through your brain *right now*! If you could perceive them, if your brain could interpret them the same way it does sights and sounds and smells, then you could pull that information right out of the air. It's there; your brain just doesn't know how to find it.

My ultra-powerful brain had learned how to receive that information.

The problem was, I couldn't turn it off.

What made things worse was that I couldn't sort it out. The images all blurred together. When I closed my eyes I might hear two or three radio stations while I watched Scooby Doo chase Peewee Herman across the bridge of the starship Enterprise.

I figured another day or two of this and I would

go mad. As it was, I couldn't think. The reputation I had started to get for being smart was going to dissolve pretty fast. People had spent years thinking of me as stupid and a couple of weeks thinking of me as smart. If it all ended now, they would figure the smart thing had been just a mistake. It wouldn't take long for them to forget it altogether.

I had had my temper under control for the last several days. But with all this going on in my head, with the constant noise and confusion and my own terror at what I had done to myself, I wasn't able to control things as well. So that afternoon, when Mr. Black asked me the kind of question I should have been able to answer in a flash, I couldn't come near the solution.

"Come, come, Duncan," he said. "Pay attention. You know what this is all about."

"How do you know what I know?" I shouted. "Until two weeks ago you thought I was a total jerk."

Mr. Black was so surprised he dropped his chalk. It shattered into a dozen pieces.

I closed my eyes, waiting for him to tell me to go see the Mancatcher.

To my surprise, he said, "Are you feeling all right, Duncan? Would you like to see the nurse?"

I blinked. There was something important going on here. But between the fact that my head was picking up *The Dating Game* and a violin concerto by Mozart, I couldn't quite figure it out.

"Duncan, I asked if you want to see the nurse."

I shook my head. I didn't think the nurse could help. An electrician might do me some good, if he or she could install an on/off switch and a volume knob somewhere on the back of my neck.

"I'll be all right," I muttered, which was the first lie I had told in several days. "Sorry I yelled."

Mr. Black shrugged. "Sometimes these things happen."

I lost my temper again that night at home, when Patrick said, "Hey, Duncan, how come you don't have your nose stuck in a book tonight? Decide to get normal for a while?"

I told him to shut up. He hit me in the head.

I announced that I had had enough of him, and I was going to run away from home. I didn't mean it, of course. But when things get this way, sometimes you say things you don't mean.

I hadn't had a good night's sleep since this started. That night, when I lay down in bed and closed my eyes, I saw Humphrey Bogart kissing John Wayne's horse while Ed McMahon was trying to sell dog food to Attila the Hun. In the background I was getting a mixture of Lawrence Welk and a rap group called Stinking Pond Scum.

I thought I was going to scream.

Then it all disappeared.

"Duncan," said a voice in my head. "Duncan, can you hear me?"

It was Peter Thompson!

"I can hear you," I whispered.

"Duncan," he repeated. "Can you hear me?"

He sounded desperate.

"Where are you?" I whispered. But he was gone. The radio and the TV programs came pouring back into my head.

I wondered if I was losing my mind. I had to talk to someone. I wished I could call Susan. But it was too late; her family would be asleep, and her parents would never put her on the line at that hour.

I got up and wrote her a note: "Susan, I have to talk to you. This is *urgent*! I am sorry about the *National Sun* article and everything else. Please, *please* talk to me today after school. Duncan."

The next morning I stuffed the note in her locker.

That day was the worst yet. I couldn't concentrate at all. I broke a bowl in home economics, and then yelled at Miss Karpou when she tried to ask if I was all right. I felt terrible.

I felt even worse when I found out that Susan was home sick that day. Now what was I going to do? I *had* to talk to someone.

Finally I asked Miss Karpou if I could see her after school. I didn't really think she could help me; she was too ditzy. But she might be able to think of someone who could help me. And I had a feeling that at least she would believe me.

After the last bell I went to Miss Karpou's room. She was fiddling around with something in the test kitchen when I got there. That was fine; that area was really private, and I didn't want anyone to overhear us. Especially not Andromeda Jones.

Miss Karpou looked up when she heard me come in. "Hello, Duncan," she called cheerfully. "Come on back."

I closed the door and walked back to where she was working, trying to shut out the whining violin music that was running through my head.

"I'm sorry about yelling this morning," I said once I was standing next to her.

Miss Karpou shook her head. "Don't worry about it, Duncan. I didn't take it personally."

I tried to smile. If only the violins would shut up!

"Miss Karpou," I said, trying not to cry, "I have to talk to someone. I have to tell someone what's happening to me. Only it's so unbelievable, I'm afraid you're going to think I'm crazy."

She shook her head. "I'll believe you, Duncan. I promise."

Then she pointed her wooden spoon at me and twisted the handle. My body seemed to lock in place.

How could I have been so stupid? I thought.

Frozen not with fear, but by some alien technology, I watched in horror as ditzy little Betty Lou Karpou grabbed her chin and began to peel off her face.

CHAPTER FIFTEEN
NO SECRETS

Miss Karpou's real face didn't look anything like Broxholm's. Her skin was a soft green-gold color—about the shade of willow trees in spring. It was also covered with scales. She had three eyes, with the one in the middle being located above the other two, sort of in the center of her forehead. It was the biggest of the three. I didn't realize about the third eye right away, since it was hidden under a protective patch.

"Ah, that feels better," she said as she pulled the patch away. The third eye opened. Its purple pupil was vertical, like a cat's. When it focused on me I wanted to shout. I wanted to run. I wanted to faint.

But I just stood there, frozen and forced to watch.

The strangest part was yet to come, for once Miss Karpou had removed the patch from her eye, she pulled something that was a little like a hair clip away from her nose.

"Ohhhh," she sighed, as her nose rolled down, "and isn't *that* a relief."

I could see where it would be, if you had a nose like hers. It looked like it belonged to a little green elephant. Only Miss Karpou's nose was flatter than an elephant's. Also, it had three prongs (or fingers, or something) on the end. When it was resting it dangled down to cover her mouth. But it wasn't resting very often. Mostly it was waving around in front of her, like some sort of snake with a mind of its own.

"Oh, Duncan, you can't imagine how good it feels to really let my hair down," she said as she pulled off a thing that had covered her head like a shower cap.

"Let my hair down" was the wrong phrase, since

most of it stood straight up as soon as she pulled off the cap. I don't know if it really qualified as hair. It was lavender, and thick as worms. Like her nose, it seemed to move on its own, each thick strand going its own way, curling, uncurling, bending from side to side.

Watching it gave me the willies. Unfortunately, I couldn't close my eyes.

"One last thing, and then we can talk," she said. "Or at least, I can talk. You'll just have to listen for a while."

She turned to the refrigerator and pulled out a familiar-looking piece of Tupperware. Lifting off the top, she said, "You can come out now, Poot."

She turned the container on its side. The glowing slug-thing oozed over the edge and onto the counter.

I figured this was either good news or bad news. If this was the same slug I had first met, it was good news, because I was glad it was still alive. If it was just an after-school snack for Miss Karpou, that was bad news, because I really didn't want to watch her eat the thing.

After a few seconds she put her hand on the

counter. The thing began to ooze its way up her arm. I figured that unless she ate with her armpit, this was a good sign.

"Well, now that I'm comfortable, let's see what we can do about you," said the alien.

She started to walk in my direction. I wanted to scream and run, but I was still frozen. I couldn't even make my eyes go wide in horror, though they were trying for all they were worth.

The alien touched me on the forehead with her wooden spoon. Then she pushed until I fell backward. I had a moment of total terror, almost worse than when she had started to take off her mask. Maybe falling backward is some basic fear built into our genes. It sure felt that way.

But I didn't fall very far, because my forehead was still connected to her wooden spoon. She made a couple of adjustments to the spoon, and soon my body was stretched out flat in the air, three feet above the floor. When she lifted the spoon I came with it, as if I weighed no more than a balloon.

Using the spoon, Miss Karpou put me on the

countertop. Then she bent down and looked me in the face. The slug oozed along her arm, as if it wanted to get a closer look, too.

It was bad enough to have the alien's three eyes staring into my two. But when her nose started examining me as well, poking and prodding around my face as if it was gathering information for its own purposes, I really, really wanted to scream—especially when one of those green feelers on the end of the alien's trunk poked its way into my right nostril.

"Had a rough week, Duncan?" asked the alien in a voice that actually sounded sympathetic.

What was I supposed to do? Nod and smile at her? I did the only thing I could do, which was lie there and stare straight up with wide eyes.

If only the violins inside my head would shut up so that I could think!

"Poor Duncan," said Miss Karpou. "Let's see if we can't improve your situation a little."

She went to the cupboard where we kept the mixing bowls. Stretching her arm, she took one down from the top shelf. When I say stretching her arm, I don't mean like you or I would stretch. Her arm actually got longer, as if it were made of rubber or something.

The mixing bowl looked like the bowls we used almost every day in class. But it must have been filled with some kind of alien circuitry, because when she sat it on edge on the counter and then slid my head inside, it blocked out the radio reception.

What bliss! For the first time in days I had silence inside my head. That was such a relief I could have kissed that hideous alien face.

"My face is not considered hideous where I come from," said Miss Karpou. "And I would not want a kiss from you anyway."

I would have blinked in surprise if I could have. (Actually, I would have jumped off the counter and run if I could have, but that wasn't even a possibility.) Had she just read my mind?

"Yes," said Miss Karpou.

She *had* read my mind!

"It's not quite mind reading," she said quietly. "The circuits in the mixing bowl are not only blocking the radio and television waves coming into your brain, they are amplifying and sorting the waves that you create within. Sorting is the big problem, of course, since your brain is doing a multitude of things at once. The task for the machine is to choose the brain patterns that are relevant, sort them into some sort of order, magnify them, and transmit them to the receiver plugged into my head. It's *like* mind reading, but it's all done with machines."

What was I supposed to say to that?

"Don't say anything. I'll do the talking. But since we are going to be working together, we might as well get to know each other a little better."

Working together? I thought in alarm.

The alien smiled. "I need your brain," she said cheerfully, just before she put me to sleep.

CHAPTER SIXTEEN

KREEBLIM

When I woke up again, I was in the alien's home. I don't remember going to sleep, so I assume she knocked me out before she took me there.

I have no idea how she got me out of the school. Lifting me was no problem, of course, since that wooden-spoon thing of hers had some kind of built-in antigravity device. But I'm not sure how she managed to get me to her car without anyone seeing. Maybe she put me in a big box. Maybe she shrank me and carried me out in her pocket. Heck, for all I know, she used some kind of alien fax machine to disassemble my molecules, then sent me over the phone lines. Who knew what these people could do?

Anyway, when I opened my eyes again, I was in a living room. Just a normal living room. It wasn't bare, like Broxholm's had been, and it wasn't filled with weird alien furniture, either. It was just a room. The alien was sitting in a kind of beat-up-looking arm-chair, looking all green and scaly. She was wearing faded jeans and a blue sweatshirt that said Cornell University on the front. The clothes didn't quite seem to go with the rest of her look. The slug-thing was hanging from the ceiling over her head, imitating her face.

"Welcome back to wakefulness, Duncan," said the alien cheerfully when I opened my eyes. "My name . . . my real name . . . is Kreeblim. Well, not quite, but it's as close as you'll be able to get with an earth brain and an earth tongue. And this is my pet, Poot," she added, pointing to the glowing blob on the ceiling.

The slug dropped down from the ceiling and wrapped around her hand. "Poot!" it said happily.

"Poot likes you, by the way," she said. "I knew that when it made a picture of your face for me."

Poot is a tattletale! I thought.

Kreeblim smiled. "Don't be silly, Duncan. I didn't need the poot to know you were the one using the mind enhancer. I was aware of it all along. Actually, I tried to arrange things so that it would be you, since you were one of the few kids in the school whom I could borrow for a while without causing too much fuss. I'm just surprised you hadn't figured out who I was. After all, you had clues."

She must have read the question in my mind. "Oh, come, come," she said. "You were in the class when I burned my finger that first day—or, more accurately, when I burned a hole in the mask I wear over my hand."

I wanted to groan, only I couldn't on account of being frozen, or whatever it was she had done to me. Why hadn't I realized what was going on? Of course, the fact that I had found Poot in the science-lab refrigerator and not in the home ec room had helped throw me off track.

"Ah, yes," said Kreeblim, reading my mind again. "But if you'll think back, you'll remember that you found the poot shortly after the refrigerator in the home economics room had broken down. I had stored the poor baby in Andromeda Jones's lab for safekeeping until my refrigerator was fixed."

I remembered how Poot had been missing the next time I snuck into the lab; another clue I had ignored.

"Don't be angry with yourself, Duncan," said the alien.

But I should have figured it out! I thought fiercely.

Kreeblim laughed. "You had a lot of other things on your mind," she said. "And you certainly didn't have a lot of experience in using that newly enhanced brain of yours. However, I *do* have a real use for it—which is why I brought you here."

That sentence had more possible meanings than I wanted to consider at the moment. On the other hand, my increased intelligence had stuck me with an incurable curiosity. *What are you going to do with me?* I thought, despite the fact that I wasn't at all sure I wanted to know.

"I need you for communication purposes," said Kreeblim. As she spoke, one of her lavender hairs made the mistake of prodding the poot. The slug seemed to absorb the end of the hair, which squeaked and pulled back in surprise, slightly shorter than it had been.

Kreeblim patted her head, and the hairs all bent away from Poot and started waving in the opposite direction. She turned her attention back to me. "You see, when your friend Susan forced Broxholm into an emergency retreat, it left me stranded here. Normally he would have come back for me fairly quickly. However, her interference created a slight crisis, and he received an emergency call to return to our home base.

"Even that wouldn't have been so bad, except for the fact that it left me without some of my basic equipment. The worst loss was my communication device. I'm sure you've read enough by now to know how fast light travels."

A hundred and eighty-six thousand miles per second, or about five-point-eight trillion miles a year, said my brain, supplying the information without me even having to look for it.

Kreeblim nodded. "And you also know that even that incredible speed is inadequate for talking across the vastness of space."

I would have nodded back, but being frozen sort of limits your nonverbal responses.

"What you probably don't know," continued Kreeblim, "is that we have developed a few ways around that kind of limitation. However, I don't have the hardware to replace my trans-space radio device. So I have to use you instead."

She smiled. "That, dear Duncan, is why I arranged for you to be connected to the brain enhancer. I needed someone to act as a communication center for me, and you seemed the most likely candidate. It was almost more than I could have hoped for when you started giving *yourself* treatments, since it meant I could delay the time when I needed to bring you here—which would also delay any fuss that might be caused by your disappearance."

When she said that I felt a little surge of hope. Sooner or later someone was going to miss me and start looking for me. I tried to clamp down on that idea, but thoughts are hard to control.

Kreeblim sighed, almost as if she felt sorry for me. "Don't waste your emotional energy thinking someone is going to come and rescue you," she said.

"After all, just last night you told your family you were going to run away from home. So no one is going to be all that surprised when you don't show up for the next few days. And by the time they decide to look for you, it won't make any difference."

"Poot!" said the slug on her shoulder.

CHAPTER SEVENTEEN

FORCED INTO THE FIELD

Something started to beep upstairs. Kreeblim kept her right and left eyes fixed on me while she rolled the center one toward the sound.

"I need to go tend to something," she said with a slight sigh. "I'll be back soon. We can talk some more then."

You call this talking? I thought bitterly.

Kreeblim made a clicking noise with her tongue. "Come, come, Duncan. Whether or not you are actually opening your mouth, we are exchanging ideas, which is what talking is all about. I'm sorry my language implant does not have a word adequate to describe the fact that your half of the conversation comes in thoughts rather than words. I rather suspect, however, that the problem has more to do with a lack in your language than in the device itself."

The beeping upstairs continued. She turned and left the room.

While she was gone I tried to move. I strained as if I were trying to lift an elephant—and with about as much effect. I wasn't cold, but I was frozen stiff as a popsicle. As I stood there, paralyzed, in the middle of the living room of an alien invader who happened to be masquerading as a slightly dippy home economics teacher, I decided that life is just so fascinating I can barely stand it.

The poot came over and rolled around my feet for a while. Then it started to climb my leg. That's when I knew that whatever Kreeblim had done to paralyze me was foolproof. I couldn't even shudder!

The poot kept climbing until it reached my shoulder, where it settled down like a small kitten. Even though I kind of liked the poot, I couldn't quite convince myself that it wasn't about to make itself real thin so it could ooze into my ear canal and suck out my fried brain.

Suddenly it reached up with a blob of itself—a pseudopod, my brain informed me, even though I hadn't asked—and patted my cheek. Then it sent me a message.

Don't worry!

If I could have blinked, shouted, jumped, anything to show my surprise, I would have.

Poot had talked to me!

Well, that's not quite the way to put it. It had sent a message into my head, but not in words. It was definitely a feeling.

It patted my cheek again. *Nice Duncan.*

"Poot, you get down from there!"

It was Kreeblim. She had come back into the room while I was concentrating on the slug.

"Poot!" cried the slug in alarm as it slid down my arm. It made it to the floor faster than I would have thought possible.

"Bad Poot," said Kreeblim when the creature wrapped itself around her foot. "Bad."

The slug made several whimpering little poots. I couldn't say for certain, but I think they meant, "Please don't put me back in my Tupperware!"

Kreeblim ignored her pet. She looked troubled.

What's wrong? I thought.

She looked at me in surprise. Actually, I was a little surprised myself. Why should I care that something was bothering her? Well, I suppose the fact that if she was in a bad mood I was in real trouble would be one reason to care. But this wasn't that kind of thought. It just came floating to the top of my mind, as if I really did care.

Kreeblim flapped her nose at me, which I had begun to recognize as something that she sometimes did in place of smiling. "Thank you for asking," she said. "Actually, it has to do with why you are here. That was an incoming message. Unfortunately it is so old it is of no value to me. I really must get you installed in the communication system. Curse Broxholm for leaving me in this situation anyway."

That brought up something I had been wondering about. *How come you don't look like Broxholm?*

Kreeblim smiled. "The universe is a very big place, Duncan. Broxholm and I come from different planets—different star systems, actually. We are part of an intercultural group performing a major study on your planet. Really, you humans are the most fascinating species. You have the greatest brain capacity of any animal in the galaxy, yet you behave like total idiots."

Hey! I thought at her.

Kreeblim just clucked her tongue. "Oh, really, Duncan—you're bright enough now to know that's true. There isn't another intelligent species in the galaxy that treats its whole planet like a sewer. No one else lets their children starve. Virtually every other intelligent species gave up war centuries earlier in their developmental cycle."

Her nose swatted at a fly that had landed on the side of her face, then tucked the flattened insect into her mouth. She chewed thoughtfully for a second, then said, "I'm sure you can see what the problem is, Duncan. Now that you're on the verge of space travel, you're making every other intelligent species quite nervous. No one knows what you people might do once you get out there! That's why we're studying you, dear. We have to figure out what to do about you."

I didn't like the sound of that. But Kreeblim wasn't willing to talk about it any longer. She tapped me on the forehead with her wooden spoon, then floated me up two flights of stairs to her attic.

She parked me in the middle of the room, then went to a panel on the wall and fiddled with some dials. Suddenly a blue beam stretched from the floor to the ceiling. I knew what that was; Susan had described it to me. It was the kind of force field Broxholm had used to hold Ms. Schwartz a prisoner.

"This is where you'll be staying for now, Duncan," said the alien.

NOOO!!

"Oh, don't be silly. It won't hurt you. Of course, it will be a little dull, since nothing happens in there. All your bodily processes will be on hold. Eating, drinking, breathing, digesting—you won't have to worry about any of them. Your body will stop aging, too, though getting older is hardly an issue for you right now. Of course, you can think all you want. It may give you a chance to put together some of the learning you've been doing. After all, facts don't do much good in isolation, do they?"

She pulled me over to the force field with her wooden spoon. My body was rigid, but my brain was fighting like crazy. Not that it did me any good. Suddenly I felt a tingle in the top of my head. I was entering the force field!

It pulled me in like a vacuum cleaner sucking up a speck of dust. As I felt myself whooshed into the shimmering shaft of blue light, tiny forces began to adjust my body, pushing here, pulling there, until I was perfectly centered.

I couldn't move my head to look down, of course, but from looking straight ahead, I got the feeling I was floating about a foot and a half in the air.

I was tingling all over.

"Comfortable?" asked Kreeblim, putting her hand against the force field.

GET ME OUT OF HERE! I thought desperately.

She looked surprised at the intensity of my reaction. At least, the eye in the middle of her forehead blinked.

"I'm sorry, Duncan, but I can't do that."

The weird thing was, I really felt like she really meant it.

She turned and went down the stairs, leaving me alone with my thoughts. That wasn't altogether bad. I had been so frightened for the past few hours that I hadn't been thinking clearly. Actually, with the radio and TV reception problems, it had been more like a couple of days since I had been able to think clearly. And what was the use of a magnificent brain like mine if I didn't use it to think?

Unfortunately, all I could think about was what Kreeblim had said—the thing about the other intelligent species in the galaxy trying to figure out what to do about us. I was frightened—and ashamed. I had read a lot of history in the past few weeks, along with everything else, and it wasn't a pretty picture. The idea that someone from outside had been watching all that, had been watching us bumble along, blowing each other up, starving ourselves when there was enough food for everyone, poisoning our own air—well, it was embarrassing.

It certainly is, said a voice in my head.

I felt a shiver of fear. Was I losing my mind? What was going on here?

Who is that?

Come on, Duncan—don't you know who I am?

CHAPTER EIGHTEEN

ACROSS THE VOID

Peter! **I thought in astonishment.** ***Peter Thompson?***

None other! Wait, let me try something here. . . .

Where are you?

Shhhh! Wait.

I was bursting with curiosity. But I waited.

"There, that's better!"

This time I actually heard his voice, which was different than thought reading. To my astonishment, I could see Peter inside my head! The same brown hair, skinny face, big eyes. Except something was missing.

Where are your glasses?

"I don't need them anymore," said Peter with a smile. "They fixed my eyes the second day out."

Where are you?

"In space, silly. Where did you expect I would be? Oh, Duncan, it's glorious. The stars! I can't tell you. But it's frightening, too. There's a lot going on. Big things. And Earth is right in the middle of it. *We're* right in the middle of it."

What do you mean?

"The Interplanetary Council—that's sort of a galaxywide United Nations—is trying to figure out what to do about us. We've got their tails in a tizzy because our planet is so weird. From what Broxholm has told me—"

Wait! I thought. *Tell me about Broxholm. Is he treating you all right?*

"Well, that's kind of weird, too," said Peter. "I'm never quite sure what's going on with him. But listen, I've got to tell you this stuff first, because I'm not sure how long I can stay on, and you have to get word out to someone. Here's the deal. The aliens are having a big debate among themselves about how to handle the Earth. And I don't mean just Broxholm's gang. We're talking about hundreds of different planets here. As near as I can make out, they've narrowed it down to four basic approaches. One group wants to take over the Earth, one group wants to leave us on our own, one group wants to blow the planet to smithereens, and one group wants to set up a blockade."

What?!

Peter looked grim. "They say it's for the sake of the rest of the galaxy. They seem to find us pretty scary, Duncan."

I don't get it.

"Don't ask me to explain how an alien's mind works!" said Peter, sounding a little cranky. "As far as I can make out, they think there's something wrong with us. Well, two things, actually. The first is the way we handle things down there. That's why they've been sending in people like Broxholm; they're supposed to study us and figure out why we act the way we do."

So Broxholm was some kind of anthropologist from space, studying the whole human race like it was a tribe in the jungle?

"You could put it that way. Anyway, the other

thing that has them concerned is how smart we could be if we ever got our act together. Broxholm actually seems jealous. Every once in a while he goes on about the human brain being the most underused tool in the galaxy. I get the impression they're afraid that if we learn to use our full intelligence before we get civilized—"

We're civilized!

"Not by their standards. Anyway, they're afraid—uh-oh. Someone's coming. I gotta go, Duncan."

Wait!

But he was gone, leaving me floating in my force field to think about what he had said. I knew that at least part of what the aliens thought about us was true; my own growing brainpower had proved to me that we had the possibility of being a lot more intelligent than we act. I was beginning to understand that everything I had ever experienced was stored inside my brain. That's why I knew words like *synapse* and *anthropologist.* They didn't come out of nowhere. I had heard them sometime in the past. So they were in my brain, but until I had gotten my brain fried, I couldn't use them because for some reason I couldn't get at them. Were we all like that, filled with information we weren't using? Why couldn't we use it? Were we like computers with faulty disk drives or something?

The second question was even more frightening. What would we do with all that intelligence if we ever did unleash it? Would we use it to make things better? Or would we just do the kinds of things we do right now, only faster? For example, would we figure out a way to save the rain forests, or just figure out new, improved ways to cut them down?

Time is funny in a force field. I don't know how long I floated there, worrying about Peter's message, before Kreeblim came back. It could have been two hours or two weeks for all I knew, though considering how urgent she seemed to think things were, two hours was probably more likely.

"All right, Duncan," she said cheerfully. "It's time you started to repay me for those brain enhancements you received. Let's see if we can get this communication system to work."

For a moment I was terrified that she would read

my mind and find out that Peter had contacted me. But as it turned out, she was too involved in her own project to worry about what was going on inside my head right then.

She started by sitting on the floor. Well, that's not really accurate. She didn't sit so much as she made her legs shrink. Or maybe she pulled them up inside of her. Anyway, she didn't bother with a chair. Once she was down, she put a little box between her feet and started to fiddle with some dials on the front of it.

I felt a tingle in my brain.

Kreeblim looked up. "That doesn't hurt, does it?" she asked.

It's scary, I thought at her.

"Most new experiences are," she replied, flipping her nose. "You'll get used to it. Ah, here we go. I've got contact!"

She ignored me and turned all her attention to the communication box. She sat there, frowning and muttering. A couple of times her nose twitched around as if she was really angry.

I thought it was pretty unfair that messages were

being passed through my brain and I couldn't find out what they were all about.

After a while Kreeblim slammed the box shut and stood up—which is to say that her legs came back from wherever they had gone.

What was that all about? I asked.

"Private business," she said. She sounded upset. Scooping up the poot, she went back down the stairs.

I was getting a little sick of everyone else using my brain, though I would have been glad to have Peter to talk to again. At least, that was what I thought—until he actually showed up again.

"Duncan," came the voice in my head. "Is there anybody there?"

Just you and me, I answered.

"Good." His image shimmered into my brain. He looked worried. "Listen, things are heating up out here. The aliens are planning something. I don't know what, but it's big. You have to get word to the government."

Well, how can I do that? Even if they would believe me, which is pretty doubtful, I'm stuck in the middle of a force field in Kreeblim's attic!

Suddenly I heard a step on the stairway. Being connected to my brain, Peter heard it, too. "Pretend I'm not here!" he said desperately. "I can't be caught talking to you like this. I'll try to hold on, but I'll break the connection if I have to."

I understand, I told him.

The footsteps reached the top of the stairs. I couldn't see who was coming, because I couldn't turn my head. But it didn't sound like Kreeblim.

Finally the intruder stepped in front of the force field.

I couldn't believe my eyes.

What are you doing here? I thought.

CHAPTER NINETEEN

PLAYING THE FIELD

Looking nervous, the intruder walked over to the force field and placed her hands against it. "Hello, Duncan," she said.

Even though my body couldn't move, my brain started to smile. If the breath of air I had taken after I climbed out of the dumpster was the best breath I ever took, Susan Simmons walking into that attic was the best sight I ever saw.

What are you doing here? I thought again.

"Looking for you, you goofball," she replied. "After I found your note in my locker, I was sure that you hadn't run away from home, no matter what anyone else said. So I started trying to track you down."

How did you find me so quickly?

Susan gave me an odd look. "Duncan, I didn't find you quickly. You've been gone for over three weeks. I've been working like crazy to figure out what happened to you. Almost got myself killed a couple of times in the process."

Three weeks! I think my brain did something that was a little like screaming, because she flinched back for a moment.

Sorry! I said when she put her hands back on the force field. *I didn't mean to do that. But you really surprised me. I had no idea I had been in here so long. Can you get me out?*

At one time I would have been embarrassed to be rescued by a girl. But with my newly fried brain, I had examined the biomechanical structures of the male and the female, not to mention the underlying historical and economic situations that had led to our relative differences, and I had come to the conclusion that women are a tough bunch. So that was OK.

Susan looked worried. "I don't know how these things work, Duncan."

Great. I was found, but still lost, so to speak. At least, that was what I thought at first—until a voice whispered in my head, "I know how to turn the thing off. By the way, tell Susan I said hello."

"Peter!" cried Susan. "What are you doing here?" She looked around. "And where are you?"

You can hear him? I asked in astonishment.

"Of course I can. Where is he?"

"I'm in space," replied Peter.

Susan looked startled. "Then how come I can hear you?" she asked.

"I think it's because we're both connected to Duncan's brain through the force field. How are you, anyway? I've missed you."

"I'm fine, Peter. How about you?"

Sheesh! I was glad they were both here, but I was beginning to feel a little like my head was a hotel room. I hoped nobody else was going to show up right away. I mean, I could understand why Peter and Susan wanted to talk, but I didn't particularly want them to use my head to do it.

Fortunately, I didn't have to complain too much. They both knew that we had to get busy.

"Susan, see if you can spot anything that looks like a control panel somewhere nearby," said Peter once they had finished greeting each other. "We've got to get Duncan out of this thing."

It's over to your left, Susan, I thought, remembering when I had seen Kreeblim use it to begin with.

Susan turned to look for it. "Got it!" she said after a moment.

"Good," said Peter. "Now describe it to me."

Unfortunately, Susan couldn't hear him because she wasn't touching the force field anymore. I guess she figured out what she ought to do anyway, because she rattled off a long list of the things she saw on the control panel, which seemed to consist more of points to push than the knobs, dials, and levers that we're used to.

I didn't have to repeat what she said, since Peter could hear whatever I heard.

When she was done he said, "Ask her if she can see a red spot in the second row of controls."

How?

"Crud. I forgot she can't hear you unless she touches the force field. Get her over here."

How? I repeated, feeling incredibly helpless.

"What do I do now?" asked Susan. Then, realizing what the problem was, she came over to touch the force field again.

Peter repeated the instruction about the red spot.

Susan returned to the control panel. "Got it," she said. "Do you want me to press it? Oh—"

She trotted back over to the force field.

"Yes," said Peter before she could even repeat the question.

She returned to the control panel again and did as he had told her. I waited eagerly for the force field to release me.

Nothing happened.

I wanted to cry, but of course my body was having none of that.

"Don't worry, Duncan," said Peter. "That wasn't the release. We're just getting started. This is going to take a few minutes."

"Nothing happened!" said Susan, putting her hands back on the force field.

"Don't worry," repeated Peter. "This is a several-step process."

"How long is it going to take?" asked Susan nervously. "I don't want to be here when Miss Karpou comes back!"

Her real name is Kreeblim, I thought.

"I don't care if it's Kleenex! I don't want to be here. What next, Peter?" He gave her another instruction. For several minutes it went on that way, with Susan moving back and forth between the force field and the control panel while Peter told her what to do. I might as well have taken a nap for all the good I was doing.

I began working an equation in my head to keep myself busy while the two of them fiddled with the force field. I got so involved with the math that I was a little surprised when I suddenly heard a soft *zoooop* and found myself sitting on the floor. I'd landed with a thump, but the pain in my rump was right up there with that breath of air and the sight of Susan for peak experiences. I was free at last!

With the force field gone, I thought I was going

to lose contact with Peter. But he was still there inside my brain.

"Of course," he said. "Your head is what we call wetware—an organic machine. At the moment you happen to be one of the most powerful communication devices in the galaxy, Duncan. Now listen, I've got some important stuff to tell you. There are big things happening up here, and you need to—oh, no!"

The last words came as a shout of terror. *Peter, what is it?* I thought desperately. *What's going on?*

CHAPTER TWENTY
HEARTS AND MINDS

I closed my eyes and concentrated with all my might. *Peter!* I thought desperately, casting my thoughts into space. *Peter, where are you?*

No answer. He was gone.

Susan grabbed my arm. "What is it?" she whispered. "What's going on?"

"I don't know. Peter was there, then suddenly he got cut off. I'm afraid someone found him transmitting to us. He said there was something big going on, something he wanted me to warn the government about."

"What?"

"I don't know! He never got a chance to tell me."

Susan looked pale. "Do you think they're getting ready to invade?" she said. Her voice was low, and hoarse with terror.

"They've been considering it," I said. "But whatever it is, we've got to get out of here. We're not going to take a message to anyone if Kreeblim catches us."

"You're right," she said. "Let's go." Grabbing my hand, she headed for the attic stairs.

I blinked. Susan Simmons had my hand. My heart did a little flip.

Well, that was interesting information. It turns out a mighty brain is no protection against emotions. *Down, boy,* I thought to my heart. *Right now we've got to get out of here.*

I followed Susan to the stairwell. "Is it day or night?" I whispered.

"Night," she said. "Miss Karpou is chaperoning a dance. I was supposed to go, but I figured this was the only time I would be able to get in here."

I decided not to ask her who she was supposed to have been going with. Instead, I said, "How did you know where I was?"

She shrugged. "Detective work. I knew you were feeling bad—we weren't treating you very well, for one thing. I also knew Miss Karpou was the one you were most likely to go to for a little sympathy, since you seemed to get along with her pretty well. I started to keep an eye on her; the more I watched, the more suspicious she seemed. Finally I decided it was time to come looking for you."

"Thanks," I said. Then, feeling daring, I gave her hand a little squeeze.

"Don't mention it," she whispered. "In fact, don't mention anything until we get out of here."

I nodded. We needed to stay alert if we were going to survive this.

We moved down the stairs on tiptoe. Only one board creaked, but when it did I felt my stomach lurch with fear.

We paused. No sound below us.

When we came down into the second-floor hallway, I began to relax a little. We had both been worried that Kreeblim might have come back into the house while we were in the attic, but everything was dark downstairs. Unless she could see in the dark (which was a possibility, I guess), she hadn't come back yet.

We moved quickly and quietly down to the first floor. As Susan began to head for the door, I got an idea.

"Wait!" I whispered. "What's wrong?"

"Listen, we need some proof that there's another alien here if we're going to get anyone to listen to us, right?"

"You're not kidding," she said bitterly. "I tried to talk about it to a few people and they just wouldn't hear me. Their attitude was, 'That's over, and we never want to have to think about it again.' I can't believe people can be so stupid."

"I can," I said. "But I think I know where to find something that will make them believe us."

"Are you sure?" asked Susan. "These guys are pretty careful. I couldn't find anything in Broxholm's house to use as evidence."

"Broxholm didn't have a pet!" I said. "Come on."

I had never had a chance to look around Kreeblim's house, so I didn't know where the kitchen was. But it didn't take long to find it. If only she hadn't taken Poot to school with her that day. . . .

I tiptoed across the room to the refrigerator. The little light inside seemed like a beacon in the dark room.

I stared inside. There it was!

"What's that?" asked Susan when I pulled out the Tupperware container.

"If we're lucky, it's a poot."

I put the container on the counter and pulled off the lid to check what was inside. After all, there was no sense in escaping with some leftover Brussels sprouts.

"Poot!" said the glowing blob of stuff inside. It sounded happy.

"Jackpot!" I whispered.

Susan drew back in fear. "What is it?" she asked.

"It's a poot," I said, putting down my hand so that the slug could crawl up onto it.

"That's right," said a voice from the other side of the room. "It's a poot, and it belongs to me."

The kitchen light came on. I spun around in horror.

Standing in the doorway, looking cute but very cranky, was Betty Lou Karpou.

"Let us go, or the poot is toast!" I screamed.

"Poot?" asked the slug, sounding frightened.

CHAPTER TWENTY-ONE

WHO WILL SPEAK FOR THE EARTH?

"You wouldn't," said the alien calmly. "I know you too well for that, Duncan. Remember, I've had a look inside your brain. You're really much nicer than you think you are."

I hesitated. I didn't know if I was really nice or not, but I wasn't at all sure I could hurt the poot.

Some hero, huh? The fate of the world is in my hands, and I can't bring myself to squash a space slug. But I remembered how it had patted my cheek and told me not to worry. How could I hurt the little guy?

"Poot?" it said again, sliding up my arm. Then it

patted my cheek again. *Nice Duncan,* I heard in my head.

I sighed. "I won't hurt it," I said.

"That's better," said Kreeblim/Karpou. "Now, if you'll give me a moment to get comfortable, we can talk about the future of your planet. I'd suggest you cooperate, because at the moment things don't look too promising."

"Susan, run!" I shouted. "I'll cover you."

"Duncan, don't be silly," said Kreeblim/Karpou with a sigh. "Use that magnificent brain of yours. You can't get away from me and you know it. Now you'll save us all a lot of trouble if you just stand still and listen."

As if to prove that was the case, she touched a button on the edge of the counter. I heard a noise behind me. I turned in time to see a piece of clear material of some kind slide into place over the door.

We were trapped.

"Now if you'll hold still, we can talk about this," said Kreeblim/Karpou. "Let's begin by dispensing with disguises."

Reaching up, she began to draw off her face. I

could feel Susan tense up beside me. I didn't blame her. Watching an alien strip off her face and let down her nose is a pretty revolting sight.

"If you can't stop judging people by their looks, you'll never get along in the galaxy," said Kreeblim sharply. "And no, I'm not reading your minds. Your faces tell quite clearly what you're thinking. Now, upstairs. We have to talk, and I want to do it where I know we won't be disturbed. Duncan, there is a chance that I will have to put you back in the force field. However, if I do—"

I didn't let her finish the sentence. *"Noooo!"* I shouted in horror.

She continued right over my protest. "If I do, I promise it will only be for as long as it takes to run a few important communications. However, it may not be necessary."

"Why should I trust you?" I asked, ignoring the more obvious point that if she wanted to put me in the force field, there probably wasn't a thing I could do about it.

"Because I'm almost on your side," she said.

"What's that supposed to mean?" asked Susan.

"If you'll come upstairs, I'll tell you!" said Kreeblim impatiently.

I looked at Susan. She nodded.

"All right, we'll go," I said.

"That's better," replied the alien. "It's about time you started using that brain to think as well as feel. Now come along."

We followed her to the stairs. When we got there, she made us walk up ahead of her so we wouldn't try to escape.

"Don't look so frightened," said Kreeblim once we were back in the attic. "It won't do anything to help your case."

"What case?" asked Susan.

Kreeblim sighed. "The case you have to make before the Interplanetary Council. I'm not entirely pleased at the role I have been assigned in this matter, but as the only emissary to your world who is currently in direct contact with the natives, I have no choice. Fortunately, I do have someone to assist me."

"I still don't get it," said Susan.

"I think I do," I said. "Let me see if I've got this

right. The Interplanetary Council has decided it's time to take action regarding the Earth. They have four options—they can take over, blow us up, blockade us, or leave us alone—and they want one more report before they make their final decision."

Kreeblim looked at me oddly.

"Why would they want to blow us up?" asked Susan in horror.

"Because they're afraid of us," I said. "Not because of what we can do right now, but because of what we might be able to do in the future."

"You earthlings are such an unstable group," said Kreeblim wistfully. "Full of promise and poison in equal measure."

"So what's going to happen?" I asked.

"The council has assigned a five-member team to assemble a report. We have one of your months in which to do so. That report, when filed, will determine the fate of your planet."

I swallowed nervously. "Just who is on this team?"

"The three of us, to start with," said Kreeblim.

"That still leaves two spots," said Susan.

Kreeblim flapped her nose. "Look behind you," she said.

I turned in time to see a beam of blue light shine down into the center of the room. As I watched, two figures took shape inside it.

The light vanished. Where it had been stood Broxholm and Peter Thompson.

"Peter!" cried Susan. She ran over and threw her arms around him.

"Hi, Susan," he said, looking a little embarrassed. "It's nice to see you."

"Good evening, Miss Simmons, Mr. Dougal," said Broxholm, nodding his green head. "I can't say it is exactly a pleasure to see you again, but since we are going to be working together, I hope that we will be able to put the past behind us."

"Working together?" asked Susan.

"We're the rest of the team," said Peter. "I told Duncan there was something big going on. When I got cut off during that last transmission it was because Broxholm had come in to tell me that the Interplanetary Council had assigned us to join the team that is going to file the final report on what they call 'The Earth Question.'"

"So it's the three of us and the two of them," I said, gesturing to Broxholm and Kreeblim.

"That's right," said Peter. He looked at me and smiled. "Kind of an odd choice, when you think about it."

I knew what he meant. Peter and I had both been pretty unhappy down here. So we weren't exactly the best choices to convince aliens how wonderful this planet was. But the two of us, along with Susan, had been given that assignment.

Talk about tough homework! We had one month to convince the rulers of the galaxy not to wipe the human race out of existence.

My brain was racing, sorting thoughts, ideas, and images. It seemed like more than I could handle.

I looked at Kreeblim. "Why did you do this to me?" I asked, tears starting at the corners of my eyes.

She closed her side eyes, so that only the middle one was looking at me—looking right into me, almost. "I didn't do this to you, Duncan. I gave you an invitation, and you accepted it. The first treatment of the brain enhancer was my choice—the others were all yours."

"Come along," said Broxholm. "The council is waiting to give us their final instructions."

"Waiting where?" asked Susan.

Peter rolled his eyes and pointed toward the ceiling. I knew what he meant. They were waiting out there, out in space. And we were about to join them. Standing where Broxholm directed, I waited for the blue beam that would lift me out beyond the planet where I had been born, out to a ship that had come from the stars.

I reached out my hands. Susan took one. Peter took the other.

The blue transporter beam began to shimmer around us. I felt myself being drawn into space.

It was going to be an interesting October.

MY TEACHER GLOWS IN THE DARK

For Tisha Hamilton, who cared

TABLE OF CONTENTS

CHAPTER ONE
I CHOOSE THE STARS

So there we were—Susan Simmons, Duncan Dougal, and me, Peter Thompson—sitting in an alien spaceship the size of New Jersey, waiting to learn how we were supposed to save the world, when Susan said, "All right, Peter, give."

"Beg your pardon?" I asked innocently.

"Tell us what's been going on! Five months ago you took off for outer space with Broxholm. Five minutes ago you showed up in a beam of blue light and told Duncan and me we had to help you save the world. I want to know what happened in between."

"Me, too!" said Duncan.

Five months ago I wouldn't have cared what Duncan Dougal thought. As far as I was concerned, he was the world's biggest snotball, a kid whose main hobbies were drooling on his homework, farting in class, and beating me up. I thought he was as likable as a mosquito, as friendly as a rattlesnake, and as useful as a screen door in a spaceship.

But that was before I got a good look at the inside of his head—which was less frightening and more sad than I ever would have guessed.

"Well, since you asked . . . ," I drawled.

"Peter," snapped Susan, "for five months every kid in Kennituck Falls has been dying to know what happened to you after you went off with Broxholm. Stop stalling and tell the story, or you're going to be very sorry!"

So I told them. But that wasn't good enough. Oh, no. Now they insist I have to write it down. "We wrote about our part," they keep saying. "Now it's your turn."

So here goes:

As you probably know, it all started when this alien named Broxholm wanted to kidnap five kids from our sixth grade class last spring. He started by trapping our real teacher, Ms. Schwartz, in a force field. He kept her in his attic while he disguised himself as a substitute teacher named Mr. Smith and took over our class.

One day Susan followed Mr. Smith home and saw him peel off his face. Underneath his human mask was a green-skinned, orange-eyed alien.

Susan came to me for help, mostly because she didn't think anyone else would believe her. She thought *I* might because I used to read so much science fiction.

The two of us spent days trying to figure out how to stop Broxholm. One night I was sitting home alone, eating a can of cold beans and wondering where my father was, when it hit me that if we *couldn't* stop Broxholm, if some kids *had* to go into space, I might as well be one of them. It wouldn't be any worse than staying where I was. And it might be better.

I was frightened by the idea, of course. But I didn't think the aliens were going to dissect my brain or anything like that. In fact, I figured *I* might learn as much from them as they did from me.

That was the key, I guess; I knew I could learn something. That was important to me, since learning is the one thing I really like. If that sounds strange, look at it like this: if other kids treated you like a nerd and a geek all the time, if you went for weeks feeling like books were your only friends—well, you might really be into learning, too.

Anyway, between being the school dumping ground for emotional toxic waste and having a father who didn't give two bags of llama droppings whether I was alive or dead, I figured I didn't have much to lose by going with Broxholm.

Besides, more than anything else in the world, I wanted to travel to the stars and explore other planets.

That's why when Susan and the school band overpowered the alien on the night of our spring concert, I slipped around back to help him escape.

After I let Broxholm out, he turned and used something that looked like a pencil to *melt* the door shut.

Oh, oh, I thought. *Now you're in for it, Peter.*

But then I thought, *Well, wait a minute. If he has a weapon like that, he* could *have fried the whole crowd.*

Since he *hadn't*, I figured he wasn't going to make me into sausage; at least, not right away.

So when he started to run, I began to run alongside him.

"What are you doing?" cried the alien.

"I want to come with you!"

I think Broxholm would have stopped running right then, if he had figured it was safe. It wasn't, so he kept going. He was in good shape; I didn't hear him pant or gasp for breath at all. (Of course, for all I knew, when people from his planet got tired it made their armpits ache.)

Three blocks from the school he stopped running.

Then he disappeared.

I felt like my heart had disappeared, too. Never mind that Broxholm was a lean, green kidnapper from outer space. He was going back to the stars, and I wanted to go with him.

"Broxholm!" I yelled. "Wait! Take me!"

"Be quiet while I adjust this!" snapped a voice beside me.

An instant later I disappeared, too. Which is to say, I became invisible because of something Broxholm did.

"Wow," I whispered, looking down at where I used to be, "that's *awesome*!"

"Shut up, or you stay here," growled Broxholm.

I shut up. I may have saved his bacon back at the school, and I may have been the only one willing to go with him, but I figured if I got in the way of his escape, Broxholm would dump me faster than my mother had dumped my father when something better came along.

"Now, follow me," whispered Broxholm.

"How? I can't see you!"

After a moment of silence, I felt strong hands grab me by the waist. "Stay quiet!" hissed Broxholm as he tossed me over his shoulder. It reminded me of the first day I had met him, when he picked up Duncan and me to stop us from fighting.

He started to run. He was amazingly fast.

When we reached the little house where Broxholm had been living, he made us both visible again. Turning to me, he said, "I have some things to do before we can go. I also owe you a favor. Here it is: you have three minutes to change your mind. Otherwise, you're coming with me."

Before I could say a thing, he walked away—leaving me alone to make the biggest decision of my life.

Back at school that decision had been easy. Lying in my bed, in my empty house, I had known for sure what I would do. But this wasn't just some wishing game anymore. It was real.

I thought about my father. Would he miss me? Probably. At least, for a little while. Then he'd probably be just as glad I was gone; one less nuisance for him to cope with.

I thought about school, where I spent most of my time trying not to get beat up by Duncan and other jerks who thought being smart was a crime.

My life would have been a lot different if it was okay to be smart in school. But it's not. It's okay to be pretty smart. But not *real* smart—which is kind of stupid when you think about it. I mean, all these guys picking on smart kids and calling them geeks and dweebs are going to grow up and want to know why *they* don't *do something* about the terrible state the world is in.

I can tell you why. By the time they grow up, most of the kids who really could have changed things are wrecked.

I'll bet you this very minute, even while you're reading these words, some kid who's bright enough to cure cancer when he or she grows up is getting hassled for being an "egghead."

Any takers?

Anyway, I had plenty of reasons to run away. But that wasn't what made up my mind. I didn't just want to run away; I wanted to run *to* something. And that something was space.

I thought about my father again, and wondered if he had ever loved me.

I thought about the stars, and the secrets they held.

Broxholm walked into the kitchen, carrying a large wooden box and two flat pieces of plastic. I recognized the pieces of plastic: they were part of his communication system. Later I found out that the box was his dressing table, all folded up.

"Well?" he asked.

My hands were trembling like a pair of gerbils that had just been dropped into a snake pit. Some of that was terror; some of it was pure excitement. Looking straight into his huge orange eyes, I whispered, "I'm coming with you."

CHAPTER TWO

THE CELLAR BENEATH THE CELLAR

Broxholm didn't congratulate me, or thank me, or say he was glad to have me along. He just nodded, said, "Follow me," and started toward the cellar door.

The cellar was pretty much as I remembered it from the times I had snuck in with Susan. But Broxholm surprised me. When we reached the far wall, he pressed his hand against a concrete block. A section of the floor tilted back. Blue-gray light streamed up through the opening.

"You first," he said, nodding toward the hole.

Swallowing hard, I approached the light. Then I

looked down, and my fear was washed away in wonder. The trapdoor led to an enormous chamber; in the chamber was a spaceship.

A stairway curved along the side of the chamber. I scrambled down the steps. Broxholm was close behind me.

This second cellar was as polished as the first had been rough. The soft light that filled it came from the wall itself. I say wall because that's all the room had—a single gently curving wall with no edges and no corners. When I put my hand against it, it felt smooth, and slightly warm.

I felt like I was inside an egg.

Still, it was the ship that took most of my attention. Staring at it, I felt such a wave of joy that I thought I might float right off the floor. This was more than my ticket off a planet where I'd never been very happy; it was the key to the stars, and everything I'd dreamed of.

The top of the ship was a half sphere. This rested on a base that looked like a fifty-foot-wide soup bowl surrounded by a ring of lights. The base tapered down in layers, a little like a kid's toy top.

Broxholm whistled three harsh notes and an opening appeared in the side of the ship. A long strip of silvery metal stretched down to where we stood. Turning to me, Broxholm said: "Enter."

I stepped onto the silvery plank. It started to move. Feeling as if the ship was about to swallow me, I jumped back.

"Hurry!" snapped Broxholm.

I ran up the plank.

Once inside, I was aching to look around. But Broxholm hustled me to a platform that floated us up to the next level.

"Sit," he said, pointing toward one of four large chairs.

I sat. The padding on the chair was comfortable.

Taking a seat near me, Broxholm pushed a couple of buttons. Part of the curved wall slid aside. He laid his hand on a glowing pad. The ship began to slide forward, into a dark area. Suddenly we started to float. I was afraid we were going to hit the ceiling. But at the last possible moment, Broxholm's *entire back yard* flipped up, like a giant trapdoor.

As we lifted away I saw cop cars racing toward the house. One stopped. The door flew open and a blond kid scrambled out.

"Susan!" I cried.

She couldn't hear me, of course. That didn't stop me from making a fool of myself. Seeing her made me remember that not *everything* down there was rotten. "Wait!" I cried, turning to Broxholm. "Wait. I want to go back!"

Broxholm didn't even look at me as he moved his hands over the control panel. "There's no turning back now," he snapped.

The ship began to move faster. I watched the earth drop away beneath us. Within seconds I had lost sight of Susan, the house, even the town.

I felt hollow inside.

"Stop that," said Broxholm. He shook his head. "You earthlings! You never know what you want. If you'd stop trying to hold on to everything, you'd be a lot happier."

It wasn't until he spoke that I realized I was crying. "Sorry," I whispered, wiping my eyes with the back of my hand.

Broxholm touched my shoulder. "Don't look back," he said softly. "Look up!"

When I did, I started to cry again—this time out of sheer joy. We were heading for the moon. Beyond it lay the void of outer space, a deep black sprinkled with stars.

The moon continued to grow in the viewing space.

"We're going awfully fast, aren't we?" I asked after a moment.

"Compared to what?"

"Well, compared to earth rockets."

"Yes."

The guy was not much of a conversationalist. I was about to ask why the acceleration hadn't pushed me into my seat when we began to make a curve around the moon. When we got to the other side, I was astonished into silence myself.

One problem with writing about aliens is that sometimes it gets hard to describe things. For example, if I say that what I saw now was the biggest thing I had ever seen in my life, that wouldn't be true. A lot of things in nature—like the sun, the moon, and the stars—are bigger.

But if I say it was the biggest man-made thing I ever saw, that wouldn't be true either, because this wasn't made by men—or women, for that matter. It was made by aliens. And it was enormous—a huge lavender sphere that made Broxholm's ship look like an ant on the face of Mount Rushmore.

"What is that?" I finally managed to whisper.

"The good ship *New Jersey*," replied Broxholm.

I blinked. "The *New Jersey*?"

Broxholm pulled on his nose, which stretched out to about twice its normal length, then snapped back into place. I learned later that this is what people on his planet do instead of sighing.

"One of the senior members of our ship's crew has a rather bizarre sense of humor," said Broxholm. "This crew member has also spent a lot of time studying your planet. When the ship was built, it decided that since the ship's surface area was equal to that of New Jersey, that should be the name of the ship. Not everyone was amused."

"The ship decided?" I asked in puzzlement.

"No, the crew member," said Broxholm.

"But you said 'it' decided."

"That's because I'm wearing an implant that translates everything I say into English, and no pronoun in your language properly describes this crew member, who is neither a he nor a she, but something else all together."

"What else is there?"

Broxholm pulled on his nose again. "This crew-person comes from a planet where it takes five different genders just to get an egg—and three more to hatch it."

My mind was starting to spin. But before I could ask more questions, a hole opened in the side of the great sphere and a multicolored beam of light extended to our little vessel.

"Docking beam," said Broxholm, pointing to the light. "Soon we'll be inside. Then the fun begins."

"Fun?"

"Sarcasm," said Broxholm softly. "I will have to explain why you are with me. That will not be fun. Not at all."

CHAPTER THREE

THE NAKED STRANGER

Sarcasm? Did that mean Broxholm had a sense of humor? The idea fascinated me. But this didn't seem like the time to ask about it, since I had more important questions in mind—such as, "*Why* won't it be fun?"

"I will tell you later," replied Broxholm. "If I am able. Right now I have business to attend to."

His hands moved swiftly across the control board, which looked like a lot of marbles embedded in a sheet of black concrete. Sometimes he pushed the marbles (or whatever they were), sometimes he rolled them, sometimes he tapped them.

Suddenly a face appeared at the right of the

panel. To my surprise, it didn't look like Broxholm. The forehead was low, the skull wide, the skin a strange shade of yellow.

"Oorbis tiktum?" asked the face.

"Broxholm, requesting emergency landing status. I have one young earthling with me."

I wondered why he spoke in English, until I remembered that his implant forced him to.

Clearly, the alien understood him anyway. "Coopla daktum!" cried the face. Its skin turned orange, and the screen went blank.

"He's not happy, is he?" I said.

"That was a she. And as I was supposed to arrive six hours later, with a total of five children, all of whom were supposed to be asleep, she is naturally somewhat disturbed."

By this time the docking beam had pulled us most of the way in. Imagine you're a flea. Now imagine you're walking through the door of the Empire State Building. That's what it was like for me going into the ship. For a while all I could think was, *This thing is so BIG!* Then my mind did a little flip, and I started thinking, *I'm so SMALL!*

Then I got sort of confused between being afraid and being excited.

Also, I had to go to the bathroom.

The docking beam pulled us into an area that had to be three times as long as a football field. The walls, which were about a thousand feet high, were lined with huge shelves. About half the shelf spaces were filled with spaceships.

None of the ships looked anything like Broxholm's.

When we were about three quarters of the way across this space, the docking beam deposited us on a shelf.

Broxholm did one of his nose-sighs. "Time to face the music," he said.

Given how much Broxholm hated music, that sounded worse coming from him than it would have from anyone else I had ever met. Or was it just his language implant, changing his words into a common English phrase?

I didn't have time to ask, because the top of the ship flipped up, and we began to float into the air. About a meter above the ship, we started to drift in different directions.

"Broxholm!" I cried. "What's going on?"

"We have to be disinfected," he answered, as a hole opened in the wall in front of me.

I struggled, but it was like fighting with air. No matter how I twisted, the invisible beam held me in its grip. Feet first, flat on my back, floating a hundred feet above the floor of the docking area, I was pulled into a small white room shaped a little like an egg that's been stood on end.

"Branna praxim pee-doongie prit," said a musical voice.

I looked around—which didn't take long, since the whole chamber wasn't more than four feet wide. I couldn't see whoever had spoken the words. I couldn't even see a device that the words might have come from.

"Branna praxim pee-doongie prit," repeated the voice gently.

A picture appeared on the wall. It showed an alien—one who looked completely different from Broxholm—standing in a room like this. As I watched, the alien took off its clothes.

I blinked in surprise. Then I remembered the last

thing Broxholm had said to me: "We have to be disinfected."

They wanted *me* to take off *my* clothes!

"Now just a ding-danged minute!" I said.

"Branna praxim pee-doongie prit," said the voice again.

"Uh-uh. Sorry. I don't do naked in front of strangers!"

Either whoever was speaking didn't understand me, or didn't care. A blue beam flashed down from the ceiling, locking me in place. It was a force field, just like the one Broxholm had used to keep Ms. Schwartz a prisoner. I tried to struggle, but I couldn't even scream. Everything stops when you're in a force field.

I heard the slightest of noises behind me. I tried to turn to see what had made it. I couldn't, of course. The force field held me firm.

Suddenly I felt something tickle down my back.

What was going on?

I heard the same noise in front of me. From the wall came a tiny ray of light. A laser beam! Starting at my chin, the laser moved all the way down to my feet. I couldn't see it all the way down, because I couldn't bend my head. But I could feel that tickle. A few more tickles—down my arms, around my legs, and suddenly the force field disappeared.

I could move again! The only problem was, the instant I did, my clothes all fell off. The laser had sliced my shirt, my pants, my shoes and socks, even my underwear, into pieces—and had done it all without touching my skin.

"Get me out of here!" I yelled. "Get me some *clothes*!"

No answer.

Did that mean there wasn't anyone there? Just as well, I decided, since I didn't have any clothes on. But how long were the aliens going to leave me here? Or was someone watching me even now—watching, but not speaking?

That made sense, in a way. If the alien mission was to study earthlings, then probably they were doing that right now—especially since I was the only one they had.

I decided if I was going to be *the* sample earthling, I was going to do my best not to act like an idiot.

So I began to take deep breaths. I felt myself getting a little calmer. I mean, it wasn't like no one had ever seen me naked before. I've been to the doctor. And next year I would be taking showers in gym class.

Come to think of it, given my choice of getting stuck naked in front of a bunch of aliens, or in a seventh-grade gym class, I'd choose the aliens any day. At least *they* won't flick your butt with a wet towel!

Unfortunately, just as I was getting calm, my little chamber started to fill with gas. Was this a test, to see if I would panic? Were they going to knock me out and do some medical exams?

Or were they going to kill me and dissect me?

I held my breath until my lungs were screaming for air. When I couldn't resist any longer I took a deep, gasping breath.

"Prandit kooma," said the same voice I had heard before.

Weird musiclike sounds began drifting into the chamber. As I felt myself begin to get drowsy, I heard a slight hiss and saw a purple mist filtering down from the ceiling. I wanted to hold my breath again, but I didn't seem to have the willpower.

The music played on. It wasn't like anything you or I would recognize as music, but it was beautiful. My eyelids drooped. Soon I slumped against the side of the chamber and slid to the floor, naked and sound asleep.

CHAPTER FOUR

CROCDOC

When I opened my eyes again, I was lying on a table in a room that was filled with soft green light. I was still naked. A tall alien who looked a little bit like a human crocodile—or at least like a human crocodile would look if it was red instead of green—was standing over me.

"Feeling better?" asked the alien softly.

Actually, what it said was, "Klaakah greebratz?" But my brain *heard* it as "Feeling better?"

I sat up, got dizzy, and lay back down.

"What's going on?" I whispered.

"I just did a little work on your head," said the

alien, as casually as if it was announcing it had gone to the corner for a loaf of bread. "I'm sorry I didn't have a chance to explain the situation before I started, but I hadn't been expecting you."

"What did you do?" I asked, touching my head nervously.

"I installed a Universal Translator in your brain. That's why you can understand me. From now on, you'll be able to understand almost everyone you meet. We all wear them; it makes life quite a bit easier. As I said, I would have explained before I did the work, but there was no way to make you understand. The only being on board who had an implant that would turn his words *into* your language was Broxholm, and he was tied up."

Did the alien mean Broxholm was busy? Or had they really tied him up, as punishment for letting some kids mess up his mission? With aliens, who knew?

"You can probably sit up now," said the brain surgeon. "You just needed a moment to let your head clear."

Moving slowly, I pushed myself to a sitting position. "Where are my glasses?" I asked.

"Do you need them?" asked the crocodile person, sounding surprised. (I would say the crocodile *man* or the crocodile *woman*, but the truth is, I had no idea which—if either—it was.)

I looked around and blinked in astonishment. I had never seen things so clearly in my life, not even when I was wearing glasses. "What happened?" I cried.

"I thought as long as I was poking around inside your head I might as well fix your eyes."

"Uh—thanks," I said. I probably should have been more enthusiastic; after all, the alien had done me a real favor. But I still wasn't comfortable with the idea that it had been poking around inside my skull without my permission.

On the other hand, being able to see so clearly without my glasses was *wonderful*!

"Thanks!" I said again, this time more sincere.

The red alien smiled—which meant that I got to see about three hundred and forty-two teeth—and said, "Don't mention it."

I heard a sound behind me. Turning, I saw another alien, though I couldn't spot the door he had come in by. He was short—probably not more than three feet tall—blue and bald. He had big eyes, a large nose, and a thick white mustache. He also had spindly arms and a potbelly. He was wearing nothing but a pair of baggy red shorts covered with pictures of jumping yellow fish.

I had seen aliens who were frightening, aliens who were strange, and aliens who were almost indescribable. This was the first one I had met who was *cute*.

"Greetings, Peter," said the newcomer. "My name is Hoo-Lan."

Actually, what he said was, "Grrgn ryxkzin, Peter, prrna-prrna Hoo-Lan." But with my new implant I knew exactly what he meant.

His ears flapped as he spoke. To my surprise, I understood that this was his version of a smile—which meant that my language implant translated not only words, but gestures and expressions. When you think about how much of what you mean is carried not by your words, but by your body, that makes sense. It's just not the kind of stuff they usually teach you in French class.

"How are you feeling?" he asked.

I thought about his question for a moment.

"I feel fine," I said finally.

The blue alien gave me another ear flap. "I'm pleased to hear that," he said, in his own language. "As you probably suspect, in addition to receiving a language implant, you have been disinfected. We had to disinfect both you and Broxholm before we could allow you to enter the main body of the ship. That was why he could not be with you when you had your operation, for which you have our apologies."

I was a little surprised to hear him apologize. It was also nice to know that the reason no one had told me what was going on when I first got here was that they just couldn't communicate with me yet.

"Can I stand up?" I asked, turning to the crocodile person.

"If you feel like it."

When I stopped to think about it, I realized that I felt terrific. Had the croc/doc tinkered with the rest of my systems, too? I decided not to ask.

"You wouldn't by any chance have some clothes I could wear, would you?" I asked.

Nose twitching, Hoo-Lan brought his hand from

behind his back and tossed me a package wrapped in shiny black material. "I thought you might want these," he said. "Especially since it's time for us to visit the captain."

The package contained my clothes, which were in perfect condition. "I don't get it. I thought these had been lasered into pieces."

"These are computer recreations," said Hoo-Lan. "We put the disinfected scraps of what you had been wearing into the synthesizer. It analyzed fabric and design, then spit out a new set. These are identical to your originals, except that they are stain proof, and almost impossible to tear. If you wish, you can design your own clothes later."

That was interesting. I had never cared much about clothes. But if I could just tell the computer what I wanted, it might be fun to try a few different styles!

Once I was dressed I turned to the CrocDoc, as I now thought of him, and thanked him again for what he had done.

He tapped his elbows together three times. According to my implant, this meant he was glad to have been of service, and he hoped that he would never have to eat my children.

Let me tell you, this multicultural stuff can keep a guy on his toes!

"Follow me," said Hoo-Lan.

I nodded to CrocDoc, and got ready to follow Hoo-Lan out of the room. The only thing we needed now was a door.

The little alien walked to a place where the wall was marked by a large circle. Next to the circle were twelve rows of multicolored marbles. Hoo-Lan tapped six of the marbles, and the area inside the circle turned blue.

"Step through," he said, gesturing toward the circle.

"Through the wall?" I asked nervously.

"It's not a wall," he replied, giving me a little shove. "It's a transcendental elevator."

"Hey!" I shouted, thinking I was going to smash my face against the circle.

To my surprise, I stepped right *through* the circle. As I did, my whole body began to tingle. The tingling got stronger and stronger. It reminded me of the "pins and needles" you get when your leg falls asleep. Only this was all over my body, and it kept getting stronger.

I wanted to shout, only I couldn't, because I had no mouth. But then, I didn't have hands, feet, or a head, either.

CHAPTER FIVE

THE CRYSTAL CAPTAIN

As quickly as it began, it was over, and I found myself—all of myself—standing in a room that looked like it had been carved out of the inside of a diamond. Hoo-Lan was next to me.

"What happened?" I whispered.

Hoo-Lan looked at me in surprise. "Did you feel something?"

I nodded. He frowned, which meant the same for him as it does for us. "You shouldn't have," he said. "We'll have to look into this."

"But what happened?" I repeated.

"The elevator took you apart and put you back together."

"WHAT?"

"Don't worry—the same thing happened to me. That's how a transcendental elevator works; it breaks you into packets of energy, sends you to another place, then puts you back together."

"Wouldn't it be easier to walk?" I asked, patting myself in various places to make sure I was all there.

Hoo-Lan gave me his version of a shrug. "It's over a hundred miles from the doctor's room to the captain's cabin."

"Oh, well in that case, sure, just send my molecules," I said, wondering if the sarcasm would translate.

"We did," said Hoo-Lan, sounding quite serious. "And now it is time for us to meet the captain."

A tinkle of music played around me. "Indeed it is," translated my language implant.

I turned in a circle, trying to find the source of the sound. "Where did that come from?" I whispered.

Hoo-Lan gestured to a clear tank that stood at one end of the chamber.

"What is it?" I asked.

"The captain."

"Come here, young earthling," said the tank.

I glanced at Hoo-Lan. He nodded, so I crossed to the tank, which looked like a huge, round aquarium. Except there weren't any fish or plants inside. A pair of cables ran from the bottom of the tank into the floor.

"Look more closely," said the voice.

I stared into the tank. After a few seconds I saw a collection of crystals, sharp-edged and many-faceted. It took me a few more seconds to realize that the shapes were slowly moving.

"This is our captain," said Hoo-Lan, adding a name for which there was no translation.

"But how . . . ?"

A sigh tinkled around me. "You carbon-based life forms are so molecular-centric. Until you meet another form of life, you seem convinced that carbon is the only way to grow."

"Sorry," I said. "I didn't mean to offend you."

The air around me filled with a sound like chimes; the implant told me this was laughter.

"Hoo-Lan," sang the crystal captain, "I need only speak to Peter. You may leave if you wish."

"I have things to do," said Hoo-Lan, nodding to me. "I will see you soon." As he turned and headed for the transcendental elevator the captain's voice said, "You do realize, my young friend, that you have created a problem for us?"

I blinked. "What's the problem?"

"In a word, *you*. By galactic law, no person of Earth is allowed on board this vessel."

"I thought Broxholm was supposed to bring back *five* of us," I said, feeling somewhat puzzled.

"For observation and analysis only. Any memory of the experience would have been erased from your minds before we returned you to Earth."

"Did you ever wonder how we might feel about that?"

"Not particularly. If I had, it wouldn't have mattered. Except for our fact-finding mission, the Interplanetary Council has banned all contact with the people of Earth. This is the first time in a thousand years this has happened, by the way."

"You mean it's the first time in a thousand years

Earth has been isolated?" I asked, wondering if the aliens had visited a lot in the past.

"It's the first time in a thousand years *any* planet has been isolated."

I didn't like the sound of that. "Should we be honored?" I asked, sounding more smart-alecky than I intended.

"*Terrified* might be more appropriate."

"Terrified?" I squeaked. The very fact that the captain *said* I should react that way came close to creating the feeling in me.

The captain's voice chimed around me, louder than before. "Earth is the greatest danger faced in the three thousand year history of the Interplanetary League. It appears to be a planet in the grip of mass insanity. We must find out why you kill each other with such reckless abandon."

The language implant was translating what the captain sang into words. But the very sound of the music filled me with fear, and with sorrow.

The crystals in the bottom of the tank shifted. "There is something very strange about your world," continued the captain. "On every other planet where science has developed, the process has taken much longer than it has on Earth. Always before, people ready to enter space have been civilized in a way you humans have avoided altogether."

The captain paused, then sang sadly, "We fear if the people of Earth are allowed into space in their uncivilized state, the results could be disastrous beyond anything you can imagine."

"Allowed?" I asked nervously.

"Allowed. At the moment, we are considering a permanent quarantine on Earth. No one gets on, no one gets off. We don't mind you exploring your own solar system; there's not much there anyway. But we cannot allow you to carry this sickness, whatever it is, into the galaxy at large."

I wanted to cry; for years I had been dreaming of meeting people from another planet. When I finally do meet some, what do I find? *My* planet has embarrassed itself in front of the entire galaxy! I felt like an interstellar geek.

"Of course, quarantine is only one option," said the captain, interrupting my thoughts.

"What else is there?" I asked, more nervous than ever.

"I would rather not say. After all, the teacher does not necessarily discuss all options with the student."

I wondered if the captain really meant "with the enemy." But I couldn't think of a way to say it that didn't sound snotty.

"Anyway," continued the captain, "you can see that your presence here creates a problem."

"Are you going to lock me up?"

The bells that filled the air seemed to sigh. "You see? Only an earthling would think of something like that so quickly. I suppose if you persisted in causing trouble, we might lock you up. But that's just not something we do. However, we do have to decide what we *will* do with you. So tell me, what is it that brought you here? What do you want?"

"To *learn*," I said fiercely.

"Admirable. However, you must realize that the more you learn, the less likely it is we can ever let you return home."

"I don't care about home. I want to see the stars."

"You could have seen them from your own backyard."

"I want to visit other planets. I want to explore the galaxy. I want to find out what it's all about!" I cried, suddenly realizing I might be the only human ever to have that chance.

"Then you are welcome to join us. You will be assigned to Hoo-Lan, who has been specializing in Earth studies of late."

"How is Broxholm going to feel about that?" I asked, though for all I knew Broxholm never wanted to see me again.

"That's not an issue," said the captain. "Broxholm has other matters to which he must attend. As do I, my new crewmember. Which means that you must leave now. The elevator will take you to your cabin."

Feeling a trifle nervous, I headed for the circle where we had come in. When I glanced back, the captain's tank had changed color. I heard the word for "Farewell" chime through the air as I stepped through the wall.

I didn't feel anything this time, none of the tearing sensation that had scared me so much on my first trip through the transcendental elevator. So I figured Hoo-Lan had adjusted the mechanism for me. But the place the elevator delivered me to was so dark I was afraid the thing had malfunctioned.

My heart began to pound. What if it had sent me someplace where no one would be able to find me, some neglected storage space or something? Rooms on this ship didn't even have doors! If I got stuck in a place like that I might die before anyone found me.

I was about to scream for help when a blue light began to glow behind me.

CHAPTER SIX
HOO-LAN

I spun around and found myself face to face with Hoo-Lan.

Well, face to face isn't quite right; given how short he was, it was more like navel to face. Anyway, he was the source of the light. And I mean that exactly. The little alien wasn't carrying a lamp or a flashlight or anything. *He* was glowing—a soft, gentle glow that seemed to come from every square inch of his skin.

"For heaven's sakes, Peter," said Hoo-Lan quietly, "don't be so skittish."

It took me a moment to realize that the words

were spoken in perfect English. I stared at him in surprise. "I didn't know you could speak my language."

"There's a lot about me that you don't know, and a great deal that I have to tell you. That's why I arranged to have you sent here, instead of your own room. I needed a place where we could speak in relative secrecy."

"Secrecy?" I asked nervously.

"Great things are happening," said Hoo-Lan, glancing from side to side. "Power is shifting, and ancient mysteries are being unraveled." His glow seemed to grow more intense. His voice, and his words, sent a chill down my spine.

"What does that have to do with me?" I asked in a whisper.

"Nothing, and everything. Remember, information travels fast, if you know how to grease its skids." He paused, then added, "I'm not sure that made sense."

"Why are we here?" I asked, trying to get him back on track. "*Where* are we, for that matter?"

"In a storage space in the lower third of the good

ship *New Jersey*, which at the moment is heading past the planet you call Jupiter."

That scared me. The last spacecraft Earth sent past Jupiter had taken years to get there. We must be moving at an incredible rate! On the other hand, it was a straight answer. Shooting for two in a row, I asked, "What did you bring me here to tell me?"

Hoo-Lan motioned toward a box, indicating I should sit. In the light emanating from his body, I could see that the room was filled with containers of all shapes, sizes, and colors.

I sat. Hoo-Lan scrambled up next to me. Reaching into a pocket in his baggy shorts, he pulled out a black box about half the size of a paperback book.

"You rat," he said, handing it to me.

"What did I do?" I asked, feeling hurt.

Hoo-Lan blinked. "What did you . . . ? Oh, you misunderstood me. I didn't call *you* a rat. *This device* is a URAT—a *U*niversal *R*eader *A*nd *T*ranslator. Press your thumb against the top corner."

I did as Hoo-Lan said. The box opened, pretty much the way a book would if it was only made of two very thick pages. Except the URAT was now stiff, as if it had never been closed.

"This will be your primary information source," said Hoo-Lan. "It contains a small library of important data for navigating your way around the ship. Also a complete listing of crew members. Now, please tell it your name."

"My name is—"

"Wait, wait! I think you need a new name."

"What's wrong with the one I've got?" I asked, feeling a little annoyed. I don't know why I was annoyed. Peter Thompson was nothing special as names go. Heck, the Thompson part came from my father, and I was as glad to be rid of him as he was to be rid of me. No loss there. As for my first name, it was mostly something people used to get my attention when they wanted to tease me. So a new name shouldn't have been any big deal. Still, I had had this one all my life, and I felt somewhat attached to it.

"There's nothing *wrong* with your old name," said Hoo-Lan patiently. "It's just that it's part of your old life. New life, new name, I always say. I shall call you

Krepta, which in the language of my world means 'Child of the Stars.' This is a good name for you, since you are a boy without a planet."

I felt my stomach twist. "A boy without a planet" sounded terribly lonely.

I hesitated. "My name is Krepta," I whispered into the URAT. "Child of the Stars."

"Greetings, Krepta," replied the URAT. "How may I be of service?"

I looked at Hoo-Lan.

"Tell it you wish to travel," he said.

"Where do you wish to go?" asked the URAT, after I had followed Hoo-Lan's advice.

"Actually, I would like something to eat," I said.

"Wise choice," said Hoo-Lan. "Biologically sound, too. When you get to a new place, always find out where to eat and where to hide."

"Will I need to hide here?" I asked nervously.

Hoo-Lan shrugged. I would have pursued the question, but the URAT had started beeping. Looking at it, I saw a pattern of colored dots. It was the same pattern I had seen next to the transcendental elevator. Suddenly some of the dots began to flash.

"It's displaying the destination code," said Hoo-Lan. "When you want to go somewhere, ask the URAT for the code. Punch the code into the control pad beside any elevator, and it will take you to your destination."

"Can I go anywhere I want?"

"Of course," said Hoo-Lan. "Why not?"

"Well, don't you have rules—you know, security precautions against spies, things like that?"

"You have to stop thinking as if you were still on Earth, Peter. We're not the same as you are. I'm the closest thing to a spy on this ship. Certainly the biggest troublemaker."

I looked at him in alarm. "Are you going to get *me* in trouble?" I asked nervously.

"Oh, probably. Anyone who tries to do something worthwhile gets in trouble now and then, don't you think?"

To tell you the truth, I didn't know what to think. I decided to get some more information, and do the thinking later. "What do you mean, you're the closest thing to a spy?" I asked. "Are you a spy, or aren't you?"

"Merely a representative of a minority point of view. As you know, your planet is currently the focus of a great debate. At the moment, I am on the losing side of that debate."

"What side is that?"

Before Hoo-Lan could answer, I heard another beeping. Reaching into his pocket, he took out a second URAT. When he opened it, a face that looked like it belonged to a purple frog appeared on its surface and said, "You are wanted for an urgent meeting."

"The main problem with these things," said Hoo-Lan, tucking away his URAT and hopping down to the floor, "is that they're great for communication, but lousy for privacy. I'm sorry, Krepta, but I can't ignore this call. We'll talk more later. For now, why don't you get something to eat. I'll catch up with you in a while."

He crossed to the wall and started to punch a code into the elevator buttons. Then he stopped, turned to me, and said, "Since you can't see in the dark, maybe you'd better go first."

That made sense. When Hoo-Lan left he would

take my only source of light—namely, himself—with him.

I stepped up to the wall. My URAT was still flashing the code for a dining area, the image of the buttons lighting up in a certain order, pausing, and then repeating the sequence.

I watched the code twice, then punched it into the control pad. Taking a deep breath, I stepped through the wall—and into the middle of a fight.

CHAPTER SEVEN

LUNCH WITH FLEEF AND GURK

"It was a bad idea from the beginning!" said an alien who looked something like a tall brown pickle with arms.

"Nonsense!" snapped the orange alien standing next to him. "A few hours wouldn't have made the slightest bit of difference to those creatures."

This second alien was only a little taller than me, and clearly female, at least by Earth standards. Though her skin was orange, her features were basically human—well, except for the fact that she had a thumb-thick green stalk rising from the top of her head. The stalk ended in a thick knob, which I took to be a sense organ of some sort, since it was constantly rotating. Every once in a while it would stop moving and go, "Neep! Neep!"

"Ah, look!" cried the orange alien, when she noticed me standing there. "We can ask him!"

"It might be nice if we greeted him first," said the pickle.

"Flog me for an oaf!" cried the orange one. "I just get too excited sometimes." Turning to me, she said, "You are the Earth child, are you not?"

Her voice was sweet and gentle.

"I used to be," I replied. "Now I'm a child of the stars."

The orange alien nudged the pickle. "What did I tell you, Gurk. It doesn't matter!"

Gurk squeezed one of the warty things that covered his pickly skin. It popped, releasing a terrible smell.

My implant told me this was his way of saying "Nonsense!"

"Euuuw!" cried the orange alien. "I told you not to do that!" The stalk on the top of her head flopped backward. "Neep," it whispered. "Neee—"

I looked at the alien in alarm, worried that the knob might be permanently disabled, or even dead. But she seemed more annoyed than concerned.

Gurk put his hands on top of his head, which was a gesture of apology. "Sorry, I got carried away. But I still think you're mistaken. Let's start this conversation over, or we'll give the young one a bad impression."

He turned to me. I got ready to hold my breath, in case he was going to communicate by smell again. But his voice was quiet, and when I looked at him more carefully, I realized that he had the kindest, warmest eyes I had ever seen.

Putting his skinny arms together in front of him, he said, "Young one, my name is Gurk. My companion is called Fleef."

"Greetings," said Fleef, who was trying to get the stalk on her head to stand up again.

"Greetings," I replied.

They both looked at me expectantly. "And your name?" asked Gurk, after a moment of silence.

"Oh, I'm sorry. My name is—" I hesitated. Was I Peter Thompson—or was I Krepta?

The aliens were staring at me. I had a sense that they were beginning to wonder if I was stupid.

"My name is Krepta!" I said defiantly.

As I said it, I felt something twist inside me. I had let go of my name and my home, and though I had a new name, and a new home, neither one of them felt like they were really mine.

I wondered if they ever would. I almost said, "Wait, I made a mistake! My name is Peter!"

But that would have been a lie. I wasn't Peter anymore. Hoo-Lan had been right. I was a boy without a planet, and the name I had carried away from Earth no longer fit me.

"Krepta!" said Gurk in surprise. "A Child of the Stars, indeed. And what happened to the name you were born with?"

"I am a different person now," I said softly.

"Well, Krepta," said Fleef, "come and sit with us while we eat. Perhaps you can help us settle a disagreement."

I wasn't sure I wanted to eat with the two of them. Still, if I was going to get along on this ship, I did need to start making friends.

"I'd be glad to eat with you," I said, hoping neither one of them was going to eat something so gross I would get sick just watching them swallow it.

"Are you touchable?" asked Gurk.

I raised an eyebrow. His translator must have interpreted the movement, because he answered the question before I could put it into words.

"Some beings like to be touched, others are deeply offended by certain kinds of contact," he explained, his wonderful eyes looking straight into mine. "If touch does not bother you, then I would put my arm around your shoulder, or place a hand on the back of your neck, to guide you to the sitting place. But it is best to ask, first."

I hesitated. My father wasn't much of a hugger. So the only person who had touched me much back home was Duncan Dougal, and that was only to punch me. Since I wasn't used to it, I was a little nervous about having Gurk touch me, especially with that pickly skin of his. On the other hand, this was a new world, a new life. . . .

"It's okay," I said. "You can touch me."

I thought about adding something about being

careful *where* he touched me, but he had been so worried about offending me at all, I decided it wasn't going to be a problem.

Besides, even though I hadn't gone three steps past the elevator, I could see a whole room full of people just beyond Fleef and Gurk. So I figured I was safe for the time being—at least, as safe as a kid can be in a room where he's the only person who looks more than vaguely human.

Taking me by the arm, Gurk led me to a table at the edge of the room. "There are many beings interested in you," he whispered, "so there's no need to draw too much attention to yourself right now."

"For once we agree," said Fleef.

"Neep!" said the thing on top of her head. I noticed the stalk was standing up straight again.

I also noticed that the room was sort of dim. I was a little puzzled about this, until I decided they had probably set the light at a level most comfortable for the greatest number of different beings.

"Where do we get our food?" I asked.

"Right here!" said Fleef, gesturing to the table.

The table was round, with a smooth black top.

In front of each of us was a set of buttons much like the ones beside the transcendental elevators.

"Do we use these to order?" I asked, pointing to the buttons.

"See, I told you they weren't stupid!" said Gurk.

"Intelligence and emotion are not always connected," replied Fleef. Her orange skin grew darker as she spoke, which my translator informed me was a sign that she was irritated.

"Could you tell me what this is all about?" I asked, trying not to do anything that was going to offend either one of them.

"Later," said Gurk. "First let's order. Have you programmed in any meals yet?"

I shook my head, trusting Gurk's implant to translate the gesture.

"All right, then we'll have to show you how. You are a carbon-based life form, if I remember correctly?"

I nodded, wondering what they would feed me if I wasn't.

"All right, first you punch in your personal code—"

"But I don't have a personal code," I interrupted.

"Gurk," said Fleef gently, "let *me* show him how."

Gurk slid some warts around, which was his way of sighing, and sat back in his chair while Fleef showed me how to find my personal code. Then she helped me tell the master computer the kinds of things that I would like. It took a while, because the food synthesizer wasn't programmed for an earthling. But by asking careful questions, she was able to help me come up with a menu that we both felt would (a) not kill me and (b) not make me throw up.

We all punched in the codes for our meals at the same time. Within seconds a hole opened in the top of the table. Three plates floated out and positioned themselves in front of us.

Gurk's plate had a steaming, writhing mess of something that looked like it wanted to crawl across the table and say hello to me.

Fleef's dinner looked like blue marbles and smelled like rotten eggs mixed with toe jam.

The stuff on my plate actually looked pretty good. That was because Fleef had showed me how to program color and shape into my order. While it didn't taste quite as good as it looked, at least most of it was edible. The only thing I couldn't get down was the stuff that looked like french fries but tasted like peanut butter mixed with rotten blueberries.

While we ate, Fleef told me how to refine my next order, based on what I did and didn't like in this batch of stuff. She was a good teacher, and I was starting to like her.

After we had all had a bit to eat, Gurk said, "Here's the question we were arguing about when you stepped out of the elevator. What would happen if—"

Before he could finish, the lights blinked three times. "Better lie down, Krepta," said Fleef, throwing herself to the floor. "You'll be less likely to throw up that way."

CHAPTER EIGHT
FASTER THAN LIGHT

I stretched out on the floor beside Fleef and Gurk. After a second, I raised my head. Almost everyone else in the large room was on the floor with us.

"Put your head down," whispered Fleef. "Quickly!"

I felt like I was in one of those stories where the king was about to come by, and everyone had to bow down. I stared at the ceiling, wondering if the aliens had some supreme high commander they treated like a god.

At first, I thought the ceiling was made of green marble. Then I noticed that the swirls of color were slowly moving. I was thinking how pretty it was when an ear-splitting squeal sliced through the room, as if some monstrous claw had just scraped across the blackboard of the universe. A low moan rose from the aliens on the floor, the kind of sound you might hear if a thousand kids all began to feel carsick at the same time.

It took me a moment to realize that my own voice was part of that mass moan. My stomach lurched. I clutched at it, trying to keep down what I had eaten. I didn't want to disgust my new friends by throwing up on them! (I was also hoping they were not going to throw up on me. I was pretty nervous about what it might smell like if Gurk tossed his cookies—or whatever it is that giant pickles toss when they lose their lunches.)

Suddenly I felt like I was being pulled apart. Only this was a thousand times worse than my first trip through the transcendental elevator. It was as if some giant had my head, another had my feet, and they were having a tug of war—with about a thousand other people pulling at the top, bottom, and sides of me just for the heck of it.

About the time I thought I absolutely couldn't stand it any longer, it stopped. I lay flat for a moment, wondering what had just happened to me.

Gurk touched my shoulder. "Are you all right, Krepta?" he asked softly.

I was so disoriented it took me a moment to realize he was speaking to me. "I'm not sure," I whispered. "What just happened?"

"The ship made a space-shift," said Fleef softly. "Galactically speaking, it's the only way to travel."

I opened and closed my eyes a few times. The ceiling didn't seem so pretty anymore. In fact, it was kind of nauseating. I wished it would stop moving.

"What's a space-shift?" I asked weakly.

"Instant transportation," said Gurk, rolling over and pushing himself up with his skinny arms.

"Like the transcendental elevators, but on a grand scale," added Fleef. She was already on her feet, holding out a six-fingered orange hand to help me up. "The ship just moved several light-years from where it was when you joined us."

I felt an unexpected sense of loss wash over me. How far from home was I now?

"Could you tell me a bit more?" I asked.

"Well, do you know about the speed of light?" asked Gurk.

"It goes 186,000 miles per second," I said, trusting their implants to figure out what miles are. "It's the fastest thing we know."

"It's the fastest thing *anyone* knows," said Fleef, patting her stalk to make sure it was all right. "Now that would make traveling around the galaxy nearly impossible, since even at the speed of light it would take you years to get from one star system to another. Centuries, sometimes."

"So the best method is to skip all that traveling," said Gurk, sliding a wart across his forehead. "Which is what we just did."

I staggered to my chair, trying to keep my stomach from providing a review of everything I had just eaten. "Could you make that a little more clear?"

Gurk punched some buttons on the food preparation device. A plate floated up, carrying a thick red noodle that had to be at least three feet long.

"How can you eat so soon after that shift?" asked Fleef.

"This isn't a snack, it's a demonstration," replied Gurk. "Sit down, Krepta, and I will try to explain." He picked up the noodle. "If you stretch out this *bee-ranga*—which, by the way, is the preferred snack on the planet Hopfner—you have a straight line. Now, if you were at one end, and the place you wanted to go was at the other end, you would have to travel the entire length of the *bee-ranga* to get there, right?"

I nodded.

"But if you join the ends of the *bee-ranga*, like this, all you would have to do is go from here—to here!" And with that he brought the two ends of the noodle together.

"What does that have to do with us?" I asked.

"That's how this ship travels. We bring two parts of space together and then step across them."

"It's the stepping across that's the hard part," added Fleef. "It makes most beings quite queasy."

"But how do you *do* it?"

"I don't know how it works," said Gurk. "All I know is the basic idea."

That seemed strange, until I thought about how

many people on Earth ride around in cars without having the slightest idea of how they work. I decided to switch questions. "If we just jumped several light-years, then where are we now?"

"How do you expect us to know?" asked Gurk, popping the *bee-ranga* into his mouth. "We're not the captain."

The sight of Gurk eating seemed to make Fleef queasy. "If my friend were feeling a little more polite," she whispered, "he would mention that you could find out by asking your URAT. I would guess we're heading back toward the center of the galaxy. If that was a typical jump, we probably moved about twenty light-years."

A strange feeling came over me. *The fastest rocket ever built on earth couldn't get this far in a hundred years,* I thought to myself.

With a shock, I realized I was homesick.

Fleef tapped me on the shoulder. "Are you all right, Krepta?"

"What? Oh, sure," I lied. "I'm fine, just fine."

I figured there was no point in telling them how I felt. To begin with, I wasn't sure I understood it myself.

Besides, years of living with my father had taught me not to bother talking about things that upset me.

"Good," said Fleef. "Then maybe I can finally ask you my question. What we were arguing about when you first met us was whether or not it made any difference if we borrowed some of your planet's children for a while."

"You mean like when Broxholm was planning to steal some kids from our school?" I asked.

"No, no, no," said Fleef. "We weren't going to steal anyone—just borrow them for a while. It's part of a research project. We would have brought them back! Which is why I don't think anyone would have minded that much. But Gurk says people, parents especially, would have been terribly upset. So—which of us is right?"

"Gurk is. Parents would have gone berserk. You can't just go around stealing—er, *borrowing* kids like that."

"See!" said Gurk triumphantly. Actually, he didn't say it, he pulled off one of his brown warts and waved it in front of Fleef's face, which my translation device told me was a sign of victory.

"But it doesn't make sense," said Fleef. She looked upset. Not just unhappy because Gurk had won the argument; she seemed genuinely disturbed.

"What doesn't make sense?" I asked.

"Oh, ignore her," said Gurk. "She's just annoyed because she wants to believe you people don't have well developed emotions."

"Why would you want to believe that?" I asked.

Fleef didn't answer. Gurk spoke for her. "Because then she won't feel so bad if we have to blow up your planet."

CHAPTER NINE

ROOM SERVICE

If you've ever just missed being in some terrible car accident, you know what I felt like. My hands were trembling, my heart was pounding, and my stomach wasn't sure where it wanted to go.

"You want to do what?" I whispered, staring at Fleef in horror.

The stalk on her head was whirling around like crazy, the little knob going "Neep neep neep!" as if someone was trying to catch and kill it. According to my implant this was a sign of extreme emotional distress.

Tough! I thought. *Your distress can't be any worse than mine.*

Sure, I'd had my problems with Earth. But these guys were talking about blowing up billions of human beings, including my father, Ms. Schwartz, Susan Simmons—and *you*.

"You'd better go, Krepta," said Gurk, touching my arm.

"No! I want to know what this is all about."

Gurk rearranged a few warts, a signal that the topic was definitely closed. I decided leaving was a good idea after all. If I wasn't going to get any more information, I needed some time and some privacy to think about what I had just heard.

As I pushed myself away from the table, Fleef reached out and touched my arm. "Please do not take this personally, Krepta. We will discuss it more later."

I looked at her in astonishment. "You want to blow up my planet, and I'm not supposed to take it personally?" I asked.

Shaking with fury, I stalked away from the table.

At the transcendental elevator I asked the URAT

to give me the code for my room. At once a pattern flashed on the screen. I punched it into the keypad, stepped through the elevator, and found myself in an egg-shaped space. Its curving wall was a soft brownish-orange color. Since there were no doors or windows, it really felt like being inside an egg.

I liked the color and the shape of the room. Unfortunately, it was completely bare, with not a stick of furniture to be seen.

Broxholm's house had been bare of furniture, too. Was that the alien style? Did they expect me to just sit on the floor, staring at the walls?

It's interesting how much little things can distract you when you have something big on your mind. What I wanted to do was worry about the fate of the Earth. What I found myself fretting about was the fact that I didn't have a chair to sit and worry in.

I decided to ask the URAT. Flipping open the box, I said, "Can I have some furniture?"

"Certainly," replied the mechanical voice.

"Well, how do I get it?"

"All you need to do is ask."

"I'm asking."

"You have to specify what you want."

"What kind of choices do I have?" I asked, trying not to sound too impatient.

"We have an enormous variety of personal convenience items on file," said the URAT. "You can also design your own. The possibilities are infinite."

"Is there a way to know what you have on file?"

Instantly the wall in front of me began to display a picture. That was neat; the entire wall was like a giant television screen—except that the image was clearer than any television you have ever seen.

The picture it showed now was actually a chart, with all kinds of furniture on it—and I do mean all kinds. Not only did it show chairs, desks, and beds, it had items that looked like everything from medieval torture devices to toilets designed for octopi.

Which reminded me: "Is there a bathroom attached to this room?"

"No."

"Then how am I supposed to go to the toilet?" I cried, suddenly feeling desperate.

"There are many bathrooms available, simply none attached to this room, Krepta."

That made sense. After all, if a transcendental elevator could move you from one place to another instantly, there was no need to have your bathroom actually *attached* to your room. It could be fifty miles away, and it wouldn't make any difference. Maybe you didn't even *have* your own bathroom; for all I knew, the elevator just sent you to the first empty bathroom it found.

"Give me the code for a bathroom, please," I said to the URAT.

"Insufficient data."

"What do you mean?" I cried, crossing my legs.

"I do not know what kind of bathroom you need. We have fifty-three different types of facilities."

I remembered the octopi toilets, or whatever they were, that I had seen on the first chart. Given the variety of aliens I had met already, it made sense that the ship needed a lot of different bathrooms.

"I'm glad I'm not the plumber for this place," I muttered.

"Yes," agreed the URAT, "that would be a disaster."

"Look, I don't need to be insulted by a machine. Just tell me how to find a bathroom!"

The URAT informed me that it needed to know more about me. After it had asked fifteen or twenty questions, some of them very personal, it finally gave me a bathroom code.

Not a moment too soon! I thought, as I punched the code into the control pad. I stepped into a bathroom that was only mildly odd—which is to say that it only took me about five minutes (five desperate minutes) to figure out how to use it.

When I was done, I returned to my own room. The furniture chart was still on the wall. I wondered if it only showed available *categories* of furniture, since there was only one chair, one desk, one octopus's toilet, and so on.

"Can you show me other chairs?" I asked.

Instantly, the image changed to a chart that held over fifty different kinds of chairs.

"Can I have one of those?" I asked, pointing to a comfortable looking armchair.

"Color?" asked the URAT.

"What do you have?"

A chart with about a hundred colors appeared on the wall. After I chose one I liked, the URAT asked about size.

Size? Chairs are chairs, right?

Not when you're on a ship the size of New Jersey, filled with who knows how many varieties of aliens.

By the time I was done answering questions, we had designed a chair that was as perfectly matched to me as a handmade suit would have been. This was neat!

What was even neater was that after I finally gave the URAT all the information it requested I heard a humming noise. Less than five minutes later the very chair I had ordered popped through the door of the transcendental elevator.

This was the ultimate in home shopping!

Plunking down in my chair, I tried to think. From what Fleef and Gurk had said, while some aliens wanted to blow up the Earth, no definite decision had been made yet.

Even so, it was clear that the planet was in danger. Only I got the feeling that since I had abandoned Earth, no one expected me to care.

But I did care. Earth was in danger. I was the only one who could save it. And I didn't have the first idea how to begin.

Suddenly I felt very small, and very frightened.

I held out my hands and stared at them. They weren't big enough to hold the fate of the world.

CHAPTER TEN

THE ALIEN COUNCIL

After I sat for an hour or so without getting any ideas, I decided to look for Broxholm. Maybe he would help me.

Of course, for all I knew, he was one of the ones in favor of torching the planet.

But somehow I couldn't bring myself to believe that.

The problem was, where to find him? The *New Jersey* had thousands, maybe millions of rooms. It seemed like an impossible task, until it occurred to me that given what I had seen so far, it was likely the ship had a way to keep track of folks.

So I asked the URAT where Broxholm was.

Within seconds, I had an elevator code. I punched a few buttons, stepped through the wall, and found myself staring at Broxholm's back. This put me in the minority; everyone else in the room was staring at Broxholm's front.

"Everyone else" consisted of a group of eight aliens arranged in a half circle. Some were sitting, some standing. One dangled from the ceiling in a sling. Another was stretched across a rack that held up its purple tentacles. At the top of the rack a nozzle released a lavender mist that kept the tentacles moist and gleaming.

"We expect to reconnect with Kreeblim soon," said the alien in the rack. "She should be able to rewire one of the earthlings so that—"

The alien broke off when it noticed me. Broxholm, realizing that the alien was looking past him, turned to see what was going on.

"Peter!" he said sharply. "What are you doing here?"

"Looking for you," I whispered. I was frightened; it was clear I had stumbled into a place where I didn't belong.

The knobs on Broxholm's head began to throb. "Return to your room," he ordered. "I will be there directly."

I nodded and turned to go. But before I could leave, the tallest of the aliens, a huge sea-green creature who towered over even Broxholm, said, "Wait. As long as the child is here, let's talk with him a bit."

He looked around the semicircle of aliens. They all made gestures of agreement, which in this case ranged from a simple nod to a triple armpit fart.

"Tell us why you are here," said the alien with purple tentacles.

I thought for a moment before I answered.

"Because I believe the human race was born to go to the stars," I said at last. "It's what I've dreamed of since I was old enough to understand the idea."

"Tell us about your school," said another alien.

I did as he asked. The aliens listened carefully, making gestures of agreement, or interest, or annoyance. Sometimes they seemed astonished—sometimes astonished and disgusted, as when I described our basal readers.

"That will be enough for now," said the sea-green alien suddenly. "Thank you for your time."

"Wait for me in your room," said Broxholm, as I walked past him back toward the elevator.

I nodded, and continued toward the wall.

When I got back to the room, I was shaking. I don't like talking in front of people. It makes me nervous.

I was using the URAT to get a better understanding of the ship when Broxholm reappeared.

I had started by trying to find out why the ship was so huge. I couldn't believe they had sent something this big halfway across the galaxy just to drop a few spies on Earth.

It turns out that the method the aliens use for skipping over huge distances requires a kind of gravity distortion that can only be achieved with an enormous ship. In fact, the *New Jersey* was actually the smallest starship yet built.

The reason the loading dock was half empty was that the *New Jersey* had been dropping off smaller vessels here and there as it wandered through the galaxy. That was actually its main job: shuttling between stars, leaving a ship, or a dozen, one place, picking up new ships in the next. That, and carrying out the orders of the Interplanetary Council.

I was so engrossed in what I was reading that I actually jumped and shouted when Broxholm came through the wall.

"What's wrong?" he cried in alarm.

"Nothing," I said. "You just startled me."

Broxholm made a sign of understanding. "I suppose anyone living on a planet as violent as yours would need that kind of reflex reaction to stay alive."

Even though I had chosen to leave Earth, I was a little sick of hearing it get dumped on like this. "And what were you and your pals discussing?" I asked bitterly. "Some nice, nonviolent way to blow up the planet?"

It was Broxholm's turn to look startled. But he took it in stride. "That *is* one option being considered," he said calmly.

My stomach twisted at his words. Out here, so far from home, it was easier to remember the good things about Earth—things like Susan Simmons, dolphins, and chocolate chip cookies.

"How can you even consider something like that?" I asked, trying to fight back sudden, unexpected tears.

Broxholm gave his nose a pull. "I didn't say I was considering it. I said it was under consideration. Peter, you have to understand that the entire galaxy is in an uproar over this situation. We've been letting it ride for a while—we even got a break from making our decision because your planet's science got sidetracked a few decades ago. But the time is nearing when we must deal with what is known *across the stars* as 'The Earth Question.'"

"Why?"

"Because while they are not aware of it, your people are fast approaching the breakthrough point in space travel."

"You mean we're about to figure out how to go faster than light?" I whispered in awe.

Broxholm nodded. "We've been monitoring your science carefully. We know, better than you yourselves, how soon you will be able to come into space."

He paused, then crouched in front of me. Putting his hands on my shoulders, he looked directly into my eyes and said, "Do you understand what that means, Peter?"

I shook my head, feeling somewhat baffled.

"It means that for the first time in the 3,000-year history of the Interplanetary League, we are going to have to deal with a people who are at once smart enough to conquer space, and foolish enough to have wars. It means a peace that has lasted for 3,000 years, a peace that extends over 10,000 worlds, is in danger. Of course we are considering extreme measures. But the fate of Earth is by no means decided. The truth is, there are four main plans under consideration."

"What are they?" I asked, not entirely sure I wanted to know.

"One group believes we should take over your planet. A second thinks we should leave you on your own and see what happens; they believe you'll destroy yourselves before we ever have to worry about you. The third group wants to quarantine you—"

"What do you mean by 'quarantine'?" I interrupted.

"Cut you off from all connection with the greater galaxy," said Broxholm. "This could be done by setting up a space shield beyond which you could not pass, or by planting agents on Earth to sabotage your science, so that you could not learn how to get off the planet."

"That's terrible!" I cried, furious at the thought of anyone trying to bar us from space, from exploring the stars.

"I agree," said Broxholm. "But not as terrible as what might happen if you actually move into the galaxy at large. That is why one group simply wants to destroy the planet. They don't like the idea. But they think it is far better than letting you loose on the galaxy in your present condition."

"But why don't you just help us?" I cried, feeling scared and angry all at once.

Broxholm closed his orange eyes. "We don't know if we can. We believe there is something dangerously wrong with your people. This belief is based on three factors. First, the way you've treated your planet. Second, the incredible violence you do to each other. Third—and this is the really amazing thing to us—there's the condition of your brains."

"Our brains?"

Broxholm pulled on his nose, then let it snap back into place. "What baffles us most of all is the fact that the human race has the most powerful brain of any species in the galaxy."

CHAPTER ELEVEN

ANTHROPOLOGISTS FROM SPACE

I stared at Broxholm for a moment, then whacked the side of my head as if I thought my hearing had gone bad. "Say that again?" I asked.

"You heard me," he replied. "The human race has what may be the most powerful brain in the galaxy." He tapped one green finger against my forehead. "Trapped inside that skull is a brain that is the envy of every being on this ship."

"But I'm not smarter than the people here," I said—which was hard for me to admit, since being smart was the one thing I had always taken pride in. I paused, then added, "Am I?"

Broxholm shook his head. "No, you're not. But you *could* be. That's part of the mystery. The human brain is not only the most amazing piece of organic matter in the galaxy; it is also the *least used* brain in the known universe. We've never encountered anything like it—nowhere seen such a gap between what *could* be and what *is*."

As he talked, I began to get the feeling that Broxholm was actually jealous of the human brain.

"Do you have any idea what the rest of us could have accomplished if we had your brain?" he asked feverishly. "Any idea how it galls us to see that potential, and know how little you have done with it?"

I shook my head, too amazed to say a word.

"What terrifies us is what might happen if you learn to use your full intelligence *before* you become truly civilized. Stars above! If you people find your way into space before you fix whatever's wrong with your spirits, the damage you'd wreak could make what you've done to your own planet look like a forest rangers' picnic."

I sat back against the wall, staring at him. What could I say?

"Why do you think I was on your planet?" continued Broxholm. "What do you think was the point of trying to bring some of you back here for short-term study? We're trying to figure out why you act the way you do. We're looking for an answer—a cure, if you want to call it that."

He was pacing the floor now, not really angry, but agitated. It turned out that he had studied for years to make the trip to Earth. He was one of a group of aliens you might call "Anthropologists from Space"—a team watching the whole human race as if it was a tribe in the jungle.

A new question struck me. "If you guys are so wonderful, why were *you* so mean to our class?" I asked, remembering the way he had acted as a teacher.

Broxholm tugged on his nose. "For one thing, I am naturally gruff. Secondly, I would point out that you earthlings have a funny idea of what constitutes 'mean.' On my world we don't worry nearly so much as you people do about talking nicely to each other. We speak the truth and get on with things. On the other hand, we don't leave people to starve in the streets."

He paused, then added, "Actually, my natural gruffness was *not* the reason I behaved as I did with your class. I could easily have been as sweet and kind as anyone might have wished. However we were making a study of your learning styles—how you respond to different methods of education. We have an agent working in your town right now who is as 'nice' as I was nasty. It's all part of our study."

"You mean you're not really a creep?" I asked.

Broxholm stared at me. For a moment I was afraid he was going to be angry. But suddenly his nose began to twitch, just a little at first, then faster and harder, as if something inside was struggling to get out.

I realized that if he was an earthling, he would have been roaring with laughter.

"Peter," he said, "where I come from, I'm considered to be what you would call 'a real pussycat.' Look, young one, what was your greatest desire in all the world?"

"To see the stars!" I said, though suddenly I realized that my heart was saying something else.

I pushed the thought away. It was too frightening.

"To see the stars," said Broxholm. "Don't you think I knew that? Do you have any idea what trouble I caused myself by bringing you here?"

I shook my head.

He paused. "Nor need you know," he said at last. "Other than to understand that I chose to ignore a powerful command for two reasons. The first was that I owed you a favor for helping me escape *without having to hurt anyone.*"

I shivered as I realized just what Broxholm meant by that. "What was the second reason?" I whispered.

He spread his hands. "I like you," he said.

I blinked. Why was I starting to cry?

"Thank you," I whispered, feeling really stupid.

Broxholm put his arms around me. "You poor boy," he whispered. Then he stood and turned away. "Oh, you poor people," he said, so softly that I could barely hear him. "You poor, sad, wonderful people, so full of love and hate, hope and horror, sorrow and need."

He made a terrible, rasping sound, and suddenly I realized that he was weeping. Weeping for a planet that wasn't his, and all the pain that he had seen there.

I ran to him, threw my arms around him.

Then the two of us stood in the center of my room, and cried until we had no tears left.

CHAPTER TWELVE

HOW TO USE A URAT

So that was my first day on board the *New Jersey*. Is it any wonder I was exhausted?

Now you may have noticed that my "day" had started at night. But time on the ship was not related to time on Earth—or more specifically, time in Kennituck Falls. The ship had its own rhythm, and while there were times when more of its inhabitants were resting than others, in general it was busy twenty-seven hours a day.

According to Hoo-Lan, days on the ship were twenty-seven hours long because that was the schedule that made the most sense for the greatest number of beings on board.

Of course, since it was easy to control light and temperature, many of the aliens had private spaces to suit their personal needs. In some chambers the days were only ten hours long, and the temperature was like Death Valley during a heat wave. Some had long hot days, others had short cold days, and so on. Even so, everyone was able to function in the ship's main area—though it did mean that some of them had to wear thick layers of clothing, while others were nearly naked.

After Broxholm left that first "night," I used the URAT to get myself something to sleep in. The most interesting thing on the chart—at least, the most interesting thing that looked like I could actually sleep in it—was a kind of hammock device. The only problem was, I couldn't figure out where to hang it, since the walls in my room were smooth, and I had a feeling I wasn't supposed to put screws or nails in them, even if I had screws or nails, which I didn't.

I should have known not to worry. Each end of

the hammock had a rope. At the end of the rope was a ball. When you threw the ball at the ceiling, it stuck wherever it struck, and didn't come down until you gave the rope three sharp tugs.

So I got myself a hammock and hung it from my ceiling.

It was like sleeping on a cloud—though by the time I got it hung up, I was so exhausted I probably could have slept on a bed of cold seaweed and hot rocks.

I had no clock, so I don't know how long I had been asleep when I was awakened by a sudden loud buzzing.

"Who—what?" I sputtered. I tried to get up, but only succeeded in rocking the hammock sideways.

"It's not Hoo-Wat, it's Hoo-Lan," said an offended-sounding voice that seemed to come from nowhere. "May I come in?"

"I suppose so," I yawned, too groggy to think of just telling him to go away.

Almost instantly Hoo-Lan came walking through my wall. His blue shorts were covered with purple, red, and yellow flowers so bright that if I had still been asleep they probably would have woken me all by themselves.

"Ready to start your day?" asked Hoo-Lan cheerfully.

"I don't think so," I groaned.

"Tish-tush. We have too much to do for you to lie abed like this. Spit-spot, clip-clop, now's the time for all good men to come to the aid of their planet."

My grogginess vanished instantly. "Can you help me come to the aid of my planet?" I asked intently.

Hoo-Lan's big round nose twitched. "A figure of speech. I'm here to come to the aid of your brain. I'm your teacher, remember?"

I looked at him curiously. He stared back at me with huge, round eyes that almost dared me to read his mind. But of course I couldn't.

At least, not yet.

"First lesson," said Hoo-Lan, after I had found a bathroom and thrown some cold water on my face. "The uses of the URAT. You have already discovered some of them. I expect you would find many more on your own. But let's speed up the process."

"Fine with me," I said, settling into my wonderful chair.

"Right, then," said Hoo-Lan. "Now to begin with, the URAT is linked by microwave to the ship's main library. This means that it can find any kind of information almost instantly."

As it turned out, this also meant that the URAT could pull up fun stuff—plays and dances and concerts—from other worlds. If I wanted to go to the trouble, I could even hook it up to a holographic projector, which was truly amazing. Imagine being able to see a three-dimensional movie acted out in the middle of your living room—even a special effects extravaganza, with monsters, rocket battles, and alien landscapes. That's what this thing could do.

Next Hoo-Lan took me to the library itself, where they had machines you could actually plug yourself into so that you *experienced* stuff. These machines fooled all your senses; you didn't just see things—you tasted, touched, smelled, and heard them.

This was great for stories—though some of those alien stories were pretty weird, I want to tell you.

But it was even better for research.

Imagine your teacher has assigned a report on Columbus's first voyage. With one of these machines, you would feel like you were right on one of his ships; you would feel the sea breezes, smell the sailors' body odor, taste the kind of food they ate.

If you're a browser like me—the kind of person who starts out looking up horses and winds up reading about ancient Greece—doing research this way is incredible.

For example: say that while you're studying Columbus, you get interested in a bird you see flying by your ship. Whisper a command, and the bird is in your hands! It's like a three-dimensional illustration you can pick up and feel. And while you examine it, the machine pours information about it into your head.

Now let's say you wonder how the bird sees the world. Say the word and you're inside its skin and *you're flying!*

As you fly, you spot an island that looks interesting. Dropping down for a landing, you leave the bird's body behind, and begin to walk along the beach.

It's hot, so you decide to go for a swim. You *feel* the water—and taste it, too. And all the while you're really just in a room, plugged into one of these machines.

Let me tell you, a guy can get lost inside these things!

In fact, I guess that's sort of a problem. From what Hoo-Lan told me, when the machines were first invented, some beings got so fascinated by them that they never wanted to come out; a few got so involved in the machines they actually starved to death. So the ship's head librarian (who was purple and had twelve tentacles) had very strict rules about how long you could use the machines. She didn't want beings to get hooked.

Of course, I didn't learn all this stuff all at once. By the time Hoo-Lan was done showing me how to use the URAT that first day, I was pretty tired. I was also exhilarated, since the possibilities were so astonishing.

I was also depressed, because the more I saw

of the alien technology, the more clear it became that Earth didn't stand a chance if they decided to do us in.

I felt like the future of the planet was in my hands, which at the moment seemed awfully small and weak.

As it turned out, I was wrong. Earth's destiny wasn't so much in my hands. It was in my brain.

However, since I considered my brain my most precious possession, I wasn't entirely happy when the aliens asked if they could have it.

CHAPTER THIRTEEN

ALIENS WANT MY BRAIN

Actually, I suppose it would be more accurate to say that the aliens wanted to borrow my brain for a bit. I found out about it a couple of days after I had come on board the *New Jersey*. I had just climbed out of my hammock, and was getting ready to go order something to eat, when my URAT began to buzz.

Flipping it open, I saw Hoo-Lan. He looked upset. "Krepta, I need to speak to you. May I come to your room?"

"Could it wait until after I have something to eat?" I asked.

"Why don't I meet you in the dining area?" he replied.

That was fine with me. So we decided which dining area we would meet at—there were several thousand of them on board the ship. I punched the code into the transcendental elevator and stepped through the wall.

Hoo-Lan arrived in a pair of brilliant red shorts covered with tropical flowers and purple butterflies. We took a seat in a quiet corner.

"So what's up?" I asked.

Before he could answer, the alarm sounded, and we had to lie down on the floor while the ship made a leap across space.

"I wish they wouldn't always do that when I'm getting ready to eat," I groaned, when I was sitting at the table again.

"Someone did a study," replied Hoo-Lan. "It showed that, for no apparent reason, most jumps are made when the greatest number of beings are sitting down to eat." He punched a few buttons on the table, then looked up and added, "Sometimes the universe is just like that. By the way, did anyone tell you about the time component of the jumps?"

"Beg your pardon?" I asked, massaging my stomach and wondering if I would be able to eat or not.

"I take it that means 'No,'" said Hoo-Lan. A plate floated up from the center of the table. In the center was a pile of something that looked like marinated eyeballs.

I decided to skip breakfast. "Yes, it means no. Tell me about the time aspect."

"It's pretty simple, really. One thing that happens when we make one of those leaps across space is that while it takes only a minute of *our* time, the time passage in the outside world is quite a bit longer."

I wrinkled my brow. "I know that the faster we go, the slower time goes for us," I said.

I had learned that from all my science fiction reading. I knew that if we approached the speed of light, time inside the ship would come to a virtual standstill. This meant that if we spent a century traveling at the speed of light, those of us inside the ship would age by only a tiny fraction of that amount of time. But I had a feeling Hoo-Lan was saying something different.

"We're really not quite sure how it works," he confessed, when I asked him about it. "We just know that we start a space leap at one point, come out at another a few seconds later, and in the so-called real world, a whole lot of time has gone by."

"Wait a minute," I said. "How much time has gone by since I came on board?"

Hoo-Lan popped one of the eyeball-looking things into his mouth and bit down on it. The squishy sound made me wish we had decided to meet in my room instead.

"Can't say for sure," he said. "I don't always pay attention to that sort of thing. The ship travels at about half the speed of light most of the time. Between that and the space leaps we've taken, I'd guess that a month to a month and a half have gone by back on Earth."

I sat back in my chair, feeling slightly boggled. I had left on the 24th of May. From my point of view, about three days had gone by. But Susan Simmons might have done six weeks of living since then. It was weird: I was three days older and Susan was six weeks older. I wondered what it would feel like to go home and find that she was a grown up and I was still a kid.

I didn't care for the idea all that much.

I decided to change the subject. "What did you want to talk to me about?" I asked, looking at Hoo-Lan's plate and wondering if I wanted to try one of the things he was eating. I figured they couldn't possibly taste as bad as they looked.

Hoo-Lan poked at one of the things on his plate and a drop of green ooze came out.

I decided I didn't want to try them after all.

"I have been asked to get your reaction to an idea proposed by one of the members of the council that you broke in on the other day."

At first I was surprised that Hoo-Lan had heard about that incident. But if they had appointed him to be my tutor, I guess it made sense that they would keep him posted on what I was up to.

"What's the request?" I asked.

Hoo-Lan looked terribly uncomfortable. "You know the Interplanetary Council is engaged in a bitter struggle regarding what we are going to do about your planet. They would like your permission to tap your mind for some additional information."

"What do you mean, 'tap my mind'?"

Hoo-Lan ordered the table to take away the rest of his food. "First, they'll want to ask you a lot of questions. Then they'll probably hypnotize you, so that you can tell us things about your past that you have forgotten." He paused, then said, "Last of all, they'd like to do some brain work."

"Brain work?" I asked nervously.

"They're hoping if they dig around in there a bit, they may be able to find out what's wrong with you."

"What do you mean?" I yelped. "There's nothing wrong with me!"

Of course, that wasn't entirely true. I knew I was far from perfect. But I didn't think I needed brain surgery to fix my minor defects—or even my major ones.

"I don't mean you personally. I mean you earthlings. We're wondering if the problem is organic."

"What problem?" I asked, knowing full well what he was talking about.

"The general human problem," said Hoo-Lan patiently. "Your race's willingness to destroy your home, kill each other, let people starve—all that stuff."

All that stuff indeed! Did they think they would find the reasons for all that in *my* brain?

Suddenly a horrible thought struck me: What if the reasons were in my brain?

I don't mean just my brain. I mean every human brain. What if the problem is that there's something wrong with the way we're wired? Would that mean the mess we've made of things isn't our fault? And if so, would that mean things were hopeless, that we could never fix the mess?

Or could the aliens do something about it? What if by looking inside my head, they could find a way to help us change? What if by examining my brain, they could learn how to help us stop wars forever?

Maybe it was no big deal. After all, CrocDoc had already done a little work on my head, and I had been able to get up and walk away from the table as if nothing had happened.

"Just how much digging do they want to do?" I asked.

"We're talking a total cut and paste job," said Hoo-Lan. "Most of the work would be done with light and magnets and atomic probes, of course. And our doctors are pretty good. But still, there's no guarantee."

I swallowed hard. "No guarantee of what?"

Hoo-Lan looked straight into my eyes. "No guarantee that you'll ever be able to think again," he whispered.

CHAPTER FOURTEEN

DISSECTED!

I stared at Hoo-Lan. A few minutes ago I was having a hard time trying to decide what to have for breakfast. Now I was supposed to decide if I was willing to risk my brain for the sake of the planet I had abandoned.

I sat without speaking for a long time. I thought about home and school. I wasn't particularly eager to b[illegible]me a drooling moron for the sake of Duncan [illegible] But then I thought about the things I had [illegible] news—kids in the Middle East getting [illegible]ellied babies starving in Africa, street kids in South America being killed just to get them out of the way.

"You don't have to answer right away," said Hoo-Lan. "And we won't force you. You are one of us now."

"Am I really?" I whispered.

It was true that I was one of them in that they had accepted me, taken me in. But had I really let go of Earth? Or did I have my heart in the stars—and my feet in Kennituck Falls?

Hoo-Lan said nothing.

I stared at the table, then turned away from him. There was so much yet to see, to do, to explore. I had found my way to the stars. I was the one—the kid from Earth who had made it out into the galaxy. And now I was being asked to risk it all for the crazies I had left behind.

I rubbed the spot on my arm where Duncan used to punch me when he had had a bad night at home.

I thought of those kids in Africa.

"When do we start?" I whispered.

* * *

Broxholm came to see me later that day. "You don't have to do this, you know," he said.

"Do you think I shouldn't?" I asked.

He tugged on his nose. "I'm just worried about you," he said.

"I'm worried, too," I replied. "But hey, one reason I left Earth was that I figured no one would miss me. So what difference does it make?"

Broxholm looked at me for a moment. "I believe you overheard that we have a communications problem. My early departure from Earth left our other agent in Kennituck Falls without some essential equipment. So I cannot prove anything to you. But I believe that if I could show you the people back there, you would find some that miss you very much. Susan Simmons, for example."

I didn't say anything. I didn't like to talk about how I felt about Susan.

Our conversation was interrupted when Hoo-Lan stepped through the wall. He was wearing green shorts covered with hummingbirds.

"They're ready for you, Krepta," he said.

I touched foreheads with Broxholm, which is his planet's way of saying farewell with honor, and followed Hoo-Lan through the transcendental elevator to the operating room.

CrocDoc was waiting for us.

"Pleased to see you again, Krepta," he said soberly. His red jaws were drawn back in something that looked like a grin, but wasn't.

I nodded to him, and he made a gesture which translated into, "I salute your sinus cavities"—something I'm sure had more meaning for him than it did for me.

Having brain surgery on the *New Jersey* is not the same as having it on Earth. I wasn't scrubbed and put into a hospital gown. I almost wish I had been; some kind of ritual might have made me feel better, or helped me take it more seriously. Maybe it was just my fear that made me feel disconnected, as if I were moving through a dream of some kind.

Anyway, CrocDoc had me lie down on a table, told me the operation was being monitored by several dozen other doctors from a wealth of worlds, and then pricked me in the ear with something that immediately knocked me unconscious.

For a while, the sense of being in a dream increased. I felt like I was surrounded by mists, and trying to swim in molasses.

Voices seemed to whisper around me. Faces floated into my consciousness, some familiar, some totally unknown to me. Sometimes the familiar and the unfamiliar merged, or a face I had known all my life would stretch and pull into a strange new shape.

I saw Susan, Duncan, and Ms. Schwartz, and most of the other kids from school. If I could have thought about it, which I couldn't, I might have wondered if CrocDoc was touching nerves in my brain that were setting off specific memories—somehow tickling the areas where those images were stored.

I saw my father. He was crying.

I saw Duncan again. He was frightened. I tried to cry out, because I was sure that something had happened to him. Only I couldn't, of course, since I was sound asleep, with the top of my head off.

Then I saw a man, a tall man wearing a suit. He was sitting at a desk in what looked like a typical classroom. It was dark, as if he had been working late and never bothered to turn on the lights.

As far as I could tell, I had never seen him before.

In my vision, the man's face began to twist with emotion; I couldn't tell what emotion it was—it could have been fear, or anger, or sorrow, maybe some odd combination of all three. It was so intense, it was hard to label. But whatever it was, it slowly twisted his face until suddenly he shoved the desk forward so violently that it fell over, scattering the stuff on top all across the floor.

Standing, he strode across the room until he was facing the television set that sat on the far counter. His features still twisted with that unnameable emotion, he reached up and began to peel off his face.

The skin beneath the mask was blue. As he slowly pulled it upward, he revealed a huge white mustache, a comic nose, enormous eyes.

It was Hoo-Lan!

Trembling now, he raised his hand. The skin

of the hand looked human, as if he was wearing a mask over that, too. But it began to glow, gently at first, then brighter and more intensely. As a howl that sounded like some unholy combination of pain and anger tore out of Hoo-Lan, a bolt of power surged from his fingertips and blasted the television set to pieces.

Then everything went black.

I wondered if I was dead.

CHAPTER FIFTEEN

BRAINS IN A BOTTLE

When I woke up, Hoo-Lan was staring at me anxiously.

"How did you do that?" he asked.

"Do what?" I asked, still feeling groggy.

"You were inside my head. I could feel it. I want to know how you did it."

I blinked. "I didn't even know I *did* did it," I mumbled, too confused to remember the dream I had had while I was unconscious.

I did notice that my words were slurred and slow. Was I all right? I couldn't tell.

"Peter, talk to me!" said Hoo-Lan urgently.

"Let the boy be," ordered CrocDoc. "He's been through a lot."

"Am I—did you—how did it go?" I asked, finally getting the words right.

"It's hard to say," replied CrocDoc, looking at me with his huge eyes. "We have to run an intense analysis on the data I uncovered. I did manage to get this," he said proudly, holding up a clear container.

Inside the container was a brain.

"My brain!" I screamed. "You took out my brain!"

I tried to grab for my head, but my hands were tied down.

"Well yes, but just for a while," said CrocDoc. "I'm going to put it back when I'm done."

I had tried to jump off the table when I first saw the bottle with my brain in it. That failed completely—either because I was tied down, or simply had no control over my muscles at the moment. Just as well, since it wouldn't have been a good idea for me to go running around without any brains. (Although I knew a lot of people back on Earth who did it all the time.)

I took a deep breath, trying to calm down. I took a lot of deep breaths before it did any good.

"How come I can see?" I whispered, when I thought I had some control over myself.

"Oh, your brain is still hooked into your head," said CrocDoc. Holding up the bottle again, he gestured to the bottom of it. "See all these wires? They run into your skull, providing nerve attachments. I'll unplug them whenever we're going to do some work that might be uncomfortable for you. But in the meantime, you can finally join us here in the world of the waking."

"Finally?" I murmured. "How long have I been unconscious?"

"About ten days, Earth time," said Hoo-Lan.

"More than a week!" I cried. "They haven't done anything to Earth yet, have they?"

"No, no. All action is postponed pending analysis of your brain."

Typical of my life. In most of the stories I've read, the fate of the world is in the hero's hands. In my case, the fate of the world was somewhere in my brains—maybe in my temporal lobes, or my corpus callosum, or my medulla oblongata. Wherever they finally found what they were looking for. Or didn't find it, since there was no guarantee that the answer *was* in my brain. Just a possibility.

A buzzer sounded from the ceiling. CrocDoc pushed a button. "What is it?" he asked.

"May we come in?"

I thought I recognized the voice, but I couldn't be certain, since I was still feeling kind of groggy. Would I ever feel alert again? Or was I doomed to a life of permanent mental fuzz?

The worst thing was, in my current condition, I didn't really care. I couldn't even *make* myself care. I wondered vaguely if this was what it was like to be hooked on drugs.

"Do you feel like having visitors?" asked Croc-Doc.

"Why not?" I said, though to tell you the truth, I really didn't care all that much at this point.

At once, Fleef and Gurk stepped through the wall.

"Oh, my," said Fleef, when she saw me strapped to the table, with my brain sitting on the counter next to me. Her face turned a deeper shade of orange, and the sphere on the stalk on her skull went "Neep! Neep!"

"How are you, Krepta?" asked Gurk. His big eyes seemed filled with worry.

"Okay, sort of," I said.

"We've been worried about you," said Fleef. "Everyone is very impressed with how brave you are."

"Does that mean you don't want to blow up Earth anymore?" I whispered.

"It means I hope we don't have to," replied Fleef, squeezing my hand.

I was disappointed. On the other hand, I suppose my being a good guy about all this didn't really reduce the possible menace of my planet. I sighed.

"We brought you something," said Gurk, trying to sound cheerful. He held up a bag. "Do you want to see?"

I tried to nod, but couldn't, because my head was strapped down. "Sure," I said. "Let's see."

He reached into the bag and pulled out a blob of fur.

"What is it?" I asked.

"It's a skimml," said Fleef. She sounded very pleased.

Gurk held the thing in front of my face. It was about six inches across, round and red—which made it look something like a big furry ladybug. After a moment two stalks rose out of the fur. The eyes on the ends of them looked at me and blinked.

"They're squishy." said Gurk. "And almost indestructible. See?"

With that, he squeezed the skimml's middle, which caused it to bulge out of the top and bottom of his hand.

"Lots of fur, no bones," said Fleef.

Gurk set the skimml on my stomach. It walked up and took another look at my face, walked back to my stomach, turned around three times, and settled down with a sigh. After a moment it began to make a noise something like a window fan.

"It likes you!" cried Fleef happily.

I named the skimml Murgatroyd. It kept me company through the following days as CrocDoc turned my brain on and off while he examined it.

I had a lot of visitors. They all seemed to like to squeeze the skimml.

Broxholm showed up almost every day, as did Fleef and Gurk. Aliens I had never seen before stopped in to say hello. The crystal captain sent me a plant whose blossoms made singing noises that reminded me of my interview in the diamond chamber. And Hoo-Lan spent hours with me every day, telling me wonderful stories about the history of the galaxy.

Every once in a while he would look at me strangely, and ask me questions about what had happened to me while I was having the operation. But CrocDoc was always there, and wouldn't let him question me too sharply.

Finally the day came when CrocDoc was going to put my brain back in my head.

"Did you find what you needed?" I asked, still feeling groggy and disconnected.

His snout drooped down. "Not yet," he said. "But we're still analyzing the data. Don't despair, Krepta. All is not lost."

And then he put me to sleep.

* * *

When I woke up, the skimml was whirring on my stomach, and my brain was back in my head. CrocDoc was leaning over me, just as he had that first day, after he had put in the language implant.

"Am I all right?" I whispered.

"With any luck, you'll be better than ever," he said.

I opened and closed my eyes a few times, and looked around the room. My vision was sharp and clear. I stretched, and realized that my hands were no longer tied down.

"Can I stand up?" I asked.

"No reason not to," said CrocDoc. "Just take it easy."

"Why don't you come up here?" I said, lifting Murgatroyd from my stomach to my shoulder. Murgatroyd snuggled in as I sat up and swung my legs over the edge of the table.

"Careful," said CrocDoc.

I waited a moment before standing up. But I felt terrific. It was as if my brain had been wrapped in fog, and now the fog was gone.

CrocDoc made a gesture that meant "I put my hand beneath your grandmother's egg," and told me how much he appreciated my help. "You may come and talk to me any time about our findings," he said. "I owe you that courtesy at least."

I gathered my things, the little gifts that aliens had brought me, squeezed Murgatroyd for luck, and prepared to return to my room.

But when I stepped through the transcendental elevator, it spit me out into a place I had never seen before.

CHAPTER SIXTEEN

DUNCAN

I was in a chamber filled with machinery. I recognized some of the devices as things the aliens used for communicating across space.

To my right was a kind of desk. Sitting on the desk was a helmet.

"Put it on," said a voice behind me.

I jumped in surprise, which caused Murgatroyd to squeak in protest. "Hoo-Lan," I snapped, spinning to face him. "Don't do things like that to me."

"Sorry," said the little alien. "I keep forgetting how skittish you are."

"I assume you're the one who brought me here."

Hoo-Lan reached out for the skimml. I handed it to him. "You assume correctly," he said, kneading the red ball of fur between his hands until Murgatroyd began to thrum with contentment.

"Would you mind telling me why?"

"Put on the helmet," replied Hoo-Lan.

I looked at the helmet nervously. "Is it safe?" I asked. As soon as the words were out of my mouth I thought, *Well, that was a stupid question, Peter. He won't tell me if it's not, so why bother to ask?*

But Hoo-Lan spread his hands and said, "No, not entirely."—Which just goes to show how much I knew.

"Then why do you want me to put it on? Haven't I taken enough risks already?"

"I ask because the possible benefit outweighs the risk," said Hoo-Lan. "Put it on."

I hesitated, then sat down at the table and put on the helmet. At Hoo-Lan's direction, I moved a couple of the control balls on the table in front of me.

And then I was inside Duncan Dougal's head. I shouted so loud that the skimml squawked and jumped out of Hoo-Lan's hands. It lay flat on the floor, stretched out and shivering, its eye stalks shooting up and down as it looked for trouble.

"For heaven's sakes, be quiet!" hissed Hoo-Lan, bending down to pick up Murgatroyd.

At least, I think that's what he said. I was too enmeshed in what was happening inside my head to pay attention to him.

I'm not sure how I knew that I was inside Duncan's head so quickly. It's not like there were any labels saying: THIS IS DUNCAN DOUGAL'S BRAIN.

Maybe I knew just because it *was* Duncan's brain, and his identity was stamped on every cell and synapse.

I felt uncomfortable about this. Little as I liked Duncan, I didn't think I had any right to poke around inside his brain. *Duncan*, I thought. *Duncan, can you hear me?*

No answer; either he wasn't aware of me, or wasn't able to answer, or was answering and it wasn't coming through.

Things happen fast inside a human brain. I started looking around. In a matter of seconds—or less, maybe; I don't know exactly how long it took—I had learned more about Duncan Dougal's life than I ever wanted to know.

Speaking from my point of view, here are some of the most important things I learned:

1) Part of the reason Duncan was such a beast was the way he got whacked around at home.

2) He was incredibly intelligent (this totally astonished me, until I found out more about it).

3) He was a sadder person than I ever would have guessed and

4) He had talked with my father not long ago, and my father was terribly upset about my leaving. Believe me, that last one was a shock to me.

Duncan, I thought again, *can you hear me?*

Still no answer. I took one last, quick look around the inside of his head, then raised the helmet from my own head.

Hoo-Lan was looking at me eagerly.

"What is going on here?" I hissed.

"You mean you got through?" he whispered. His voice sounded almost hungry.

"What is going on?" I asked again, tired of giving more answers than I got.

But Hoo-Lan wasn't ready to explain yet. Instead, he looked at me for a long moment, then answered my question with another question. Namely, "How would you like to visit another planet?"

I knew he was changing the subject, but I couldn't help myself. "When can we go?" I asked eagerly.

"How about now?" Passing Murgatroyd back to me, he led me to a circle printed on the floor. "Stand here," he ordered. "And as you value your life—don't move!"

He crossed the room and fiddled with some dials, then crossed back and positioned himself next to me. Almost instantly a blue beam shone down from the ceiling, and the room faded from sight.

When I opened my eyes, I was on a tiny bit of sand in the middle of a huge body of water.

It was night, and the sky above us was unlike anything I had ever seen—a vast sheet of black filled with stars. All right, that's not so weird. But their patterns were unfamiliar, and their light was so bright you could read by it. In the sky to our right floated a small green moon. A ribbon of shimmering, changing color stretched from horizon to horizon.

"All right!" I shrieked.

"Shhh!" said Hoo-Lan. "There are some very big animals around here. We don't want to attract their attention if we can avoid it."

I squeezed Murgatroyd and looked around nervously. I couldn't see any big animals. But who knew what form they might take here? For all I knew, the island we were standing on was actually some enormous sea creature. I looked down, half expecting to see a huge mouth in the sand.

"How did we get here?" I whispered.

"We took a ship-to-surface elevator," said Hoo-Lan. "It's like moving around inside the ship, but on a grander scale."

"Why didn't Broxholm use one of these when he came to Earth?" I asked, remembering our trip from Kennituck Falls to the *New Jersey*.

"Because first you have to set them up," said Hoo-Lan.

"Why would anybody set one up out here in the middle of nowhere?"

"I set it up, to be a private place. I like to come here to think."

I glanced at Hoo-Lan, who was easy to see because he was glowing again. "Who are you?" I asked.

"Your teacher," he said, as if that answered everything. "And as your teacher, I want you to see some things here."

He pulled a thin tube out of one of his pockets and blew a little tune on it. A moment later I heard the tune repeated somewhere across the water, as if it were being sung by a bird—or, for all I knew, some strange kind of fish. Or something else altogether, for that matter.

I turned to Hoo-Lan. He put his fingers to his lips and motioned me to silence.

We waited. The tune was repeated again, off in another direction, and then again, and again. Suddenly I saw a commotion in the water, as something bright and huge rose from the depths to the edge of the island.

"Our chariot arrives," said Hoo-Lan.

My eyes were fixated on the green thing waiting just beneath the surface of the water. It was at least a hundred feet long. If it was a chariot, it was a strange one, because it was clearly a living animal—

either that, or a very good imitation of one.

Hoo-Lan played another little tune. The creature rose to the surface and tipped back its head, which was the size of a small room. Its huge silver tongue extended to the shore like a gangplank.

"Go ahead," said Hoo-Lan. "Step aboard!"

CHAPTER SEVENTEEN

RHOOMBA RIDE, HOO-LAN'S HOME

Have you ever walked on a tongue? It's an odd feeling. The surface is firm but squishy, and it's a little hard to keep your balance.

I glanced behind me, to make sure Hoo-Lan was coming. Not that I didn't trust him. But walking into a mouth is pretty scary.

He nodded to me.

Clutching Murgatroyd, I walked on.

Hoo-Lan caught up with me as I reached the creature's teeth. They were taller than me, and made me think of huge icicles. Once we were clear of its fangs, the beast drew in its tongue, pulling us so far into its mouth that I was afraid we were going to be swallowed after all. Then it closed its mouth, and for a moment we *were* swallowed—by darkness.

That ended when Hoo-Lan began to glow. The blue light reflecting off the beast's silvery tongue made everything look strange and ghostly.

"Where are we going?" I whispered. Not that I thought the beast would hear us. It was just one of those places that made you want to whisper.

"We're going to my home," Hoo-Lan replied. He looked happy.

"Are we going across the water—or under it?"

"Oh, under. Definitely under. Rhoombas don't like to go on top of the water if they can help it."

"Rhoombas?"

"That's what you're riding in now," said Hoo-Lan. "They're one of the best ways to get around on this world."

"Do they ever, well—you know, do they have *accidents*?" I asked. I couldn't quite bring myself to come right out and ask if they ever made a mistake and swallowed their passengers.

"No one's perfect," said Hoo-Lan with a shrug.

I realized he was speaking in English again.

"Why are you doing that?"

"What did you see inside my head?"

I looked at him for a moment. "What do you mean?"

"I mean if you tell me what you saw, I'll tell you why I'm speaking English."

I hesitated, for two reasons. First, I wasn't sure just what I *had* seen when I was in Hoo-Lan's head; I needed a moment to think about it. Second, any time someone wants to know something *that* badly it makes me a little nervous.

"I've spent a lot of time studying the Earth," said Hoo-Lan, still in English. "Fascinating place."

Something Broxholm had said when I first came onto the spaceship floated to the top of my memory. "Hoo-Lan, did you name the *New Jersey*?"

"You get a cigar for that one," he said, putting his finger beside his nose.

"Who are you?" I asked, for the third time since I had known him.

"All take and no give makes for a lopsided friendship. Tell me what you saw in my head."

I closed my eyes and thought for a moment. "You were in a classroom. Only you didn't look like yourself. You were in disguise—sort of the way Broxholm was, when he took over our class. It was night. You were angry about something, angry enough that you began to glow until it was so bright it showed right through your mask. So angry you blew up a TV set."

He stared at me with a look that was something like horror. "Have you told this to anyone else?"

I shook my head.

"Please don't."

"Did it really happen?" I asked.

Before he could answer, a low, groaning sound rumbled around us. "Ah, we've arrived," said Hoo-Lan. "We'll talk more about this later."

"Arrived where?"

"At the city under the sea."

"But how are we supposed to get out?" I cried.

I didn't mind getting wet, but I knew if we were deep enough, the water pressure would crush us.

"Step back here," answered Hoo-Lan, leading me farther into the Rhoomba's throat. After we had gone about ten feet we came to a kind of chamber, a round area that went straight up.

Once Hoo-Lan was sure I was standing in the right place, he slapped the wall of the chamber three times. The Rhoomba roared and a mighty gust of wind sent us flying straight up, as if we were being shot through a whale's blowhole.

I landed on a padded surface, inside a small room. I was still trying to recover from the surprise when I saw a being who resembled Hoo-Lan drop something down the Rhoomba's blowhole, which was pressed against an opening in the floor. You could see the Rhoomba's leathery green flesh all around the edges.

"Reward," said the stranger, when he saw my questioning look. Then he drew a trapdoor shut across the opening, sealing off the little room.

No sooner was the trapdoor shut than a door in the side of the room opened and three more beings who were clearly of Hoo-Lan's race came running into the room. They wore light green togas, not brightly colored shorts. One by one, they clapped Hoo-Lan on the back, then gave him a big hug.

When they were done greeting Hoo-Lan, they turned to me and cried "Welcome, Krepta!"

"Thank you," I said, feeling a little shy.

Clutching Murgatroyd for comfort, I followed them out of the little room, still wishing Hoo-Lan had finished telling me why he was so wound up about what I had seen inside his head.

My questions faded when I passed through the door of the little room and found myself standing in the center of a great city of tree-lined streets, soaring buildings, and busy markets.

Something about the city struck me as odd. It took me a few minutes to figure out that the place had almost no sharp edges. The buildings, even the tallest ones, were smooth and rounded, and had a soft, almost gentle look. Some of them were covered with decorations. I don't know what they were made of, but the colors were mostly soft shades of blue and green and yellow, with here and there a deeper, stronger color that kept things interesting.

Even more striking than the buildings was the fact that the city was completely encased in a clear dome that stretched far above the top of the tallest building that I could see.

On the other side of the dome, above and all around the city, was water.

"Hoo-Lan," I whispered. "It's wonderful!"

"I'm glad you like it," he said, patting a six-legged animal that happened to be walking by. "I'm very proud of it."

We spent the whole day touring the city. It was beyond anything I had ever imagined. The rhoomba that delivered us was typical of the way things worked here; much of what needed to be done was taken care of by animals that had been trained and bred to the task. My favorites were the trash munchers. Every home and store had one—a fat little beast that loved to eat all kinds of garbage.

"Cuts down on the mess," said the little blue woman who first explained them to me.

All the animals seemed happy and well cared for.

All the people did, too.

After a while I began to get suspicious. I knew enough about cities to feel like something was missing.

"Don't you have anyone hungry here, anyone without a home?" I asked at last.

"Why should we?"

"I don't think you *should*," I said. "I just didn't know there could be a city without people like that."

"There can't, on your planet. The difference is that we've made a decision that it's not going to be that way. There's enough to go around, you know. Enough here, and enough on Earth. It's not like people *have* to be cold and hungry. You just haven't decided it's a bad idea."

"Of course we think it's a bad idea!"

"No, you *think* you think it's a bad idea. If your people, all your people, really believed it was a bad idea, they would stop talking about it and change things so it didn't happen anymore."

I squeezed Murgatroyd, trying to keep from getting angry about what Hoo-Lan had said. I had a feeling he was blaming me, personally, for everything that was wrong on Earth.

We had this argument outside a huge building.

"Come on," said Hoo-Lan. "There's something in here I want to show you."

People in the building greeted him as if he were an old friend. That was nothing surprising; it had been happening all day. One of the weirder things about the visit was the feeling I got that the whole city knew my teacher.

A series of long, snakelike creatures lifted us from floor to floor, until we were near the top of the building. On every floor, people shouted greetings to Hoo-Lan.

"Who are you?" I asked again, when we were standing outside a door on the top floor of the building.

Hoo-Lan smiled. "Why don't you look into my brain and find out?"

CHAPTER EIGHTEEN

CONTACT!

Hoo-Lan led me into a room filled with all sorts of fascinating equipment.

"You know," he said, as he began tinkering with some machinery, "I've spent a good part of my life trying to crack the secrets of telepathy."

"You mean direct communication from one mind to another?" I asked.

He nodded. "The thing is," he continued, staring at me intently, "*you've* got it. You went into my brain while you were being operated on and pulled out images. Jumbled ones, of course," he added hastily. "But you did pull them out of my head, and you did it without training. I think something that happened on the operating table helped unleash the ability in you."

He took the skimml from me and began squishing it back and forth. "You can't understand what this means, Krepta, unless you know that we've been trying for lifetimes to create this ability in some of our people. By *we*, I mean the Interplanetary League. The best we've been able to do so far is piggyback on thought transmission with some of our machines. That's the situation with your friend Duncan, by the way."

"He's not my friend!"

I regretted the words the instant they were out of my mouth. They made me sound small and petty. "What do you mean, anyway?" I asked, trying to cover up my stupid remark.

"Well, one of the early problems we had with star travel was that radio messages only move at the speed of light. Of course, this made it almost impossible to communicate between places that were light-years apart. We finally managed to invent a hyper-space transmitter, which gave us nearly instant contact between stars. Unfortunately, Broxholm had the only one on your planet. So when he was forced to flee, our remaining agent in Kennituck Falls, a female named Kreeblim, was left without a way to communicate with the ship after it had moved out of your solar system.

"To get around this, she used a brain enhancer on Duncan."

"You mean she made him smart?" I cried. That explained what I had found when I connected with Duncan back on the mother ship.

"No, she didn't *make* him smart," said Hoo-Lan. "She simply unleashed some of his basic potential. You humans are so much smarter than you act, it's appalling. Anyway, since thought is instant, by sending her messages through his brain, she is once more able to communicate with us."

"So what's the big deal about telepathy? Sounds like you already have it."

Hoo-Lan shook his head. "No," he said, passing Murgatroyd back to me. "It's not the same as direct mind-to-mind communication. *That's* what I'm after. That's what *you* managed when you tapped into my head. And when you got through to Duncan Dougal today, before we left the ship, you managed it without the brain treatments and mechanical connections we have to use for such a communication. Only three beings on the *New Jersey* could have made that connection. And each of them has had extensive training and repeated brain stimulation, and has to be *in* a force field with hardware attached to do it."

He looked at me. "But you—you did it without even trying. The secret is in there," he said, pointing at my forehead, which he was too short to reach. "Just like the reason for Earth's violence."

I was sick of everyone thinking I had all the answers. "This isn't the *Encyclopaedia Britannica,* you know," I said, tapping my head myself. (Though I must admit I'd read quite a bit of the *EB*.) Then another thought struck me. "You don't want to do more brain surgery on me, do you?" I asked, taking a step backward.

Hoo-Lan took my hand. "I just want to see if we can talk to each other," he said, leading me to a machine that looked like the one I had seen in the communication room on the ship.

"You stand here," said Hoo-Lan, positioning me under a metallic pyramid. "And I'll sit over here, where I can get some readings on what's going on inside your head. If you make contact, try using these dials to fine tune things. If things get too intense, punch this escape button."

The whole thing had happened so fast I didn't have time to think about whether or not I wanted to do it. I clutched Murgatroyd, feeling frightened and hopeful at the same time.

Hoo-Lan turned on the machine and said, "Now concentrate! Try to read my mind!"

I did as he asked. But instead of connecting with Hoo-Lan, I found myself back in contact with Duncan!

I couldn't believe it. Light-years away from Earth, visiting a distant planet, and who do I end up in a psychic link with? Duncan Dougal!

I mean, gimme a break, folks.

Duncan wasn't much happier than I was, though he didn't know I was there yet. Actually, he was feeling something that I had felt more than once since this all started: unhappiness that other worlds had been watching us as we bumbled along, blowing each other up and starving ourselves when there was enough food for everyone. *It's embarrassing,* he told himself.

It certainly is, I thought at him.

This time he heard me! I knew, because I was so linked to him that I could tell he wondered if he was losing his mind. *Who is that?* he thought.

Come on, Duncan—don't you know who I am?

Peter? he thought in astonishment. *Peter Thompson?*

None other! Wait, let me try something here. I fiddled with the dials Hoo-Lan had showed me.

Where are you? asked Duncan.

Shhh! Wait!

He was bursting with curiosity. But he waited while I tinkered with the machine, which was a little like adjusting the antenna on a television set. Suddenly I got complete focus: not only was I inside Duncan's brain, but Duncan was inside *my* brain.

To tell you the truth, I wasn't sure I liked the idea. I mean, in the past about the only way Duncan had communicated with me was through noogies and black eyes. But here we were, worlds apart, linked solely by our minds. So it was pretty exciting, even if it *was* Duncan. I could hear his thoughts as clearly as if he were speaking to me, instead of merely thinking.

"Where are you?" he asked.

"In space, silly. Where did you expect I would be? Oh, Duncan, it's glorious. The stars! I can't tell you. But it's frightening, too. There's a lot going on. Big things. And Earth is right in the middle of it. *We're* right in the middle of it."

"What do you mean?"

"The Interplanetary Council—that's sort of a galaxywide United Nations—is trying to figure out what to do about us. We've got their tails in a tizzy because our planet is so weird. From what Broxholm has told me—"

"Wait!" he replied. "Tell me about Broxholm. Is he treating you all right?"

"Well, that's kind of weird, too," I said. "I'm never quite sure what's going on with him. But listen, I've got to tell you this stuff first, because I'm not sure how long I can stay on, and you have to get word out to someone. Here's the deal. The aliens are having a big debate among themselves about how to handle the Earth. And I don't mean just Broxholm's gang. We're talking about hundreds of different planets here. As near as I can make out, they've narrowed it down to four basic approaches. One group wants to take over Earth, one group wants to leave us on our own, one group wants to blow the planet to smithereens, and one group wants to set up a blockade."

"What?"

"They say it's for the sake of the rest of the galaxy. They seem to find us pretty scary, Duncan."

"I don't get it."

"Don't ask me to explain how an alien's mind works," I snapped. "As far as I can make out, they think there's something wrong with us. Well, two things, actually. The first is the way we handle things down there. That's why they've been sending in people like Broxholm; they're supposed to study us and figure out why we act the way we do."

"So Broxholm was some kind of anthropologist—?"

"You could put it that way," I replied. I was astonished Duncan knew the word, until I remembered what had happened to him. "Anyway, the other thing that has them concerned is how smart we could be if we ever got our act together. Broxholm actually seems jealous. Every once in a while he goes on about the human brain being the most underused tool in the galaxy. I get the impression they're afraid if we learn to use our full intelligence before we get civilized—"

"We're civilized!" cried Duncan in indignation.

"Not by their standards. Anyway, they're afraid—"

I didn't finish the sentence. Someone had entered the chamber. I heard a lot of scuffling and squawking.

"Uh-oh," I said. "Something's happening. I gotta go, Duncan."

I pushed the escape button. Only I wished I hadn't, because the sight that greeted me when I came out of my trance nearly broke my heart.

CHAPTER NINETEEN

THE FADING GLOW

Hoo-Lan lay on the floor, stretched out straight and stiff as a board. Several of the little blue people were gathered around him, squawking in dismay.

"What is it?" I cried, rushing over to him. "What's happened?"

"The leader!" cried a green-haired woman. "What have you done to the leader?"

"It was the machine!" cried one of the men. "He knew he shouldn't use the machine!"

"No, it's not the machine," another one shouted. "It's him. It's the earthling!"

"What do you mean?" I asked. "What's wrong with Hoo-Lan?"

Before anyone could answer, the room was filled with a loud buzzing sound. It took me a moment to realize that the noise was coming from both Hoo-Lan's URAT and mine.

"The ship!" cried one of the men. "The ship is leaving. You must get him back to the ship!"

"But he's sick!" I said, nearly sick with fear myself.

"Yes. But he must be on the ship. Besides, his doctor is there. You must go back to the ship."

Gathering around Hoo-Lan's stiff body, the blue men and women picked him up and carried him to the room next door. The buzzing of the URAT grew more urgent.

"Stand here!" said one of the women, motioning to a circle on the floor. "Stand here!"

They put Hoo-Lan next to me. The men were pulling on their mustaches—a sign, my translator told me, of extreme grief.

"But what happened to him—?"

My words were cut off as a beam of blue light shot down from the ceiling, and we were sucked out of the city beneath the sea, through space, and back into the *New Jersey*.

I blinked. We were back in the room where we had started. "Hoo-Lan!" I cried, kneeling beside him. "Hoo-Lan, talk to me!"

He said nothing, only groaned a little. He was glowing, but only faintly.

Suddenly the alarm sounded. The ship was about to make a jump. I threw myself on the floor beside Hoo-Lan. Clutching Murgatroyd, who was chittering in alarm, I braced myself for the jump—and hoped that Hoo-Lan would live through it.

The horrible, high-pitched whine tore through the room, drowning my own moans of nausea. The tearing feelings began, became unbearable, and then ended. I lay next to Hoo-Lan, trembling and trying to recover, wondering how many light-years we had jumped, where we were now.

When I could push myself to my knees, I stared at Hoo-Lan. His glow was even fainter than before. I knew that he was dying.

I grabbed my URAT. "Give me the code for CrocDoc!" I cried. The moment the colored dots began to flash on the screen I raced across the room and punched the destination into the elevator. Then I ran back and tried to pick up Hoo-Lan. He was heavier than I thought, and his body was rigid, but I finally managed to get him into my arms.

Worried that I wouldn't get back across the room before the elevator did an automatic shut-off, I struggled toward the wall. The shut-off alarm sounded just as I pitched forward, falling through the wall and into CrocDoc's office.

Only CrocDoc wasn't there.

"Find him!" I shouted at the URAT. "Find Croc-Doc."

The machine gave me another code. Leaving Hoo-Lan on the floor, I hurtled through the wall. Interrupting a meeting of some sort, I grabbed Croc-Doc by the arm and said, "Your office! Quickly!"

To my relief, he didn't try to brush me off; instead, he immediately followed me back through the wall to his office.

I slumped against the wall in relief. I had done what I could do. Or so I thought. CrocDoc asked me to help him get Hoo-Lan onto the table. He was examining him while I watched in fascinated horror when Broxholm's voice came from the ceiling.

"Peter, you are wanted in the Council Room. The elevator is programmed. Please step through the wall."

"But, Broxholm—"

"Come at once!"

"Better go," said CrocDoc. "I'll take care of things here."

"But is he—will he—?"

"I make no guarantees," said CrocDoc. "However I believe he will still be here when you get back."

Be here? What did that mean? Still on the table, but dead as a tubeless television? I started to say something, but Broxholm's voice thundered through the speaker.

"Now, Peter!"

"Best go," whispered CrocDoc.

I went.

Broxholm was waiting for me when I entered the chamber. So was the rest of the alien council, the eight beings I had encountered the first time I entered this room.

"Peter Thompson—Krepta—Child of the Stars—" said the sea-green alien. "The time is fast approaching when we will make a decision regarding the fate of the Earth."

I considered bolting right then, racing off to the communication room to see if I could get one last message off to Duncan, somehow get him to warn the government, someone, anyone, who might be able to do something. Then at least the Earth might have a fighting chance.

"We offer you a chance to speak in Earth's defense," said the alien who hung on the rack. "Tell us something we do not know, something that might give us cause to think again as we deliberate."

"You need to ask someone else," I said desperately. "I'm only a kid! What can I tell you?"

"Then you refuse to speak on behalf of the planet?" asked the purple alien.

"No! That's not what I mean! I just don't know what to say. I haven't lived enough, seen enough. I know there must be more good things out there than I have seen, things worth saving, things too wonderful too lose. *I know it!*"

"Yet you chose to leave," said one of the aliens who had not spoken before this, a dark creature who looked more like a shadow than anything real and solid.

"I chose to leave, not to destroy it," I said.

"All leaving involves a kind of destruction," said the shadow. "The chick destroys the egg in hatching. No home is the same once someone has gone from it."

"Why don't you help us?" I cried. "You have answers, you can fix things."

"You don't need our answers," said another alien. "Your problem is not shortage of food, or land. You live on one of the most blessed planets in the galaxy—or at least you used to, until you fouled it so. What could we offer you but technology? And what would you do with it but create new problems? The technology is not the problem. Hearts and minds, those are the problem."

"Send me back," I said, hardly able to believe the words were coming out of *my* mouth. "Let me find a reason for you. I won't run away. I'm not afraid for myself. But I don't want you to hurt my friends. I don't want you to hurt my father!"

I stopped, astonished at what I had just said.

"Leave us for a time," said the sea-green alien. "We need to deliberate."

I looked at Broxholm. He nodded.

I left the chamber.

CHAPTER TWENTY

HOO-LAN'S WISH

I didn't even program the elevator, since I figured the aliens would send me wherever they wanted me to go. Somewhat to my surprise, I found myself back at CrocDoc's.

Hoo-Lan lay on the table, rigid and unmoving, his glow dimmer than ever.

"How is he?" I whispered.

"Not good," said CrocDoc.

I stood for a moment, staring at my friend, my teacher. "Can I do anything for him?" I asked quietly.

"No."

"I'll be back," I said.

Moving quietly across the room, I instructed the URAT to send me back to the communication chamber where I had first made contact with Duncan. Glancing over my shoulder, feeling guilty for leaving, even though there was nothing I could do, I stepped through the wall.

What had happened to Hoo-Lan when he tried to make mental contact with me? Was this my fault? Was my human brain so poisonous it had done something terrible to his mind?

Once I reached the communication chamber, it took me a while to make contact with Duncan again. I wondered if he was still in the force field. After all, even though it had been only a couple of hours by my time since I spoke to him, the ship had made a space-shift since then. How much time had passed on Earth?

I fiddled with the controls, until I made contact with Duncan Dougal, my old enemy, my new ally. As I began to fine-tune the connection, it occurred to me that if this Kreeblim character they had mentioned had put Duncan in the force field, it might not be a good idea for me to say too much until I knew whether or not she was there.

"Duncan," I thought. "Is there anybody there?"

"Just you and me."

"Good." I finished focusing the connection, so we could see each other. "Listen, things are heating up out here. The aliens are planning something. I don't know what, but it's big. You have to get word to the government."

Duncan was explaining why he thought that was a stupid idea when we heard someone coming up the attic stairs.

"Pretend I'm not here," I said desperately. "I can't be caught talking to you like this. I'll try to hold on, but I'll break the connection if I have to."

"I understand," said Duncan.

But the person who showed up at the top of the stairs was no menace. Well, aside from the fact that the sight of her did something strange to my insides.

It was Susan Simmons, and I suddenly realized I had missed her more than I had guessed. I sighed. Why couldn't the aliens have hooked me into *her* brain?

With the URAT to help me, I told Susan how to free Duncan from the force field. Once she had him out, I was a little surprised to find that Duncan and I were still in contact.

When he said that he was surprised as well, I replied, "Of course. Your head is what we call wetware—an organic machine. At the moment, you happen to be one of the most powerful communication devices in the galaxy, Duncan. Now listen, I've got some important stuff to tell you. There are big things happening up here, and you need to—oh no!"

The last words came out as a shout of terror, because a pair of hands had just grabbed me by the back.

"You shouldn't do things like that, Peter," said Broxholm, turning me around and picking me up so that I had to stare straight into his huge orange eyes. "It makes it harder for us to trust you."

I wondered how much Broxholm had heard of what I had just told Duncan and Susan. Then I realized he couldn't have heard any of it, since it had all been done inside my head!

"The Council wants to see you again," said Broxholm. Carrying me across the room, he stepped through the transcendental elevator and back into the council chamber.

"What do you know about the fall of Hoo-Lan?" asked the sea-green alien, as soon as I was standing before the council again. He seemed sterner than ever, maybe even angry.

I hesitated. "He tried to connect himself to my mind," I said. "It happened to him then."

The other members of the council stirred restlessly. I got the sense I had said or done something wrong.

"Hoo-Lan was a fool," said the alien with purple tentacles.

Something inside me snapped. I had had enough of their superiority, their all-powerful lording it over me. I liked Hoo-Lan. No, I loved Hoo-Lan. He had been kind and gentle to me, taught me things, cared for me.

"Don't you say that!" I cried, rushing toward the alien.

I suppose it wasn't the best demonstration of how earthlings might be expected to control themselves. It didn't make any difference; I ran right through him without touching him.

I stopped, turned around, blinked in dismay.

I walked back toward the alien, waving my arms. They passed back and forth through his purple body.

"Broxholm!" I cried. "What's going on!"

He looked startled. "Did you really think they were here?" he asked. Then he blinked and said, "Do you realize who these beings are?"

"The people in charge of the ship?" I asked uncertainly.

Broxholm's nose twitched. The images of the other eight aliens responded with their various forms of laughter.

"These are the chief leaders of the Interplanetary Council," said Broxholm.

I ran back to his side, stunned at what he was saying. I had just tried to punch out one of the rulers of the galaxy!

For a kid who considers himself an intellectual, this was not the high point of my emotional life.

"What are they doing here?" I whispered. "Or not doing here?" I added, trying to salvage some dignity with a little humor.

"We generally meet via holographic projection," said a red alien, who looked sort of like a pile of seaweed. "It is simplest that way, as it allows us to stay on our own planets, and yet remain in contact. That way, we can hold our meetings anywhere we wish."

"As to your defense of Hoo-Lan," said the purple alien I had tried to clobber, "the emotion is admirable even if your way of expressing it is deplorable—and totally typical of your kind."

For a moment I had a terrible feeling they were going to blow up the planet because I had lost my temper. That was more guilt than I wanted to deal with!

"However you misunderstand our relationship with your mentor. Hoo-Lan was once a *member* of this council. He chose to resign, to pursue other interests. We have the utmost respect for him. We merely think he is wrongheaded."

"He has sent us a message," said the shadow. "I fear it may be the last message we will ever have from him."

I felt a lump begin to form in my throat. Had being in touch with my brain killed him? Were the people of Earth *that* terrible?

"Ever so gloomy," said Red Seaweed to the shadow. "Hoo-Lan may yet rejoin us."

"May and may not," replied the shadow. "Nonetheless, while you know that I favor the destruction of the Earth, I am willing to hold back in favor of what may be Hoo-Lan's last request."

"What was his last request?" I asked, my voice trembling.

"That we perform one final study of the Earth before we make our decision," said the shadow. "Personally, I think this is an enormous waste of time. But out of respect for a fallen comrade, I accede to his wishes, which specifically call for you and Broxholm to return to Earth and, with the help of the agent who is already in place there, file a final report."

"Those in favor?" asked Sea-green.

The vote was unanimous.

CHAPTER TWENTY-ONE
HOME TO HOME

Once these aliens made up their minds, they weren't ones to dillydally. Within minutes Broxholm and I were riding a blue beam from the ship to the Earth.

One reason we could do that was that the last space-shift had brought us back into Earth orbit. The transporter beam only had a range of a few hundred thousand miles.

I think that the funniest thing I ever saw in my life was the look on Duncan's face when Broxholm and I shimmered into place in Kreeblim's attic.

That was the funniest thing. The most beautiful thing (I can't believe I'm saying this!) was Susan Simmons's face.

Of course, part of what made it so lovely to me was how glad she was to see me.

"Peter!" she cried, running over and throwing her arms around me.

I was a little embarrassed. "Hi, Susan," I said. "It's nice to see you."

Gak! "Nice to see you." How stupid! That was a tenth, a thousandth of what I *wanted* to say to her. Only I didn't know how—especially with everyone else around us.

Broxholm broke the awkwardness of the moment in his own stiff way. "Good evening, Miss Simmons, Mr. Dougal," he said, nodding his green head. "I can't say it is exactly a pleasure to see you again, but since we are going to be working together, I hope that we will be able to put the past behind us."

For Broxholm, it was a pretty gracious speech.

"Working together?" asked Susan.

"How would you like to save the Earth?" I asked, trying to sound casual and heroic.

We didn't give them much chance to answer,

to tell you the truth. Within minutes I led the way back to the takeoff position. Duncan positioned himself between me and Susan, which was annoying. I told myself to ignore it; from tapping into his brain, I knew what he had been through in the last month.

Of course, I had been through a lot myself.

The blue beam shimmered around us. We were dissolved into electrons and hurtled into space, then reformed inside the great alien ship that I had ridden to the stars.

Somewhere below us was the planet we had to save.

Somewhere below us was my father.

Somewhere in the ship was a little blue alien who had made a dying wish that the Earth would have a final chance.

We had to honor that, try with all our hearts to save the planet.

We had to honor him.

I hoped that somehow he would live, so that Susan and Duncan could meet him.

Seconds later Kreeblim and Broxholm arrived.

"You're lucky," I told Susan and Duncan. "Traveling by transport beam saves you a trip through the disinfecting process."

"Disinfecting?" asked Duncan, wrinkling his nose.

"I'll tell you all about it later."

"You can tell them now, if you want," said Broxholm. "Kreeblim and I must go in for a meeting with the Council. You'll have some time while we're gone."

With that, the two of them disappeared through the transcendental elevator.

"All right, Peter, give," said Susan.

"Beg pardon?" I asked innocently.

But you know all that part. I told her and Duncan the same story I've just told you.

About the time we were done, Broxholm and Kreeblim returned. "The Council will see you now," said Kreeblim, her nose waving in front of her.

Nervous, excited, terrified, we followed them through the transcendental elevator to the room where the images of eight aliens were waiting to give us our instructions.

There was something different about the chamber

this time. Floating in the center of it was a huge, holographic image of the earth. Think of the globe you have in your classroom. Now imagine it eight feet across, created in perfect detail.

I felt Susan's hand slip into mine. "It's so beautiful," she whispered.

I didn't say anything. From out in space, the planet *was* beautiful. But I knew what was happening back on the surface, what people were doing to each other.

What would happen to *us* when we went back down there? Could we find some way to convince the aliens not to destroy it?

Suddenly, I realized Duncan was standing close to me. To my surprise, he slipped his arm around my shoulder. "We can do it, Peter," he whispered.

I nodded, still staring at the image before us, the image of Earth, the planet I had abandoned, and now must try to save.

My home.

READ ON FOR MORE
OUT-OF-THIS-WORLD ADVENTURES
IN AN EXCERPT FROM BOOK FOUR:

MY TEACHER FLUNKED THE PLANET

Broxholm's orange eyes were glowing. The leathery, lime-green skin of his face was stretched tight in a look that I could not interpret. The viewscreen behind him showed an image of the Earth, floating in the dark glory of space.

Broxholm pointed to a red button that glowed more brightly than his eyes. "This is it," he said. "*The* button."

My throat was dry. "What would happen if you pushed it?"

His lipless mouth pulled back in something like a smile, revealing rounded, purplish teeth. "Nothing.

At least, not now. It takes a complex series of secret commands to activate it."

"And if that series of commands is used?" asked Susan Simmons, who was standing beside me.

Broxholm turned and gazed at the image of Earth. "Stardust," he whispered.

"Whoa!" said Duncan Dougal. "Major bummer!"

Another being entered the chamber. Turning, I saw Kreeblim, the alien who had fried Duncan's brain and made him super-smart. Her lavender hair, thick as worms, was writhing around her head. "The council is ready to see us," she said, gesturing over her shoulder with her long, three-pronged nose.

I swallowed. The Interplanetary Council was trying to decide how to handle what they called "the Earth Question"—which was basically, "What do we do with the only species on ten thousand planets that is bright enough to figure out space travel, yet dumb enough to have wars?"

That species was human beings, of course, and I didn't much care for any of the aliens' current plans, which I had explained to Susan and Duncan earlier that night when I told them the story of my experiences since I had gone into space with Broxholm.

"If we start with the least nasty option and work up," I had said, "then Plan A calls for the aliens to leave us alone for now."

"That's not so bad!" Susan had said.

"Unfortunately, most of the aliens who favor it do so because they figure if they leave us alone, we'll destroy ourselves before we make it into space. That way the problem is solved, and they don't have to feel guilty."

"That *stinks*!" Duncan had cried.

"Agreed. Now, the aliens who support what we'll call Plan B would like to take over the planet."

Susan's eyes had widened. "An alien invasion, just like we feared from the beginning!"

"Not quite. This group wants to fix things. They would cure diseases, stop wars, end poverty, that kind of thing."

Duncan had blinked in surprise. "Sounds great!"

"It would be, except they'll only do it if we give them total control of the planet."

Duncan had started to ask why, then nodded.

"They're afraid once they give us their technology we'll use it against them."

"You've got it," I'd said, reminding myself not to be surprised when Duncan figured things out.

"So what's the third option?" Susan had asked.

"Plan C: restrict us to our own solar system, either by sabotaging our science so we never develop faster-than-light travel, or by setting up a military blockade."

Since I have always believed it is our destiny to go to the stars, I hated that idea more than I can tell you.

"Most aliens think that wouldn't work," I had continued. "They figure sooner or later we'd get out anyway. So we have Plan D—D for destruction, you might say. The group supporting this wants to blow us up now, before we can get into space and really make trouble. They believe if we make it out of the solar system, the final cost in lives and destruction will be *far* greater than if they simply wipe us out today. They look at us the way we would look at a group of monkeys that accidentally learned to make atomic bombs: interesting, but too dangerous to be allowed to live."

The bad news was, the aliens seemed to be leaning toward Plan D. The good news was, they were going to let us try to change their minds.

We followed Kreeblim to the wall. She had her pet poot—which was also *named* Poot, for reasons I didn't understand—riding on her shoulder. Poot was sort of an alien slug that oozed and changed shape. I had noticed that Duncan seemed to be very fond of it. I guess it was fond of Duncan, too, since when it noticed him it raised a blob of itself and cried, "Poot!"

Kreeblim stopped in front of a large circle. Mounted in the wall next to it were twelve rows of multicolored marbles. She punched six of the marbles. The circle turned blue.

This was what the aliens call a transcendental elevator. It could transport beings from one place to another instantly—which was just as well, since the *New Jersey* (that was the spaceship we were on) had thousands of miles of corridors.

I followed Kreeblim through the circle and into the meeting chamber of the Interplanetary Council.

Susan gasped when she came in behind me. I

didn't blame her. Each of the eight beings on the council came from a different world. Seeing them all together was plenty strange.

Actually, what we were *seeing* were holographic projections of the council members. The council members themselves remained on their own worlds. However, the three-dimensional images were so realistic, I rarely thought about that.

First to speak was an alien who looked like a pile of red seaweed with thick green stalks growing out of the top. It made a series of popping, bubbling sounds, then wiggled the squishy-looking pods that dangled from the end of each stalk to indicate that what it had said was a question.

I understood the gesture because the aliens had installed a Universal Translator in my brain, and it interpreted whatever any of them said. In turn, I was to translate their sounds (and gestures) for Susan and Duncan.

I turned to Susan. Her hair, usually blond, had a green tint from the odd light of the chamber. Susan is very pretty by Earth standards, but I had seen so many versions of beauty since I joined the aliens

I didn't think about that much now. "He wants to know if you understand why you are here," I said.

"I do," she replied, speaking directly to Red Seaweed. "Peter told me all about it."

"And do you accept this task?"

Susan took so long to answer that I began to fear that the alien might get upset. I understood; it was a big job. But even so . . . I gave her a nudge.

"I accept!" she said, more loudly than I expected.

"And you, Duncan Dougal?" asked an alien who looked more like a shadow than anything real and solid. It spoke by changing the way light reflected from its body.

Duncan's round face was serious. It was hard for me to imagine a kid who had bullied his way through grade school, a kid who appeared to have all the sensitivity of a brick, being responsible for the survival of the planet. But I was prejudiced. Duncan had been picking on me—and everyone else in our class—for so long that it was hard to remember how different he was now that the aliens had unleashed his natural intelligence by frying his brain.

When I translated the question, Duncan nodded. "I accept," he said solemnly.

"And you, Krepta?" asked a tall, sea-green alien.

I hesitated for only a moment. After all, the mission had been partly my idea. "I accept," I said. Though I meant to say it proudly, my voice came out sounding small and scared.

Next to speak was a purple alien whose long tentacles stretched across a silvery rack. A nozzle mounted above the rack sprayed lavender mist over the tentacles, keeping them slick and shiny.

"Broxholm ign Gnarx Erxxen xax Scradzz?" it asked.

That mouthful of syllables represented Broxholm's full name, including his family group (Gnarx Erxxen) and his planet (Scradzz). Broxholm was standing behind me. I turned to look at him. Putting a hand on my shoulder, he wrinkled his high, green forehead—his way of signaling agreement.

The final member of our party to be sworn in was Kreeblim. Her thick lavender hair was rippling with so many conflicting emotions she looked as if she had a colony of confused worms climbing out of her head. I began to wonder if she had changed her mind. But after a moment she closed her third eye, the one in the middle of her forehead, and said, "I accept!"

The council didn't ask us to swear on a holy book or anything; the aliens expect that if you say you'll do something, you'll do it. Only I wasn't entirely sure what we had just said we would do.

Basically, they had given us the last three weeks of October to put together a report on the state of Earth and its people.

But what was supposed to be in the report? How could we make them think better of us? At the moment, the aliens viewed us the way you and I look at flu germs—insignificant, yet nasty and dangerous. Or worse. I think they considered all of humanity as a sickness threatening to overtake the galaxy if something wasn't done about us.

"The newcomers will need translators," said a large, batlike alien who dangled from the ceiling in a sling. Its voice, which I had not heard before, was like nails scraping over concrete. I could feel it in my spine.

After Susan and Duncan took their hands away from their ears, I translated the alien's screech. Duncan looked puzzled. "Why do we need translators to go back to Earth?"

"Because your planet, which has yet to figure out the benefit of true communication, has hundreds of different languages," screeched the batlike alien.

The other aliens made sounds of sorrow and disapproval at our backward ways.

When I explained Bat-thing's answer, Duncan's eyes lit up. "You mean these translators will let us understand any language on *Earth*?" he cried eagerly.

"They would hardly be Universal Translators if they didn't," said Red Seaweed, adding a gesture that meant something like, "Is water wet?"

"Wow!" said Duncan. "This is going to be great!" Suddenly his smile faded. The blood drained from his face. "Wait a minute," he said, his voice quavering. "Are you going to do brain surgery on me?"

In my opinion, brain surgery on the old Duncan would have been a good idea. He'd had nothing to lose, and it might have improved things. But now that I had been inside his brain a couple of times (as a result of being hooked into some alien communication machines), I understood why he was so upset. Since the aliens had fried the thing, it was pretty amazing. I wouldn't have wanted to take a chance with it, either.

I was trying to decide whether to tease Duncan or reassure him when a wave of dizziness swept over me. My own brain felt as if it had come loose inside my skull and begun to spin.

"Nikka, nikka, flexxim puspa!" I cried.

As I was wondering where the words had come from, everything went black, and I collapsed in a heap on the floor.